THAT AUTISTIC CHILD AND THE DARKNESS

Where Does the Darkness Go When the Light Comes On? She queried

A Novel

by

Al. A. Ewen

Chapter One

THE OLD WOODEN VIADUCT

The Promise Land community was before a peaceful picture of rustic charm when a startlingly loud and impassioned noise suddenly plunged it into a state of bedlam. And then it attracted the attention of residents from far and neighboring districts; thus, they all passionately hurried over to look at the horrifying state of affair. And on their way, out of their arrested curiosity, they made their way to the scene in the form of a procession; and as if it had been planned, the moment they got to the scene they suddenly shouted in one accord, “Oh my God!” But to the less merciful ones, it was as if a relentless God had turned his head away. The light for them had suddenly become dimmed and placed one member of an entire family who became the sole living creature thereon, as the rest were plummeted into another world… the valley of death. And the bad thing about their death is that it doesn’t only transform the living; it leaves the sole survivor and the poor little infant with all the sad memories, with a fragile mind, and in a condition that is so hard to endure more so to overcome.

The time was 5:30 pm, and the only shining light was the sun slowly sinking behind the horizon. And the place was Willodean, where the old wooden viaduct spanned the sometimes dry and rocky bed of the yellow creek.

“What happened?” asked the frightening voice of an old woman leaning on her cane.

“I don’t know!” replied another. “I think…oh my God, I cannot say anymore!”

Her utterance ceased; her voice subdued under the overwhelming influence of her emotion.

"I think they may have met their mom and their dad on the viaduct on their way, and were standing on the viaduct when it suddenly collapsed. There were screams before a rush of cold silence.

The baby shower should have been in full swing, but they left for something; the remaining portion of prepared victuals. Twice before, Nora had gone to fetch some of the things she should have brought to the event, but not seeing her returning the third time, although nine months pregnant, her sister Clara decided to go and see what had become of her. And out of curiosity, she went; her two other sisters, mother, father, aunt, and their two cousins joined in. The path was lone; only a flack of blackbirds was frolicking in the air, and after circling, they pitched on the leafless branches of the giant birch tree leaning in obedience to the wind blowing easterly. And with the evening cloud slowly drifting on high, there too was a chill and sprinkles of rain amid the elongated shadows stretching across the vale.

It was unreal to believe there could be such a difference within twenty minutes, and it was hard enough to look at the devastation with bodies lying about on the protruding rocks. It was gruesome, too gruesome to look at. The creek's bed was bone dry, except for the verdure on the banks that was withering away. Nora, who was not on the viaduct, had missed it by seconds. Her eyes had just witnessed the tail end of the tragedy. It was a tragic loss of life. And in that single act, two more family members were further cast into a pitying need, as for a time they were wailing and groaning, their pain must have been unbearable that they succumbed to their injuries.

And nobody right away was present even to seek to work in the half Darkness on all the exposed bodies. The females' dresses are raised above their heads; the ripped pants of her dying father, the protruding shin bones, and indented skulls, alone tell the gruesome tale.

Then in the midst of all this, there were the unkind utterances of the few that spurred the comments of a nervous aged widow echoing from the pherefry, who tells her disgust as she exclaimed: "In this community, people are usually closer and nicer to each other than those in the city, so I do not know why they speak like that about these unfortunate people," she said in her compassionate tone of voice. "Who would have thought this could happen?" another voice echoed.

The closing evening of the month will never be forgotten by many. At first, Nora heard that her sisters Olga, Clara, and Rosalie perished among the planks, then worst, she was just in time to see the sad end of her mother and father as they heaved their chest, took their last breaths and empty it as if they had silently sighed. And similarly, she saw two of her in-laws, a brother, and a cousin followed suit. Now that they are all dead, what grief it must have been for her, the only survivor of the family. She beholds another, her infant niece between her mother's legs amongst the rocks. "Help!" she shouted.

The ghastly tale took place on this day, the twenty-seventh of November 1936, when nature, in its intelligence as it had before, induced the falling of colorful leaves; and the half-bare limbs of the undergrowth, the giant birch trees, and the oaks spread themselves carelessly: Their naked branches in an unnatural and ungraceful manner, shading measly portions of the already un-cheerful landscape. Then in the midst of all that happened, it grew extraordinarily frightening cold that evening; and under a fast-appearing overcast that made the heartfelt gathering onlookers shiver. Some, however, braved the chilly wind, drizzle, and the threat of sudden downpours with no imagination of what next to follow. And it may be worse, as, in the yonder, the cloud had become darker and heavier, hanging low, almost to the tip of the bending grass blades in the distant pasture.

At this time, there came a bright hue in the atmosphere amid the cries of the ill-at-ease crowd. The frightened voice of a compassionate old woman in a granny print dress blaring at the top of her lungs: "Take the infant away to the hospital," she shouted. "You mean no one to have a little mercy upon the infant!" she yelled.

"Oh God, may you help the innocent little soul!" said another voice coated with a little more tenderness.

The moment came when other frightened spectators from the faraway vales rushed in. And in their fright, they trampled the already withered vegetation as gusts of raw wind helplessly whistled by while the echoing sound of their wailing carried across the valley.

And in the middle of the hubbub came other curious onlookers who witnessed the surviving in-laws and friends, this time covering the bodies. Then the screaming voice of another old woman asked: "Is the infant dead?"

"It doesn't seem so," replied another.

"Goodness gracious! you mean that nobody is going to help her!" an aged woman shouted again. "Will someone please, please!" she beseeched.

It was like a parade when other people with their fierce, widely opened eyes and rapidly pounding hearts poured in, while some uttered through their unbridled lips--- their voices saying their part for the rescue of the infant.

"It's breathing!" Another voice bellowed.

And while some caressed themselves and trembled in dismay, some embraced each other and gnashed their teeth. And one other asked out of curiosity: "Who is that woman lying there with the infant between her legs?"

"I don't know," an angry voice replied.

"And look, a pool of blood settled at her feet!" a voice shouted.

"Who is she?" Another frightening voice queried.

"Rosalie," another voice replied, then it went silent.

There were tears from some who left.

"How this happens?" a trembling voice from the pherefry queried.

"That's not important; she is dead, save the infant," replied another.

"Did anyone call a doctor or the Marshall? It's full-time now for some authority to be called. For there is life in the poor little infant!"

A little old man walks in, his right palm shading his awed jaw that fell below the ordinary when he looks at the devastation. "I can't believe it. How could this happen?" he asked.

"I believe they were crossing the viaduct when suddenly a crack, and that's it. It happened so quickly!"

"You mean just as quickly as that?"

"Yes, as quick as that."

"Goodness me!" he shouted, "and you mean several dead?"

"Yes, the infant trampled from her mother's womb, it seems."

"Gracious God, it's hard to believe!" said the little old man.

"Sever the umbilical cord. It is still intact; will someone please? No scissors, knife, or anything around?"

"None, it seems."

"You mean that there isn't even a midwife amongst us?"

"Oh God, will somebody please help!"

"It's a slim chance it will ever live, and it's such a fine little soul; it's a girl at that!"

Several anxious moments slipped by minutes by minutes, unchanged.

The community pastor finally arrived, dismounted his sunken spine and muted old gray horse, and straight away made some strange gestures before he passed the rein to a helping hand of a young fellow who hitched it to a nearby stake. "The Lord giveth and He taketh--- life is a gift, and death, as it is known, is the most unwelcome process of all transitions. And worst, it is how they had involuntarily made their transition. However, they took a road we all will take some time or another. It is another regrettable and most unfortunate that this mother and the rest inadvertently and unwittingly elected to take it before," the highest holy spiritual leader said in his effort to console the grievers. Then, with the gesturing of his religious belief and ritual, though he hesitated sliding down the ravine before, he first wet his index finger on the dewdrops; and made the sign of the cross upon the infant's forehead. Then with the accompanying voices of a few, they sang: "Every morning the red sunrise, it rises warm and bright, then the evening cometh on to a still dark cold night." Following this, he advised that the infant be rushed to the hospital. And swaddled in a pink blanket of swollen layers of wool, the infant was placed on the lap of her sole surviving aunt, sitting at the back of an open farm cart. Hope then piled and filled the air that the infant would make it to the hospital. The horse-drawn farm cart soon races off. "It is too late now--- that should have been thought of long before," said a voice in the crowd. "It would have been only in the non-feeling of a person's insensitivity to the life of the infant who would not have wished for her to survive," the voice added.

In the meantime, there were those plaintive moaning sounds among some warm hearts as they surveyed the horrifying scene; and that expression of grief for the dead was heard in solemn tones. There were those, though, who said too many people should not have been on the flimsy viaduct to celebrate a child who was to be born within the next two to three weeks. These were the utterances of the haters with reckless comments; and a few carefree with no marginal care, concern, or empathy for anyone, more so for the dead. And so, they went on with all their unkind utterances. Nevertheless, with some humanitarian feelings, there was a slim to the bones middle age blue eyes, blond woman who said: "I think they were returning from somewhere up the road, a house where I think they went to celebrate the coming of another innocent soul into this sinful world of ours. And crossing the flimsy old wooden viaduct, it just collapsed."

"How could that have happened?"

"You know, that old wooden viaduct had spanned the ever-shallow yellow creek for years, which should have been changed long ago, but you know, government. Then it suddenly gave way--- sending all to their tragic end, timber and all fell upon them."

Sad enough, some people had not had much well or anything kind to say, while some openly snubbed them even though they were dead. Some say they were too poor to be given so much attention, while some said they should have had better sense to know that the viaduct was too flimsy for their weight.

"Who cares!" Another uttered: "They were not nice people, and they are getting out of order," the utterance of their cantankerous immediate neighbors, who must have had their grievances.

"It has always been forbidden to disrespect the dead, but these people have no heart," said a strong and stern voice from the periphery. "Never was it as difficult as it is in our days to foresee anything as this, much less to prevent and control this incident or anything of such from happening. It was like an unforeseen act of nature. What is to be must be," another said to silence the mongering.

Rosalie, her parents, and the rest must have raised their heads and turned in their states of death when they heard all the unkind remarks passed about them.

"If any modules of nature had done this to them, the living, I bet they would have placed the blame upon God," another voiced.

Troubled by the gruesome task of removing the bodies from the rubble, a couple that braved the condition flung their hands across their faces against the ghastly sight, grimaced, and then uttered: "that's awful." The woman was vexed, and vexed to the point that she jammed her hat on her head and commented: "People are too cussed unkind to others. If I had not been for this sad occasion, I would not have known how humans treat even the dead," the woman said as she shivered in the drizzle.

In the winter, the streets were usually cloaked with snow, and little by little, the sinking sunlight seeped in now and then, but not even now that the few more prosperous self-respecting were present. They were too wealthy to see the debacle of the poor, even now that they were all dead and so tragically.

"I cannot bear the sight of them, bodies still lying on the rocks and blood all over the place."

It was cold and overcast at the beginning of the day, but the sun held on to its promise that better would come. So, with that apparent promise, they took the chance and gathered themselves as the sky peeled naked of all the hanging dark clouds. And what appeared to be the coming of a severe snowstorm disappeared. The cold and constant disturbing drizzle with the occasional threats of heavy rain persisted in its annoying form. So, they needed to hurry before the rolling down of mud inflate water seized the course on which the bodies lay.

At last, the rescuers finally came and climbed down the ravine. Some, though, were afraid and passionately sought that the worst would come. This then opened the allay for the pastor to say his piece:

"Impossible, that's what I first thought. I was afraid and still afraid," he said. But he added, "The ravine is too steep, and I mean steep. I don't even know how I got down here in the first place and how I will get back up. In any event, I won't say anything more, only that I will beg you all to pray with me for their souls and that of the innocent infant," he beseeched.

Minutes following, he called aside a couple and asked in a whisper to them. "How many of you need help? I'll give you two, but you two over there seem to need it more. I'll be right back, but I beg you all to stay strong; I won't be long," he said, walked away, and fought to ascend the precipitous ravine.

The pastor, though, held it that a person's liberty may, unfortunately, be legitimately curtailed, perhaps cut short the rights of others through neglect. And since these rights include specific claims to help and sustain the rights of life and freedoms, it is just that by God's doings, some have to depart this life as they were so destined," said the pastor, speaking in his proverbial tongues to them. Then he ascended the rugged ravine while tears rushed from his eyes.

Chapter Two

THE AMALGAMATION OF THE SNEAKY DARKNESS

And it so happened that in a single act of Nature, there brings with it dusk, as the sun got closer to the line between the ocean and the sky. And with a pleasant formation of the clouds slowly changing their faces, several long streaks of red and orange stretched across the sky, ambling in the complete twilight. And as they acted by the dictate of Nature, there came some changes. The mixture of the disappearing beams while the sun is in its setting motion finally leaves the gradual amalgamation of the sneaky Darkness as it slowly creeps in. Then within the further authority of Nature, the slow coming of the winter season there were the hurling raindrops with their unvarying behavior that drove the unmerciful away. Most of them had already scampered for shelter from the threat of the torrential rain which was to follow.

And soon, the creek bed was fast filling with hurrying and flat water; all the bodies must now be removed from the dry edges on time. And while the rain was bearing down fiercely on even the heartless, there was an old woman in a tightly fitting pink and black dress gazing into the heavens as if to say, Lord, why are you doing this to us? She lifted her hands above her head, and in a loud and uncontrolled voice, she cried, "Have mercy upon us!"

Later on, as the rain abated, in the shadows of the dusk, Nora Saunders, the sister of the infant's deceased mother unnoticeably returned from the hospital, before entering the now empty hovel, she frantically took another look at the tragic sight where she bawled openly. Then she returned to the open and empty dump that death divested. And the moment she entered, she straightaway, though temporarily, unfrocked herself before hauling onto her trembling body a half dry -dirty corduroy skirt and a grey blouse with beige embroidery sleeves. She knew too well that all known members of her already small family were dead, all perished amongst the buckled timbers. It is now her responsibility to care for the infant she took to the hospital with all her hopes hanging on her survival.

Although giving no information on the infant's condition, deep in her aunt, rest the feeling that there was no prospect of such that she will live, she feared. And so, she turned to a crested mountain of her prayers, and in her surprised audible plea to God, she prayed: "May the Lord God of heaven have mercy upon the soul of this little." This was a surprising prayer that came from the lips of a woman who never liked to use the word Lord and had favored not the sound or presence of God. Strangled by her tribulation, the word God unwittingly flowed through her lips and became the conduit to the solace she sought.

The following morning, she returned to the hospital, where she was allowed to rest in a room the hospital provided for the counselor or grievers of dead loved ones. Three days now had unnoticeably gone, and it was now on the eve of the burial. And for her, the next thing to consider was the infant's survival. And as she thinks of assisting in the preparation and attending the funeral of the infant's mother, she dares not to overlook her sister, parents, aunt, uncle, brother, and cousin.

And with limited cash in hand and her boundless problem, she was further faced with the troubling task of finding enough money for other things. In the meantime, she sought to maintain that she needed to travel to the home of her surviving cousins-in-law some distance away. She is anxious to see him because she wants to pick up whatever money is available. Failing this, she would hate to know that her parents would have to be buried in the paupers' row.

Nora needed to pack away something for her trip and purchase her ticket for the overnight express train plying through Stone Mountain. She had only remembered the moment she heard the hooting of the steam engine echoing through the woods far outside the boundaries of the hospital. And as she pondered, the train raced by at full speed, leaving her with her mountain of problems and shivering body in the twilight hours of rain, dust, and mist.

At such an instant, she felt she understood why her life was so miserable and considered putting herself in order and together within. Nora thought of unloading her burden by surrendering her deplorable ways and taking on an attitude that would be more acceptable to God and man. And so, from her reckless ways, she quieted down a little, though only for a while. And only in her anxiety that she rested her head against the wall as rivulets of tears raced down her slender cheek.

She spent the entire night at the hospital, where she worried about her situation and fretted over the uncertain fate of her infant niece. She cried cheerlessly throughout the night without abatement to her mountain of trouble.

Nothing was more evident than her fear that the child would die. At this stage, Nora must have made quite a few unquestionable visits, but there was something special about this particular one, although there was one exception.

The following day, she got up, expecting to hear something, at least something, from the doctor. Still, amazingly, under the influence of doctor Patrice, a hospital staff member brought her what she thought would have been more comforting news. Instead, it was something that was prepared for her hungry stomach, but as her fretfulness prevailed over her appetite; she refused the offer with a dreary no, a reply she gave by the cross shaking of her head, accompanied by a cynically half cock smile that came in the space of verbal gratitude.

It was unusual and extraordinarily comfortable that morning. The only window in the room the hospital permitted all grievers to use was on the ground level adjacent to the mental health unit. On top of the mountain of her trouble, she could barely see from that limited comparatively vantage point, a skimpy view of the meticulously kept landscape. It was in the yonder, partially obscured by the simple curve of the entrance driveway and the shrubbery that got lost in one of the corners of her eyes. She gazed into space as she pondered.

The minor release of her heightened pressure came only from the feeling that doctor Patrice must have been a good pediatrician and that he was concerned about human lives. Hence her hope was raised. She also hoped that nothing terrible had happened to her infant niece. And the moment she saw the black smoke oozing from the chimney in the distance, it told a different story. It was her feeling that the furnace emanating the burning of possibly rubbish was also with the flesh of something. And to her, in the burning there is that pungent stench emanating from somewhere---carrying with it the familiar odor of burning flesh. It was a scary moment for the already wringing heart of a grief-stricken woman who felt the burning of meat could be the flesh of her infant niece.

"I hope that was not the flesh of my dear niece!" she said fretfully and groaned each time she reflected on that ill-fated evening--- a traumatic incident that would be with her for some time to come.

Nothing on the makeshift cot could offer her any promise of comfort. And in her state of trepidation, she restlessly twisted and turned with regularity. She did not wink her teary eyes, not even for a second. And what made it worse was a sudden push to the window open by a puff of wind. And with several chilly gusts, after that came a drizzle along with the threat of more rain in the distance, and with the leafless branches swaying to and from, there with it, the intermittently stirring wayward wind engagingly whistling by.

Nora will forever recall her frantic moments during her wakeful night hours when the pediatrician, doctor Patrice, came by. And after a gentle knock, he peeped in without an utterance. “Come in, doctor,” she said, which it was to no avail.

The room was already cast into half-Darkness as the silvery crescent moon peered intermittently and softly through the half-closed translucent window panes. Her roving eyes caught the pink frazzled half-cut curtain flapping yet gracefully in the seeping wind. And in her frantic emotion, she clasped her hands as she thought the doctor had entered. And further, in her anxiety, she settles down to listen to whatever good news he may have brought. She remains still as though on military attention; and as if on guard, she awaited that which never came. They had a brief conversation through the ad-jarred door, which was disrupted by the periodic short spells of announcement over the public system.

The passing night now stirred her anxiety and propelled annoyance, she displayed all the visible frown that brought out the rugged contours on her forehead. Still, despite her frustration, it had become necessary for her to again wait beyond the afternoon for some unmeasured time regardless all her pleadings. Another day dawn, the doctor came. He tried with all pleasing effort to comfort her, but all actions fell only on the flaps of her barren ears. She was upset. In the end, he placed his hand on her shoulder: “I must rush back to the unit,” he said. And to comfort her, he further placated her… touching her with a couple of gentle patting on her shoulder before leaving. “I will be right back with you,” he said. “I’m very sorry,” he added, assuring her.

Nora’s forehead remained creased; the several contours carved in her brow remained with all the promises of permanence as she fretted.

She was sweating profusely, accompanied by tears racing down her long cheekbone. Now with the pain of her dead loved ones taking its grip on her, she gazed anxiously through the window in a vacuum, a space filled with anxiety.

With nothing on warmer than her thin sweater, she hurried to the door of doctor Patrice, who got up; in his haste and anger, he slammed shut the door before her. She half opened it and poked her head in to glimpse what could have caused him to act in that manner. She knew that she had acted out of her anger, and her curiosity, married anxiety, but with all her aching efforts, they provided no ease or comfort to her troubled mind and her ever-growing concern, she was left with no alternative.

Again, several fretful hours had long passed, and there was no trace of the doctor. A flood of activities engaged him, as it would seem. And along with the low vision of what was happening, and with her starving of knowledge of the condition of her infant niece, nothing Nora could do, say or see except for the shiny bright floor with a porter swinging his waxing mop down the corridor, all that was presented before her. And from her disquieting point of view, to her it was as if the entire hospital were in recess from all actions. She rolled her eyes about and became more terrified in her anxiousness. Her voice echoed beneath the ceiling and off the walls of the corridor as she cried. She did everything she could to get some attention, but it was only her anxiety and her action that undoubtedly depicted her unspoken quest.

The lone Orderly, in the meantime, could only look at her. And in his powerless mind and his feeling, he shook his head pitifully. Nora was now strained to know what was going on with her infant niece, if she was dead or still alive. Turning over and over in her mind was the possibility that her niece must be dead, and when doctor Patrice came, he had only come to give her the impression that all was not well. 'Perhaps he was too afraid to tell me what had happened,' Nora mused. 'In fact, I am quite sure that was what he had come to tell me. Or, maybe, my dear niece had almost died, and perhaps came that blessed moment when her condition turnaround,' Nora pondered with much optimism.

She recalled that when the doctor came, there was that deep sense of pity written on his face, the result of her further stirring her curiosity which was virtually heard. How she felt showed that her grip on reality was becoming increasingly tenuous. In any event, despite all her whispering hopes and her views, they carried no answer to her wondering challenges, all of which she had set in her cheerless anticipation and anxiety.

Several dreaded and nervous hours had passed, much longer, before doctor Patrice finally got back. His steps could be heard as he walked briskly down the corridor and with the ruffling sounds of his papers as he rifled through them. Nora's first feeling was to get ready and braced for whatever the news he may bring. So, she wailed a little, and with all her preparedness for the negative about what to expect, she set herself ready to accept any information relating to the non-survivability of her niece.

"I would have loved to head for the road to spread the news that my niece is alive, but nothing I heard, nothing can I say," she mumbled.

Nora was truly afraid that her niece must have died because one could have saved her life but God, the God with whom she is personally having a problem, according to her belief. And whatever the news would have been, she would have ended in tears, given that ultra-ecstasy and ultra sorrows from time-to-time induced tears.

It came at the end, a very somber moment when doctor Patrice finally delivered the report on the infant's condition to her. The instant she got the news, she collapsed to the floor and worked herself up almost to insanity. The emotionally charged and tortured Nora got up, slumped herself onto the cot, and again stumbled to the bed. And acting in her third antics, she again suddenly sprang to her feet, hugged doctor Patrice, and cried uncontrollably. The doctor tried in vain to control her, but in his effort to control her, all fell on the unfertile ground. It however, didn't take any time before all her anger, her antics, and tears eventually ended an eventful day.

Chapter Three

THE FATE OF THE INFANT

Things weren't always the way they had turned out. When it came to Nora's realization, her problem seemed unending and will be carried on into another dimension, all through the next night and into another day. And it was then that another unpleasant situation developed. The child's survival seemed to have made a turn, but this time turned for the worst. Nora must now go home both to refresh herself, change her clothes and prepare for the funeral of her mother and father and the rest the next day. In addition, she will have to stay at the hospital for yet another night. During all this time, there was that annoying glaring glow of the silvery moon peeping in feverishly from behind the branches of the dancing willows and pines, which seemed to mask the open ambiance and the condition from that which was to come.

By this time, it was much past twilight, and the 6: O'clock train had long gone for the evening. The next and last one would have been at 11: O' Clock the night. And with the nearest station down the road and less than two chains from the hospital south, it could be a dangerously steep venture for a lone woman to walk that night. And what would have made it even worse is that she is a woman with a broken heart and troubled mind ever to attempt; for even though she is a virago, there is no way that she alone will ever able to manage a single hoodlum with a pistol.

In her state of confusion and restlessness, she gazed from the window toward the slow sinking quarter moon. And there she stood for some time as if watching it as it shuffled and danced behind the big pines peeling softly their trembling pre-winter straws. And as she watches, it becomes apparent that she intends to forego or minimize her tension, nervousness, and her house of piling trouble. So, she watches as they incessantly fall in the intimate foreground of a usually miserable autumn evening.

And as her teary eyes twirled with the falling pine straws, so were her thoughts as she delved into her thinking about her infant niece. However, she knew that even if her wishes could stand, and it would all appear as if it has been a blessing, it would most certainly take a miracle to bring the infant back to life. Nora's faith in the form of her religious point of view and her belief, she has always been in limbo regarding her faith, God and Christianity. However, on approaching what could have been her dreadful end, she was surprised even though she voluntarily, half-heartedly, surrendered her belief, calling upon God for his immediate intervention.

In the meantime, the weather sudden changed, which was unseasonably different. It got much colder that Wednesday evening, and to the extreme that everybody passing outside the window was tightly hugging themselves---walking briskly against the stiff autumn wind.

The moment the presence of the crescent moon finally disappeared from her sight, though nervous, she instantly pulled the strings of the window shutters. Her first impulse was to try and get whatever little nap she could. Then in her state of edginess, she first sat down and again raised herself upright. She then again sat before she finally lowered her body, her palms intimately flanking her jaws. And as she leaned forward, with her breast resting upon her knees, she fretted for the better. Her tears did not cease, at least not for some moment. They flowed continually until her tired body at the end drifted off into an unmeasured time--- the beginning of her fitful slumber…

During the night's wee hour, doctor Patrice visited the room and told her: "The infant has made another change." He again tried to comfort her in her scream, but his efforts were to no avail. She sobbed affectionately and went back to the window, peering toward the direction of the heavens. She was troubled, afflicted. And in her state of severe physical and mental suffering, she again shifted the curtains, which revealed the slow breaking of a new day. The dawn whispered in, giving her its assurance that there are better times ahead.

First, some orbs in the element caught her eye. The stars were twinkling faintly in the distance. There was a weak sunbeam painting the azure in a most welcoming manner. At times, it was in bright colors, peering from behind the horizon, which had lifted her spirit the moment it caught her teary eyes.

And as usual, a few streaks of dawn gradually came following the passing hours of the night. And as the beginning of another morning broke, it brought with it several chilly hours that had soon disappeared. And there came, at last, a brighter beam in the eastern sky, showcasing the pleasing splendor of Nature. Although Nora was pondering what next, they had offered her all the comforting feeling of the promise of anything as her trouble piled. The only interruption of the silent spell for those solemn moments was a shivering but soft breeze that had passed within reach of her temple, offering all the comfort to her weary mind.

During those moments, she had reckoned that if three days passed and the fourth-day breaks came, and the dead were not buried, if reported to the authority, it could be more trouble for her and her in-laws. For although the bodies were not in the public dead house, with her being the only next of kin, it still would be trouble for her. It is customary for the government to become aware on a timely basis in order for them to bury the dead of paupers in pauper's row. Therefore, it must be reported to the government authority promptly. And if this didn't happen, she would be in trouble. And on top of it, although they were poor, it would leave further a bad taste in her mouth and on what was left of her family's integrity, but most of all, the name of her deceased mother and father.

Nora was now advised that even though her parents were comparatively pauperized, everything should be done to preserve, at least, the family's good name, their honesty, and their noble character. And remembering her father's wishes, at the break of dawn, she hurried off to catch the first train even without knowing of the infant's condition. The train scheduled to arrive at 7: O'clock was a little late. So, she raced to the station the morning, and both she and the train arrived simultaneously.

Other passengers were filing in, some as if they were common laborers, and some were believed to be executives amongst them, she observed as she boarded. Twenty stops down the track, the train came to a halt. She disembarked in the presence of a hand full of sympathizers who had come to wish the mourners and grievers well. Her in-laws were already financially prepared to bury their side of the dead. A few of the graves were dug by then, but at the back of the shanty dwellings while they waited for her to determine who should be buried in the family plot or the old Churchyard.

Nora narrowly recalled when her parents were alive, there were occasions that she heard her father say that his grandfather no longer wanted any dead to be buried in the family plot because it was too dangerously close to the house. However, he never stated the reason beyond the nearness. It is a pity she did not know that apart from the City's ordinance, her great-grandfather had long abandoned the tradition of plot burial; and long before he said so, he knew it was because gravediggers were no longer digging graves the six–foot–six. In addition, whenever it rains and if heavy, it creates severe soil erosions all over the place, which can cause many things to happen. It was only now that it was revealed when one of the in-laws who knew that her father had tried vainly to readopt the tradition. Her father, no doubt, wanted to change her great-grandfather's wishes because his wife has always been sicklying, and should she die before him, he said: "I would like to have her still closer to me." So, it is unfortunate that now both are dead; there is no dictate from anyone but of the authority.

And even now that some understanding has been established, Nora, however, had bypassed the ordinance and gave the go-ahead to have her brother, sisters, and parents' grave dug in the plot but some distance from the hovel. And she even insisted that the graves must be dug to what is believed to be the equal depth of their savior's height. And if this was done, she might be forgiven by the authorities, all of which were in her belief.

It was now more than three days since they died. In fact, on the fourth, if not the fifth day, and with no known established funeral parlor in proximity, the bodies begin to emanate unbearably and most unhealthy foul odor. With little to contribute but love for her family, Nora had mainly depended on her in-laws for all the help they could afford.

And now she must, due to circumstances, use the opportunity to patch up things with them after years of malice of unknown cause or reason.

All eight graves were dug at their savior's height and ready while they awaited the coming of the officiating pastor from the distant A. M. E. Church. In any event, there was a foul odor emanating even though they were in their coffins, lids closed, nails were driven home, and screws tightened. Despite all those, the absence of flowers dictated, by their usually severe financial deficiencies, while the bodies were all dressed in their Sunday best.

The pastor arrived late on the back of his old grey, sunken backbone horse without a pair of stirrups. But it was not too late for him to have prayed for the souls of the dead. And then, with the accompanying voices of most of the people gathered, he sang with them: "Abide with Me," then he led the short and slow procession from the open yard to the graveside. And at the gravesides, they sang: "In the Land of Fed fewer Days," as one by one, the bodies were lowered into the earth, all interred for their eternal rest. The mourners then filled their palms with grave dirt, and in one accord, they recited, "earth-to-earth, ash-to-ash, and dust-to-dust." The volunteered shovel men soon labored, raining dirt upon the pine boxes.

It was an afternoon of the fourth stage of sadness that lasted until sunset. This leaves Nora with still another challenging task she cannot ignore. Her infant niece was still in the hospital, and she might've another funeral on her hand; she doesn't know. And if her niece survives, she would not want her to be taken care of by strangers—a promise she had made to herself.

As much as she was so cantankerous and dubbed the black sheep of her family, she was accustomed to growing up in one bond within the immediate family structure, and such change will be devastating to her. She, however, must find her way back to the hospital against the background feeling of her just seeing the burial of her cousins, sisters, a brother, and her parents… a feeling that gave her a weary body with a further troubled mind and a broken heart.

In any case, it seemed that her spirit remained halfheartedly strong, fostered by her belief that while there is life, there is hope. She believes that so long as her sides are going in and out, her chest is heaving, and her pupils are dilating, all are indicative of life, and while there is life, there is hope.

"All these thoughts came to my mind when I was on my trek to the train station. And the most troubling part about the whole thing was, I was alone on the evening, some moments just after the funeral. They all remind me of the time in my early childhood when I was confronted by several terrible things that led me back to my kindergarten days. It was even up to my primary and high school years. I hate to remember those painful things I encountered," Nora said as she expounded on the things she would never forget.

She recalled that times were very hard, and things were extremely tough with her parents. And she also remembered her days in Mississippi before her parents moved to Promised Land, when racial tension and segregation were high, and how her grandfather, who was working as a sharecropper, labored occasionally in storehouses and storerooms; and how he struggled to make ends meet before and even after changing place of abode. So, there in her, she anchored some sorrowful moments that will be in her for the rest of her life.

And she also remembers how she was sometimes forcefully transported to work on the cotton farms with her father instead of transported to school. "And I also remember my grandfather's favorite Negro spiritual song: "Better days are coming by and by...," a song he always sings while laboring sometimes in the cold, and at times his raw back in the baking heat of the sun; and at times in the shelter of the half-darkness in exchange as rent for the little old two-bedroom house he later bought from the white property owner," expounded Nora. "Now after remembering all those, I would not want my niece, if she survives, to be transported and treated the same way," she added. "I am fort year-old now and haven't a child, so I am going to take her as my own and do for her the best for the rest of her life. I love her very much, maybe because of how she came into this world," Nora declared.

During those tragic moments of reflecting, she saw a flock of birds as they suddenly lifted themselves, their flopping wings echoing some hooey sounds in the mist and the clustered towering pines along the way. And on some other trees in the distance, were some husky ravens and some turkey-like vultures perched on branches that were naked of leaves. They were also on other trees with low limbs, sprouting buds, and maybe dying branches.

Then to shrink her fear, she cast her eyes to the heavens and to the construction site, which was approximate to the adjoining neighborhood. It was here that her eyes came upon quite a few newly built homes on the plain that brought out a little more life to the community.

"It was pleasing to see them," she said and carried wishful thinking that did not last for too long. For all in her admiration and wishes, they were soon to be absorbed into her consciousness that her parents were indeed too pauperized to own any of the homes.

"They would have been proud to own one of them, but they would have been still too poor even if they were still alive," she said grimly.

Too many unbelievable happenings for her to forget. They will always be indelible in her. She has tried to ignore some of the things as she chugged along the rugged path to the train station, but having been pregnant with a host of incalculable and unbearable ideas, she found no way out of her unanswerable burden. She then set herself to forge the tides and scale all the hurdles of grief while weathering the torment and uncertainty of her life. Where she is going and what will happen to her beloved infant niece have yet to be determined.

She got to the train station eleven minutes before 8: O'clock the evening, just when the steam coach engine came clattering in. And soon, there were no visible traces of the rocky road or the tracks. They disappeared in the slow seeping Darkness, exercising its authority, leisurely capturing the ambiance without forewarning. And with nothing on but her same light sweater, she shivered nervously and restlessly in the unusually drifting and chilly wind while the Darkness sneakily crept in with its opaqueness.

The train's lone conductor's face was mysteriously lit up when she embarked, which was one of those well-pronounced acts of hypocrisy. And in fact, it was as if he had heard that she had married to the Nawab of Pataudi, but she remembered what she had been through, and as a result she employed a dreaded facial decorum. And she also handed him a crown of halfhearted smile that had smartly lacked the presence of any sincerity. She had ignored or otherwise forbade all that should have been equal to his. There was something that stood sentinel within her that she forbade her every joy of fully meeting his smile. "Every horse knickers at his fillies. I do not stand for hypocrisy. I do not want any grin from anybody who is not genuine," she remarked.

The conductor seemed to have made to believe, maybe afraid, that she was someone or a woman of grand repute. His feeling soon reverse, and before long it sunk deeper and deeper within when her smile did not meet fully with that of his. He did everything possible to impress her, but nothing he could do that could invoke her interest. Nora's focus on her niece did not shift. She continued on her direct path of concern about her infant niece, and her state of mind was unbendingly fixed with stress, anger and sadness abound.

And so, again, it ended in tears when the train pulled out of the station. The next ten stops came slower to her than usual; it would appear. She disembarked, breaking the focus of the conductor's gaze, as she turned the first corner using the shortest path to the hospital where she started her long walk under the faded guiding lights of the whole but delaying silvery moon. And as she walked along, frightening sounds were echoing from the bushes; some in the sounds of screech owls and possibly, things like bloodsucking nocturnal creatures. And as she battled with her fear and feeling, her well-fought and adopted self-control feelings stayed within. Then suddenly, all her apprehension seemed abated. It also appeared as though she had put out her hands to thwart the flashes of lights that came across her face. And with that, her confidence shifted significantly as if it were built on the feeling that her niece was alive.

Several nervous hours had passed, and she was now closer to learning the fate of her gravely ill infant niece. Thus, she raised her head and lifted her hopes when such a feeling came to her. So, she entered the hospital compound through the side gate that led her through the narrow alley and then through to the lonely corridor, she found herself. Somehow, as she strode along the corridor, she avoided seeing the worst that would have come to her sight. She leaped across the lawn and marched across the next hall aisle, showing signs of mental fatigue when her apprehension had her believed to have been wholly shifted; there, she came upon two porters pushing a stretcher; a sign ahead of them read: "Mortuary."

On a trolly were some white cotton sheets uniformly folded with precision edges and corners, all neatly and casually resting at the bottom of the corridor. And a little further down were two nurses' aides wheeling another stretcher draped with white linen shaped with an oval heave in the form of a mini tent. The moment Nora saw these, she frantically leapt into the air; her heart raced as they passed.

"That one is dead I bet," she said in a whisper, "and is going to the dead house," she added, her heart racing even faster. And with her imagination leading the way to a hasty assumption, she re-engaged in fretting as she headed to the reception desk.

"May I speak with doctor Patrice, please?" she asked in a controlled tone.

"Doctor Patrice isn't available at the moment, ma'am. Can anyone else help you?"

"Oh my God!" she said, disappointment showing upon her face. After a long pause, she broke her muted stance and made some awkward gestures before she blurted: "No, thanks. Oh my God!"

"What is it, ma'am? Can I help?" asked the receptionist at the desk.

"Will he be coming back anytime soon?" Nora asked in a calmer tone.

"He is here, ma'am, but he has an emergency, and I do not know when he'll be available."

"Okay, I'll wait. Thank you."

"Quite welcome. Have a seat; I'll try and get him for you if I can."

"Please. I'd appreciate that."

Struggling to maintain her composure, Nora made several nervous but lazy-like strides to the waiting area. And rifling through her handbag, she brought up a quarter ream of tissues she held between her trembling fingers. Then even though she was so tense that her shoulders ached, she casually sat before wiping away whatever mucus she could from her nostrils, her teary eyes in a similar fashion.

"I think she'll be fine anyhow," she said in her formed consolation.

The clock on the wall was ticking; the hour hand could only be imagined moving, while the second hand raced around the face of the dial several times since. Then before long, it was showing 10:30 am, doctor Patrice should be on his way. And it did not take long; his footsteps in fast-moving strides drowned out whatever chimes the clock may have made.

"Doctor, Patrice! Doctor Patrice!" she called in a nervous but controlled voice.

With his head buried in his orbited thought, he pivoted like a top to her frantic call and responded: "Oh! That's where you are! I was just about to go to the other waiting area to look for you. Come with me."

Nora sprang from her sitting position and trailed him to the grieving room.

"Oh no, don't tell me!" he said, rifling his coat pockets.

"Wait here…!"

"What's wrong, doctor Patrice?" she asked.

"What have I done with it?"

"Something wrong, doctor?"

"Oh no, nothing is wrong; I'll be right back. I must have left it on my desk."

"What is this?" Nora asked but kept her self-assurance.

The time of the day was 11:45 am, which had advanced an hour and fifteen minutes since. She was driving mad inside at the doctor because she could not see him again until he returned, but when and at whatever time, and in her added consolation, she said to herself: "At least, I believe he would have had the courtesy to tell me that the poor little infant did not make it, something he should have told me by this," as she crafted her consolation she said, "but why would he be looking for anything written to give me any negative information about her? I think he would have just told me straight out, oh yes, the death certificate; I forgot."

It was another testing moment of faith for her flustered mind laden with nervousness, apprehension, and frustration, in mixture with her half-suppressed anxiety. She jerked her shoulder in dissatisfaction and utter contempt, and then she gave a hissed--- followed by a curse. "What the cursing else can I do? What is to be will be," she added, then leaned back, her head resting against the freshly painted wall, and released a hefty sigh.

Chapter Four

DOCTOR PATRICE BLUNDERED

The glaring sun was still less than half way in the sky, its needlepoint beams peering in intermittently between the dark gray clouds and the half-naked branches gently swaying to the order of the wind. The chill of the morning sends the janitor to close the window, while the dancing gladioli in the massive plant pot in the corridor slowly quieted down the second it was shielded from the once ferocious wind.

Time went… doctor Patrice hurried in.

"I am sorry about that, but the busy night has its toll on me. Forgive me."

"That's ok, doctor."

Rifling through his papers again, several things had slipped his memory.

"How do you relate to the infant?" he asked.

"That's my niece, doctor! I thought you saw it on the document. And I told the girl at the desk that when I first came in."

"Oh yes, her mother died in that awful tragedy. Now I remember."

"I know I also told you too, doctor, that I am not her biological mother."

"Yes, it's right here. Forgive me."

"I remember telling the clerk that I'm the child's aunt."

"Well, your niece had pulled through a little, but…,"

"What doctor?" interjected Nora.

"She is not quite out of the woods. I am particularly concerned that she might show signs of a mental problem later in life. I cannot assure you that she will not because there were moments when her poor little heart had stopped beating. And I think she'd stayed too long in her mother's womb after her mother died. And on top of that, they waited too long before she was brought to the hospital. Surprisingly, those few moments without oxygen can cause much damage to her brain," explained doctor Patrice.

"She is alive, though, doctor?"

"Oh yeah, very much so as I told you…."

"Okay, doctor, don't bother to repeat. I cannot take it anymore."

"However, she will not be coming home anytime soon. I have to keep her for some time to see what we can do for her. She is such a sweet little infant. It's a pity."

"That's okay, doctor; all I want to know is that she is fine."

"She is not fine. She is now under acute care, and you will only be able to see her once within the next couple of days, maybe weeks; who knows? And again, she might well be in the hospital for some unknown time. So, you may go home now, and I'll see you then. Bye. I have a lot to do."

"Why, doctor, why?"

"As I have told you before, her condition is not looking all that good, although she appeared to be."

"Are you serious, doc?"

"Yes, but I think she will be okay. It will take some time before she comes to my satisfaction."

The moment Nora heard those words, she sluggishly lifted herself with her hopes and confidence, stretching out whatever delayed anxiety. Then she looked once around her personal space before picking up her belongings and heading through the door. She did not bear even the idea of seeing the infant and left without a harboring thought. But in her consciousness, she secretly wished things had been the other way around.

"I'm looking at that poor little infant as I walk out this door. And I'm praying for her poor little soul," she said self-consolingly, passing her hand through her platted salt and pepper hair. "Perhaps I should look in the mirror at my hair, not even that I remember," she said, pounding the turf to the train station for home. She forged the rugged unpaved path, and as she did so, her thoughts ran mainly on the bits and pieces she must now pick up. She has no religion; in fact, she has forsaken any religion but began to think along that line. To her, faith and man are to be kept aside—a belief she firmly holds.

"They are both too difficult to fathom, although serving their purposes at times," she muttered as she trod along the lonesome path… holding well her belief that her view of them was adequately justified. "If the little infant lives, she will be my sole friend," the weary Nora added.

As she got closer to the train station, in the fog she spied before her something; an object that had increased her fear. A lone little old man was standing when she got there. They did not say hello to each other at the instant. Still, there were glancing at each other in periodically, with frequencies of equal half cock smiles that later born a moderately informative conversation.

"The next train will come only at 12:30," the little old man expressed. "At this time of the day, it runs every hour on the half hour, which I can understand since not very many people taking the train this time, a good number of them travel by horse-drawn coaches, for many of them cannot afford a motor car," explained the old man, volunteering every ounce of the well-needed information.

"Really!" she replied.

"Oh yeah, that's the way it is here."

"Thank you, sir."

"You are not from here, eh? I can tell."

"No, not really. How do you know that, sir?" Nora asked.

"That hospital over there where I think you are coming from, brings many strangers in the neighborhood," explained the little old man. "And many of our kind are now living in the neighborhood as well," he added. His right-hand clutches the handle of what looks like his lunch pan, and in the left corner of his mouth dangles his white chalk pipe, which billows some slight but delicately curling gray smoke that emanates the friendliest of tobacco aroma. And there was that hallmark of contentment displayed on his face.

"The aroma of the tobacco is not too bad; it is the most pleasant thing that has ever passed through my nostrils in a long, long time," Nora said.

"Thank you, it is expensive stuff. It is always good to buy the best," he replied.

"I can imagine," she said. "Who is the owner of those farms over there?" she asked, feeling more at ease with him.

"I really cannot tell. I have only seen people going and coming there, some of your kind sometimes over their tilling the soil and often picking the cotton. I don't know anymore."

Nora did not take kindly to what the old man said, but out of respect for his age, she just said, "Okay! Thank you."

"Das all right," said the little old man, leaning against the shed post. "I think the train will be here anytime now. The sun is a little away from the center of the sky, meaning it is some minutes after noontime. We missed the eleven thirty-one."

"How can you tell, sir?"

"That's not hard to tell," he replied.

"How do you know?" Nora asked, "I used to hear my father say the same thing when he was alive, and I have always been wondering how he knows!" she added.

"You never asked him?"

"No, it has never dawned on me. Then again, he was a very rough man. I could not ask him many questions."

"You see, I don't know if he would have told you the same thing, but let me tell you what I know. On a clear day when the sun is in the middle of the sky, if you look down or around for your shadow, you would have problem finding it. Why can you tell me?"

"Frankly sir, no."

"Because it is beneath your feet, and because you are standing on it makes it difficult to find. Does that make sense?" explained the old man.

"Yes, a lot."

"So, with that, I use my imagination to determine the time of the day. Mind you; it depends now on where you are, for on the short days, the distance of the sun and the position of your body makes a difference," the old man explained.

"Are you saying that when it is noon, we are standing on our shadow, sir?"

"Yes, that's exactly what I am saying."

"That's interesting!"

"How do you think the people long ago, and even before my time, were able to tell the time of the day?"

"I don't know, and I never gave it any thought," replied Nora.

"You are young, so let me teach you something. It is what those ancient explorers had used to tell the time of the day by looking in the sky for the position of the sun and the casting shadows on the ground. Columbus, for example, did not have a watch as far as I know or can recall! Have you ever heard that?"

"No, sir. Never," Nora replied.

"Just think."

"That's clever!"

"You must think, young miss, start thinking."

The half an hour unnoticeably elapsed.

"You have taught me something, sir, thank you, thank you!"

"The next one is now coming."

"How do you know that sir, and you haven't seen it?"

"I can tell you it is coming, and you have all reason to wonder."

"That's another thing you younger folks need to know. You will hear that little crackling on the track if you listen keenly. What does that say?" the old man asked.

Amid their conversation, the train burst from around the shaded bend some seconds from when they spoke, giving Nora no time to prove his reasoning wrong. And as the train slowly rolled in at the station, she stared at him, amazement written in her eyes. And in the little old man and his gentle manner, he outstretched his right hand; with his kind gesticulation, he made way for her to first embark. "Ladies before gentlemen," he said. With a simple nod, they boarded the train. Only the unavailability of seats separated them after they embarked.

"Nice talking with you," the old man said, allowing her to take the first available seat. "If we see each other again, I will tell you the rest about the train and the crackling on the track. Have a nice day."

The train pulled out; he went his way to the next available seat.

"It was not necessary for me to seek to sit beside him. More so, there wasn't a seat even if I wanted to. He is a knowledgeable little old man. Not very often that I run into anyone like him!"

Nora was fascinated by the old man's analysis of the shadows and the sun, something she had never paid much if any attention to. However, as she previously stated, she had often heard her father talk about it. So, engrossed with the idea, now and then, she would give a half-diluted smile dictated by her troubled mind.

As the train sped along, funnels of black smoke puffed into the air, and soon it got lost in the woods and mist leaving the delayed crackling in its trail.

Chapter Five

NORA AND HER AUTISTIC NIECE

Nora, at least, now seemed to be settling in with that concealed burden she wrapped in the ambit of her thinking and her troubled mind. The amazing information she heard from the old man warmed her heart a little. Considering, though, her mental strain and troubled mind, how long after she can sustain her memory with all those information is anybody's guess.

All along, her problem remained a heavy burden to think of it. She had only a part-time job cleaning the house of a wealthy couple twice a week. She believes that for that reason, she should not have much of a problem finding time to do her cleaning job and take care of her niece if and when she is discharged from the hospital. But there was still an added problem of much concern to her. Who will be with the child when she goes to her cleaning job? Was it something for her to consider before the child is discharged to her care? First, she must have some form of gainful employment that would give her sufficient income for her to offer or provide the optimum care the child would need, and she must be present almost at all times --- considering that the child, according to doctor Patrice, "'she is inclined to be autistic, or maybe epileptic.'"

My other concern is the little pittance they are paying me. Will it be sufficient for me to give the care I would have liked to give my niece? she mused. "After all, even though I may not be a religious fanatic, I do believe that the Lord will provide," she said openly. "He has provided for the birds of the air, the fish in the sea, the cattle on the land, and the very worm in the soil. So why should he not provide for me and his little angel?" she expounded.

Now using those words, and with such frequency, Nora seems to be getting closer to accepting Christ. And with those mirrored images in her, she had created her consolation that her feelings have been heightened. However, there was always the question that she had locked deep within her double-folded thoughts, and she reflected to the hospital. Her mind moved all the way back to the doctor's uncertainty about the infant's possible brain problem if she lives to be three years old, which promoted some unsettling moments for her. Inasmuch, she unwittingly mumbled to herself that it conveyed an unbroken spell of annoyance to the passengers closest to her.

And in her continued state of restlessness, the passengers looked at her when she snapped of her fingers, and her loud hiss and her ceaseless and inarticulate utterances. And beneath their vexed cries, they voiced several unkind lexes: 'here comes another crazy bastard,' a feeling she assumed they said. And in her state of guilt and a snap sense of her conscience, the troubled Nora felt they were saying things about her, suddenly unleashed a barrage of profanity that polluted the quiet ambiance of the clustered train.

Several dismayed eyes amid surprises had then cast upon her. And the moment she saw their facial expressions while looking down at her, she temporarily ceased her antics and angrily asked: "What is it? What the curse everybody looking at me for?" her voice and angry tone carried across to others. "All I said was schools, and that was after I got it that I have an idea how to work out my problem. So, what the curse you are all looking at me for!" she bellowed in an unkind tone, showcasing the deep furrows of her brow.

"It is because of your strange behavior," the woman in the seat beside her replied.

"After all, that's our damn eyes, and we, therefore, look at whatever we like," said one of the passengers.

Nora reconsidered her behavior and focused on working on her newly found idea for the rest of the time.

The woman in the seat in front of her twisted her neck when she heard the constant mumbling.

"What is it? Something happen?" Nora furiously asked.

"Excuse me!"

"Something wrong? I am asking you."

"Yes, and it's quite annoying."

"What's annoying bitch?" replied the rambunctious Nora.

"Your constant mumbling and restless shuffling behind me, that's what annoys me. And I should tell you that you are even bouncing on the back of my seat, which I find very disgusting, and now that I have voiced my annoyance, you are calling me a bitch. You are obnoxiously rude."

"I'm sorry big mama, but if you are so offended by my bouncing on the back of your seat, perhaps you could relieve yourself by taking another seat, or maybe you should think of riding on the back seat of your limousine, you cursing bastard."

"I will not get up to please you. And I do not need you to tell me by what means I should travel nigger."

"And I will not stop talking to myself to please you either, sucker."

"That's what happens when you are given too much privilege."

"Given too much privilege!" Nora screamed. And with her thunderous voice, she again instantly arrested the attention of the other passengers. "Given too much privilege! "What do you mean, woman? You better don't let me grab your fat curse; you bitch."

The woman then ceased her verbal attack when she realized that this growing spell of heated words was turning into something more significant. She then got up as was annoyingly directed and went to the front of the car.

"That's where you should have been in the first place," Nora said, whose flaring temper had just begun to rise above her control. "I would have ripped your cursing ass to rags if you had only continued with me," Nora growled. And she was so incensed that residue of her verbal venom was still spewing, and for many minutes after her unsettling temper was comparatively abated.

"Nora, for a moment, wanted to spring on the woman, which would have been an act of supreme courage," another passenger muttered.

"I know that the skin of my teeth would have hung me, but what the hell! Many have died before me by lynching, so what is it that would be new about my dying that way?" said the angry Nora. "There was one thing for sure, though, I have nothing to live for, just my little niece, whose life and my situation are yet to be determined without any worthwhile promise. So, what the hell would I care," the aggrieved Nora added.

The conductor walked over and spoke to her, whose utterance and gentle patting ultimately placated her, but for a short time. There were numerous evil eyes, and amongst them were some anchored nasty boiling feelings trapped behind their sealed lips as another woman also got up and walked to the front of the car. This action of the woman was what infuriated Nora even more.

The train pulled into her station; Nora got up but took another dirty crossed-eyed look at the woman before getting off.

"You bitch," she said, "Just come off the train let me rip your cursing ass to rags?"

The steam engine slowly pulled out from the station, but while standing on the platform, Nora made some unbecoming gestures at the woman; she called big mama to have her final fiercely crossed look and the raising of her middle finger.

For some thirty chains of unpaved road, Nora walked to another surviving in-law's house, to whom she gave a detailed account of her verbal tiff with the women on the train.

"You did the right thing putting her in her place. You had the guts to do it, so you did it! You did not touch her, though, did you?"

"Oh no! I did not touch the sucker, and she never dared to touch me either."

"Okay, for word is wind but blows are unkind."

"I know that. But what did I care anyhow? I would have naturally dealt her some blows if she had continued with me. I would have given it to her so bad."

"Good that you did not," said her in-law. "So, now, tell me just what's going on."

"That's what I came here to tell you."

"What's the score with her?"

"Well, there are some ifs and buts about her and if she lives."

"What's the problem?"

"She is still under that what is called the close watchful eyes care list. And I believe the doctor also said there is every possibility that if she survives her ordeal, she will occasionally exhibit some disgusting mental setback. And if she starts showing signs of autism and with autistic behavior, he must be immediately contacted."

"Autistic behavior!"

"Yes."

"Such as?"

"She may be low functional since there is some possible brain damage."

"Why brain damage?"

"I cannot talk about that right now. Let's wait for the next three months and see what the Doctor says."

"Sorry to learn of that. Unfortunately, such a thing happens to that infant."

"What can I say other than it is one of those things!"

At this instant, an apparent feeling of composure found a place in Nora, at least for the moment. Dressed in her blue taffeta skirt and white long sleeves linen blouse, Nora pivoted her body to look at the sun's position. Her move was to get the time as had been explained to her by the little old man she met at the train station.

"What happens? It seems as if it's going to rain?"

"No, not really. I don't think so."

"It was threatening earlier on, but it now seemed to be no more."

"May I have a drink of something, even water? I am a little thirsty," she asked.

Her in-law offered to her a long jug of fresco his brother Charly had made days before he passed.

"Perhaps it's too old now, and must be stale and flat."

"That's a must."

"You know, he used to do a little peddling too, such as selling at the square during the summer, but now that the temperature has changed, not many are asking for it. Then again, he is not with us anymore. God blessed his soul, and may it rest in peace."

"That's something I always like! Let me have some. You make it too, do you?"

"Oh yeah, I think I know the concoction."

"Well, get me some, will you?"

"If you can wait, I'll make some fresh ones for you. I think what I have here is too stale."

"I'll wait; more so, I came to discuss matters with you."

"Ok, I'll try and see if there is more of what he put in it to make it."

"Not offering me a seat in the meantime?"

"C'mon, Nora; you are not a stranger. You can sit anywhere."

"No, but I think it is the proper thing for you to do."

"You always have that lady-like thing about you when you are ready, eh!"

"I'm not so sure about that. I would not want you to hear me when I am in another mood. You know me well. You know I can get raw whenever I am ready, don't you?"

"You could fool me."

"Rufus, stop shooting your bullshit. You know that I don't play around."

Rufus brought a chair from inside the house and placed it at the front door. Nora, however, thought for a moment that it would be best for her to remain standing. "I want to stand and watch the children next door playing a most dangerous game… throwing things at each other, that I will not get hurt."

"Sit down," Rufus said.

"No, it's ok."

"What's the matter? You asked me to let you sit!"

"I want to ensure that nothing they play with flies over here and hits me. That would have made things worse, for I can't take any more than what I am going through now."

"You will soon get over your grief, Nora; I'm still struggling to cope with the passing of my brother myself and the way he died. Now comes the passing of your two sisters, one who is my wife, as well as your parents, who died in such a tragic fashion. Although my brother died sometime before the accident at that same damn viaduct where my wife died, don't you think I have some feelings too? Anyhow, sit. Don't let those children add anything to your misery. They will not allow anything to fly over here."

Rufus hitherto held pleasant memories of his wife, Clara. He remembered the days, although they were poor from those times when they were young people holding hands everywhere they went---spending most of their after-school hours in the Stone Mountain Park. Nora was then a little girl.

He tried to catch his sister-in-law's eyes all this time, but Nora tried avoiding them. She would only occasionally gaze at short spells that had directed into a half-full vacuum, preoccupied with her niece's condition as she was still battling for life in the hospital. Rufus finished making the fresco and handed her a mugful, frothing to the rim like a breathless racehorse. There he sat down, trying to make eyes with those of hers as many times, watching her as she gulped the fresco.

"You could now take up where your brother left off," Nora suggested. "Mm, it tastes so good."

"What do you mean?"

"This thing tastes perfect, man! Perhaps you would do well on the square like your brother did before he died."

"Thank you, that's something I must think about. Good idea."

It was Nora's first good conversation with Rufus in a mighty long time. She hadn't had one with him long before her sister died. They never seemed to get along too well because Nora has always been an artificially standoffish, cantankerous, and saucy woman from birth. In any event, death always seemed to bring families and in-laws together, and faster than any professional counselor can.

This discussion made them begin to think differently. And for the remaining time they have left on earth, they pledge to contact each other more often, and all have now been knitted and hopefully solidly patched. Nora enjoyed the little talk with Rufus, according to her. The brief conference allowed her to look at herself in another frame; the two are now looking forward to a better understanding each other.

Just before she left, Rufus could not avoid making his negative built-up feeling about her known to her. And in his ceaseless tries, he made eye-to-eye contact as he unleashed his personal opinion of her. The moment Nora heard those things, she bit her lips, gritted her teeth, and in the firmness of her character, she gazed at him steadfastly in an envelope of utter silence.

"You will always be a rambunctious woman," Rufus said. "It is only for now that you are behaving or making it appear as if you have changed since your parents, sisters, and cousin died. You gave the impression in your calmness because they died just days ago," Rufus added.

"I can only hope that you will forever change, and I think you should; it would be best for you."

"You are stretching my tongue Rufus, but don't bother. Let me start. I am a changed person but don't stir me. I beg you not to," she blurted.

Rufus gave a witting smile at her utterance that said nothing different from what he knew about her, which he already stated in his relative scale of value about her. And then he closed the chapter of his admonishment he handed her.

The evening was slowly drawing night, and a stiff and nippy wind took the place of a moderately comfortable day of sunshine that lasted up to the moment. The strength of their friendship now seems cemented. She looked to the heavens and then at her shadow. She observed it stretching to the east, which told her that it must have been after 6: O'clock and she needed to catch the 7:30 p.m. train before the thick Darkness cloaked in.

"Come, it's getting late, and I must go," she said. "You can go on with all your lip service. I refuse to pay any attention to you."

"Let me walk you to the train station."

"Oh, that's very kind of you!"

"You know it is part of my duty as a man, don't you?" said Rufus.

"You have always been the kind of gentleman I know."

"Oh, thank you." Things had progressed, however. There were few details Rufus spoke of regarding Nora's behavior that he was not altogether comfortable with. These feelings she hid in the ambit of her conscience, acknowledging that they were true. She did not feel obliged to reply, knowing that she would have been stirring up another upheaval, and there would have been no doubt about the outcome. Nora was mentally exhausted from the three days of ups and down, which added to her general deportment. One after the other, the street lights came on, then started to drizzle was the condition. The twilight descended, and slowly, it was creeping into the opaque spate of Darkness. "Let's go, Rufus before the entire place becomes too dark. And as you know, there are those crooks around the place," she said.

"Calm yourself down," replied Rufus.

"I beg you, for I am afraid of the dark and I am dead tired."

"We'll be off soon; just be patient."

Suddenly a silence… her lips automatically sealed. Several moments passed, and not hearing from her caused a cynicism like Rufus's spasmatic cough. He peeped through the window and craned his neck in the fast-seeping darkness to see what had become of her. At first, he could not believe she had left; his roamed about as his torn heart contradicted his feeling about her. It was a force that came with fright and concern because he knew too well that the path to the train station could be perilous.

Unbearably concerned, Rufus came out with a lamp, and he looked in the direction where she was standing. "She must have left," he said. "I know she is thinking greatly about her niece and future. I am sure she could not have been standing in the rain all this time!"

Rufus finally got out of the house with an open torch that blew out as he exited the door. "Where are you?" he queried. His query aroused his curiosity when he received no answer. The barn door to the horse stable was wide opened; Rufus spent a few moments there thinking if whether Nora got vexed and so vexed that she challenged the condition alone on the dangerous path to the train station, as his calling yielded no answer.

Speaking in the same spirit as his heart, Rufus went back inside the house and, this time, brought out his lit shade lamp, which guided him through the path inside the stable. Unfortunately, there was no Nora. Her whereabouts were still unknown. "Where the hell this woman went?" Fergus queried, and the sudden trembling of his voice said enough. He was as nervous as a mouse and had shown all the anxiety and distress no one would imagine. And for another time in his determination, he went around the house, and to the rear he found Nora standing---gazing in the open sphere. "What are you doing here?" he asked,

"Sheltering from the rain until you finished powdering your damn face."

"Nora, Nora, Nora, you'll never change. What you just said was not necessary."

"What else should I have said after it took so long for you to come out of the damn house. You are worse than a cussed woman!"

"All that was not necessary."

"Are you going to walk me to the train station or not?"

Rufus knew perfectly well that a storm was coming but did not care. He had a good excuse for her to spend the night. The same idea had occurred to both of them, but Nora kept hers under her bushel of problems. "Frankly, if it hadn't been for those thugs on the street, I would have been gone."

Chapter Six

NORA FURTHER RUMINATED

In her younger days, she usually pinched the buds of wild berries at the side of the road as she walked and still does so occasionally whenever she walks alone. At this hour, the darkness had already cloaked her path and the berries along the way. Nothing to say to Rufus and no berries or buds to pinch; she reflected on her days as a young girl. "It bled my heart when I remember those days, but what can I do now? Nothing. To think of such dark and cruel days when life was like nothing when the life of anybody with dark skin meant nothing. You could see the bodies of men, women, and children hanging about the place like carcasses in a meat market," she lamented.

"It is not a good thing to be laboring on Nora; those things stir bitterness, which is not of good taste to the tongue or lips."

"I know that, but it is the truth, and the truth floats like oil on top of the water."

It was still hard for them to keep their eyes steadfast on each other for a long time. At the moment, her heartfelt feelings promoted by her fading memory all seemed to be wrenching their guts except for those moments she spent under the cantilever. There were still some feelings of apprehension resting equally between them.

They frequently annoyed each other with most of their views that came up in their discussion, but Nora's talking over Fergus breeds all the annoyances. It was not until the coming of the train, and after she boarded and turned around, that they made, if any, direct eye-to-eye contact and at which time she waved her fingers, twisting them in the air-indicating bye as the train pulled out in the powdery mist, smoke, and fog. The long grudge between them appeared to have been banished, and the goodwill of their minds and character stands to prevail over all future misunderstandings.

Nora left, and within herself came the assurance that from now on, she would be a much less cantankerous person, and she asked the Lord in her jiffy silent prayer to guide her through all the perils of her life. This was after looking back at how close she had come to her death some days before. She hinted that it could have been a sign for her to break up her folly ground. In any case, for her character, which is innate, it would need a whole lot more than hardship and prayer to transform her.

"Your cussed sassy lips and your rowdy behavior must first be changed," Rufus had warned her, she recalled, and "hoped that I will soon get over my stupidity," she recited, with a smirk that came upon her face.

With not many friends around and just a few remaining in-laws, she considered moving out of Promise Land to some other place where in her feeling, she would be more easily transformed among strangers. She acknowledged that her errant personal attitude was not right, especially among members of her in-laws. And more so, now that every member of her family died, leaving alone her niece, who is with no assurance that she will make it in life, made her more troubled. Nora needs to take another look at herself and make peace with them. They all said that her limited learning caused her behavior. But the tragic passing of her family should make her take the first examination of herself; perhaps it is something that she would not have thought of before, and sadly, it took such an unfortunate thing as a tragedy and of such for her to become aware of her behavior. I hope that she will learn and change for good, Rufus mused while returning.

The trip she made to Rufus's house was just about the second since her sister had married him a little over five years before her tragic death.

"She was really out of hand. She is one terrible cantankerous and conniving soul."

People now begin to wonder if she will ever be able to care for that little infant if it lives. Some even said, "she is only creating excitement to fool those who do not know the type of person she is."

As time passed, she heard the rumor that people were saying nasty things about her, which infuriated her. When she first heard it, everything went smoothly right in front of her brother–in–law's eyes. She kept it in her head until she again heard it from dead strangers before she exploded and raised draws.

"Whatever they want to say, they can say, but I hope they will never say anything in front of me and let me hear," she said. She huffed and puffed with blared with herself. "That's the main reason I want to leave this damn place," she said as the train raced along the chattering track.

Her guilt-ridden conscience had prepped her to think about her future, which is her responsibility, and it is only she who knows where in life she wants to go. And it did not take long before it appeared that she had taken on another view of life. Then what seemed to have happened began to show significant differences since the passing of her parents. In any event, along with all the changes she may have made, her ideology about man and religion, she would have to be more cognoscente of the fact that she must be a completely changed person, and she must start thinking of getting closer to God and a companion and settling down. In addition, she must begin to think wisely, dream, and plan for her tomorrow. Nonetheless, with that unsettled mind that had her confused with her naughty behavior, she had enforced her estranged relationship with her late mother's religious belief, which has made it a pretty further hefty task for her to change entirely. She knew well enough that it would have been imperative for her to make all the adjustments she could.

Therefore, her keenly sought idea should stir logically that she must agree with all the fine-tuning she must make to change her situation. And she would want to do it as soon as possible, knowing that the core of her problem lies within her indecisiveness and her disagreeable disposition. With all the apprehension, come what may, the only thing she was sure about was, she did not flout her voluntarily adopted responsibility to take care of her little autistic niece and her determination to help her throughout her lifetime.

With all that, Nora remained confused. So, let's now watch and wait until, and if and when she gets or takes the infant, what will she do, and how well will she stick to her promise to change in life? It is a must for her to keep the child if it lives.

She was accustomed to enjoying life's freedom when she was no longer forced to work on the farm with her late father. And she remembered, as his last daughter, the special attention her dad would some time pay her. She even remembered that, although they could not get along, her mother always referred her to people as her "wash belly" (my last child) in almost all her discussions. What her problem now is, she does not have the level of tolerance and the sense of value her late mother and father had. And most certainly, she was not blessed with the same gift of taking everything with a smile as they did. And even though she can express her thoughts, she does so with utmost irritability. That is why she believes nobody likes her and grumbles silently about this, all within the boundaries of her inner feelings. In the end, all eyes will be waiting to see the outcome of her niece and the foundation she hopes to set in keeping the promises she made to herself.

Time passed; the train roared at 9:30 pm at the cock picks station. She disembarked on a platform that was naked of any prospective riders or company, leaving her the usually long and lonely walk along the rough dark track to her hovel. As she strode along, she heard the plaintive barking of dogs in the yonder and the footsteps that got closer to her by the minute. Her curiosity then rose. She stopped and braced herself against a fence post, making way for whatever the bearer of the footsteps was. They became silent the moment they got closer to her. And with her overpowering fear, she began breathing with difficulty; she then took a deep breath and recited the 23rd psalms, her late mother's favorite scripture passage.

"I wonder what on earth this is?" she said fearfully. "Daddy, if it is you, please reveal yourself. And if it is a vagabond, I am appealing to you that you think wisely, for I am a poor single woman who just lost my parents. And I'm with all the distress in the world that you may think of. I have nothing you will get from me but my life, and what would it profit you?"

Suddenly there was utter silence; only her racing and heavy pounding heart could be heard. All plaintive barking of the dogs had ceased after those frightening moments; the footsteps were again heard in the distance---leaving in their wake the stale odor of perspiration and the familiar aroma of burning cigars. She wondered if it could be the spirit of her dead father!

"That's not strange, for three days have passed since his death, so his spirit must have been raised by this. What was the most astonishing, though, was that same smelly perspiration that allowed me to harbor the feeling and that strong belief that it was he. But what was puzzling was that tobacco aroma I could not understand. It was never his custom to smoke that type of tobacco, at least not for the years I knew him as a father. I remember him smoking shag in his white curved pipe, but it never smelled like that."

Several nervous minutes elapsed, her nerve half calmed now that the footsteps had silent and the smell had vanished. She resumed her strides along her narrow path of the still daughter of Darkness with the added company of a thick column of a dark threatening rain cloud. She could only harbor the strong feeling that it was the spirit of her deceased father in the company of someone else, but who! she could not tell.

"I am glad he is taking care of me anyhow, even in death."

Although it was not a most welcome feeling at first, she now drowned the fear and employed an attitude: "what the hell, he was here to protect me," she said consolingly.

Moments went by, and much of the distance had then erased. She was now near reaching the hovel when suddenly a strange hand laid its weight upon her right shoulder. She tried to scream, but the hand found itself across her mouth. And in her fright, with quick thinking, she sunk her teeth deep into the flesh of whoever. There were no scream or groan to the imagined pain it should have caused in the pitch darkness, but the tension eased, and the intruder scampered in the dark, it would appear.

She soon came to Nora's consciousness that it must be a natural person. So, guided by her memory, she scrambled in the dark of the rugged path until she came upon the old maple tree under which, as a young girl, she had hanged out with her first date. Nora knew too well that it would have been unwise for her to go right away to her hovel since no one would have been there, and it would not have been one of the wisest things to do for various reasons. Instead, she hid between the two massive half-sunken tubers that left an opening to the elements in which she temporarily rooted herself the night. She could only briefly hold her breath to muffle the pounding of her frightened heart. And in the state of her brief self-imposed imprisonment, several things came into her thoughts.

It could have been that damn stupid boy Nelson, who has been messing around me for years, and now he heard that my parents are dead; he believes that it is now the time to get me, Nora surmised, "but not in the dark! He is more than a damn jackass," she added. "Anyway, I'll know tomorrow if it was that brute, that damn brainless jackass. I'm sure I'll see him with some bandage or something on his hand. And if it turned out that it was that son of a dragon, I'll have him suffer for it."

Not quite sure what to do next, Nora tried to make herself as comfortable as she could between the two massive exposed tubers and with her hope that someone of good character and some form of light would come along. Otherwise, she would be forced to be content with staying there for the next six hours until the sum entirely broke from behind the morning clouds.

And while there, in her wishes, she looked forward to seeing somebody of her gender and with whom she would feel more comfortable. And as she pondered, she heard another sound of lighter footsteps stamping against the gravel. Her eyes rolled in the pitch Darkness of a night filled with frightening spells and troubling tight spots, but after realizing her trepidation, she thought of turning her soul to God.

"I hate any man who throws himself upon a woman, whether in the dark or even at day time," she muttered contemptuously under her self-restricted breath. With so much happening around her, she was as tormented and restless as an ocean in turmoil.

"What is this again?" she shouted, "these steps are light enough to think that it's a female as I have wished," she said. Her fear again stirred. "And it could have been that son of a dragon that came up beside me earlier, but he did not have the guts to do what he had intended. Undoubtedly, he did not dare to tell me directly that it was him. And then me with my stupid self, thinking that it was my father, I allowed him to get away with it," she said in her grumble.

Fatigue from the previous days of ups and down, she could not wait long enough before she unwittingly dozed away until the coming morning hours, when the sun would break through with its frightening beam that should brighten her path. She shuffled herself, intermingling with the trash and dry leaves and, in her restless paused, assurance as the night slowly dwindled.

Chapter Seven

AS THE MORNING BROKE

Several nervous hours came and went with the passing of a densely opaque, darkened night. With Nora's unfailing anxiety and high expectation, the night slowly transformed into a morning that came with the expected bright casting beams of the blazingly red sun. Observers of nature must have scrutinized for themselves the heavens as the Darkness that had cheatingly stood over the element slowly disappeared. And soon, the sunbeams begin to peer in more between the trembling leaves of the high-reaching evergreen. The nightingales and their singing with the swallows had long begun chirping among the willows that had awakened her. And when she heard those sounds, she looked her situation over and how blessed she was and mused over what could have happened to her.

"Thanks to mercy of God, the night, after all, was not that cold. And it was a good thing. It was chilly yes, but I exercised my will to conquer all evil that came upon me and those who would have liked to do whatever," Nora said "And I'd made sure that I blocked off any disturbing sound that would have disrupted any of the little comforts I later found. I was tired," she expounded. "Thank heaven, here I am. I have lived the night through to see the dawn of this, another troubling day, and with the breaking of dawn, the sunbeam fiercely piercing its way through the morning clouds before me," she said with all the glee in her trembling voice. The beaming sunlight showed her hair dampened from the overnight dew, and with the dust off the unpaved track the day before, she presented herself to the open element. And with her badly crushed and soiled dress, it made her innocently depicted the appearance of a derelict. Frustrated and tired, she disgustingly looked at herself for another time and then shook her shoulders, and using the back of her palms, she gingerly brushed herself off before showing any signs of thankfulness that her life had been spared to see the breaking of another dawn.

"What the hell," she said and hissed; a streak of silence followed as she pondered her next step as she walks along. She then wet her palms on the top of the half-dried vegetation that collected the overnight dew and passed them across her face--- removing deposits of overnight residue from the corners of her mouth.

"I always hear my grandparents say that it is good for your eyesight," she said as she dried the remainder of the wetness off with the hem of her dress, continues walking in the cool of the morning hoping to complete her journey with the bright glare of the sun bearing down around her.

It was still over a mile to Promise Land. With this knowledge and the presence of the rising sun, it lifted her courage that it even rose above the horizon. She was now expecting to hear something positive about her niece, for she was contemplating if she should go home and rest or refresh herself right away before heading back to the hospital.

Instead, as if to heal her bleeding heart, she stopped and straightaway took a look at the ravaged viaduct as she pondered her next step before entering her hovel. Still, one other level of concern needed to be dealt with. She must let the Cordovans, for whom she works, doing days- work; cleaning, dusting, and walking their dogs, but does not know when she will return.

Running out of money had now become another matter of her concern; her financial reservoir for years continued to suffer from severe drought. She needed money to buy things such as milk and all the nutrients for the child, and also need warm clothes and diapers for the infant if and when she is discharged from the hospital. And after she is released, she will need money to take the next train to and from for regular follow-ups. With these in mind, Nora's only knight in shining armor is to hear doctor Patrice say the infant is not ready to be sent home. More so, preparation must be made for the coming home of the child at whatever time.

"To think of it, though, what would I do if I'm told I can take her home?" Nora questioned herself. Her question then fell into the sphere of the silent void and took the upper shaft until she found her consolation.

"After all, I think it would have been best for me to go and secure the little pittance I was earning before going back to the hospital."

With her mind now ticking like a clock, she trumped up several ideas: "In real sense, it would have been a much better idea, I think," she said, making her decision at the instant. And minutes before refreshing herself, she hauled off the soiled dress, and hauled on an old half-pressed polka dot dress she reached from behind her late mother's bedroom door. She then took another glance in the mirror pasted on the wall at her hair before heading out to another troubling day ahead of her. And in the ebb and flow of her thoughts, a new idea came to her mind before the next step was made. Then with the fast dwindling of cash left in her position, she ransacked her late mother's bureau drawers for whatever little change she thought she would find. She did not remember that she had before scraped out whatever change she had in it for their funeral. Her alternative, then, was, considering her plight, to walk the couple miles to her employers' mansion to see what assistance they may give her. She followed her sense and abided by her thoughts.

"The one dollar and seventy-one cents I have on me can only take me to the hospital and bring me back. I did not even check if those people had brought anything for her the evening; they came to the little pre-welcome gathering that later ended so tragically," she said. "I have not seen such; neither have I heard of such. Food for me is the least. I know that if my employers continue to use me, I can get a little something there to eat. I do not know for the child because they are too narrow-minded and insensitive to the need of the poor."

It is a pathetic situation for any middle age woman without a husband to find herself in. With no immediate relief or promise in sight, there is every possibility that things will get worse later on, for a with no gainful employment and an attitude that can cause an angel to shed its wings, it was something to think about. She is very rambunctious and could make life extremely difficult for herself. And as a woman with all those negative dispositions, it would be better if she took another look at herself and promised to change before things could change for her.

"These people are very funny, some of them are nice, but some I cannot understand. My only hope now is, will Mrs. Cordovan understand my situation that I have no phone, and that is why I could not get in touch with her and did not employ someone else. For it is now what, four weeks since I was not able to communicate with her or go and clean her mansion and walk her dogs."

As Nora contemplated what to do, there was a threat of a severe storm forming. And for her to catch her employers' home before they go away, she must hurry. She must be there by noon to see them before they leave for their regular bridge tournament.

"After all, it's no use standing here contemplating and fretting myself about the rain and talking about these people. They usually leave their home at midday, so let me get going, for I need to be back home before it gets too late and dark. And to think about it, perhaps I may get something from them; who knows? Even a small token I'd accept. They are very mean, near, and stingy, but I would be happy with whatever little they might give me. And on top of that, I will never want to experience such a miserable night again like what I had experienced before, and certainly not what I'd experienced just last night," she said.

And while in her haste to get there, she employed her spurred superstition and spun a coin she tossed in the air with the hope of its help in her decision-making. Nature which seems to have listened to her agonizing and dire situation temporarily abated the threat of what appeared to be a severe storm. Not comfortable with her hair, she quickly turned back and tucked her late mother's church hat that serve dual purposes on her head. It shields slight drizzle off her head and masked her sore-eyed uncombed salt and pepper hair. "On the other hand, the information I gathered said that they don't keep workers very long; they change them as often as they change their clothes. In any case, I am forcing the issue to prove for myself all those disgusting things I heard about them, things I have never witnessed. One should not listen to too much gossip."

Then based on the strength of her feelings and her pathetic situation, she forced the issue and took to the road. She completed the two ¾ miles and got there just on time, minutes when she got there to see just then--- a lone black girl clothed in a blue dress and white apron with white frill-edges cap, walking away from the lawn with a tray with two empty glasses and a goblet. Nora walked up to the coach and, without hesitation, alerted her misses that she was back.

"I am back, Mrs. Cordovan," she said half gleefully, a half-crack smile locked in the shell of her troubled mind. At the moment, she had no idea if Mrs. Cordovan would even listen to her or entertain seeing her, but propelled by the gravity of her situation, she mustered the courage to state her case.

"I am sorry, Nora, we must leave now, we are running late. I cannot talk with you now. I think you should come back early tomorrow morning for us to talk about you continuing to work for us again, for I am not so sure if I any longer need your service."

"You mean ma'am…!"

"I cannot talk with you know I said. Come back tomorrow morning."

Minutes went by, and before the coach could move a trifle, Mrs. Cordovan and her husband had a brief heated discussion; her husband yanked the horse rein; the coach rolled off but halted six feet away when he suddenly pulled on the harness, the horse halted. "Come here, Nora," he said.

With just twelve looping strides, Nora was at the coach's side.

"Yes, sir?"

"My wife and I have conferred on the matter, and we have arrived at the conclusion that you should go and stay with those girls and see what is there to be done until we get back."

"Thank you, sir."

In her state of semi-glee, Nora went to the mansion's front door, but what meted out to her upon entering was more than alarming. She was greeted with much indignation by the two maids who were new to her. They must have felt threatened by her presence, which led to a few unforgettable verbal tussles. And it was to the extreme that Nora had to resign herself to the idea that she should do nothing until Mrs. Cordovan returned. In any event, she first contemplated whether she should go back home or hangs around, even though whatever she does, apart from carrying out her order, could be construed by Mrs. Cordovan as an act of disobedience and could well be penalized.

Caught up in a state of quandary, she tried to explain herself to the girls, but their interest to talk with her was never present, and their ears offered no yield. Their attitude was quite different and overbearing. "I'm very concerned that maybe if I stay here, with their attitude towards me, they could well plot something against me, a lie that Mrs. Cordovan would well believe. In fact, think I know her well enough. She always has that passion for listening to news and tale."

Alternatively, she strolls to the edge of the sprawling lake behind the mansion, where she watched the sparrows and gulls frolicking in the air, while the vast spread and well-manicured landscape encircled the mansion on the steep mound of Lithonia. With that, Nora pondered, and pondered, and even thought of going in and manhandling them. In her though, there rose some sense of her consciousness, her thinking that spoke harshly with the other inner spirit that led the path to the rebuking of herself; she was advised that she should control herself and abandon such thought.

"I do not know how long can I stand here watching these cussed birds frolicking in the air and the little terrapins crawling aimlessly about the place? I am getting hungry and all that. Maybe I should even brave the unpleasantness and ask one of those brutes for something to eat, but at the same time, they may well poison me; who knows? After all, I should go home and come back. Then again, to think of it, would the latter part of my thinking make any sense? What I do know, though, is that the two of them together could not consider matching with me if I really get raw. So, you know something, I think I better go home or to the hospital to see my sick niece," she said.

She then took to the road after leaving a note at the top of the banister for Mrs. Cordovan, just in case. And in her haste, she trotted along using all the available short passes.

There had not been any abatement of the rain that had long threatened. And with baseball size hailstones joining, the pelting rain falling in droves and out-of-the-ordinary chill whistling with the wind had made the task more difficult for her.

Minutes went by, and in a burst of extra courage and strength after she had stepped inside to catch her breath, she returned; her courage grew, as it was this cleaning job that she rested her hope that one day she would be lifting herself out of her pit of penury. And if the child dies, it would be only in the morning before she will know. She was left in a state of quandary and shattered hope.

Chapter Eight

NORA IN HER SEARCH FOR CHANGE

The only change that marked a difference in Nora's life is that she came from this other community, where she searched for a better life, such as a man whom she can depend on financially, and help deal with her autistic niece. Anyhow, up that side of the hill is where the battery-powered radios continued to blast under the grumbling tone of bass with their antenna running alongside the outside walls of the houses. And there are no laundries on the clotheslines that continue to flap fiercely on any lines as they are teased by even the gentlest of wind. And there were the usual number of black maids in their bibs and caps peering through the windows from inside the mansions, but who will not venture outside through the front door, and not even to pick up the newspaper. They know their places. And not even the chief chef or the apprentice pastry chef dared to make such mistakes to show their willingness. All the -in-house workers were forbidden from going to the front according to the dictate of a system, custom, and practice of their masters and mistresses. There they walk through the back gate where the needs be in either going and coming. Taking quick glimpse through the windows and the door from outside, shows the glossy appearance of the hardwood floor, and hear the constant howling of the giant dogs of crossed breed Ridgebacks to elephant size like Great Danes. And when they bark, one must be prepared to yell or speak at the top of his lungs if he wants to talk with anyone inside. And it made no difference when it comes to the adjacent mansions except for the different breeds of dogs, from Ridgeback Labrador to Golden Retriever. This should be enough to tell Nora that up there, she would not find the husband she is looking for.

She could only picture herself relaxing in any of these homes in a regal lifestyle according to and resulting from promises she made to herself in her wishes. She only later found that her wishes and imagination went like a butter bar in the blazing sun.

And while now looking in retrospect, she got to her hovel minutes after 3: O'clock the afternoon to an arousing sound of panic. She was bending over in front of her bed when came a sound. She also acknowledges that she was not quite the woman she would have liked to be, and admitted that she was vexed, and vexed with herself to the point that she was blowing enough steam that would have been more than enough to propel any overladen freight train. "I am a rambunctious person yes," she said, "but why do I have to be suffering like this?" she added.

'I will not live this way any longer." Those were her words, words, that she need to explain. "Perhaps my good thinking left me with all the pending responsibilities of caring for that little child, knowing that I have no source of a substantial income."

With her now speaking in a calm and collective voice, her demeanor changed but a little; she is now in a different frame of mind. She has drawn into her shell now, at least, with penitence written on her face; she lowered her head in remorse. "I do not know what came over me. I am sorry. I am very sorry," she apologized profusely, but to whom, only she can tell.

Thoughts are now being gathered on the next step that she should take. "Should I go back to the hospital to learn more about my little autistic niece, or should I go home or abandon her?" She then slothfully threw her little brown handbag over her shoulder, and fretfully she headed to the train station.

It was not unusual for the temperature to be so miserable this time of the year, changing every now and then from chilly to extreme cold and often freezing before daybreak. Some people had their hands in their pockets, some in gloves and their ear muffs on as they shivered in the soft southerly drifting breeze. And on top of that, there was that threat of rain lingering in the low-hanging black clouds.

In the meantime, what seemed to be an endless and risky situation, had caused Nora to ponder all along the way. She thought about many things as she pounded the turf to the train station. Long before this time, while she was at home, in her thoughts she had yet to show any true promise of transforming herself. It was only now that she realized that something is wrong. With that, she said, "Most naturally, it's not good, but what can I say! There is nothing I can do about it," as she entered the hospital. At this point, she took a gloomier view of the situation. And it was only at that stage that she said to herself, "I should not be blamed for anything I may do that is wrong when considering my plight with my niece and my financial situation, the compensation to a child being the product of abused paupers."

She did not think that her overly aggressive approach could have well set the stage for a protracted problem. She approached the reception desk and asked for doctor Patrice, and in an unbecoming manner. As a result, the receptionist hesitated to let her in or the doctor know she was there. And even though while she waited, her negative thoughts and her behavior continued to mount. "It is my strongest belief that the bait was set," she said as she fumed.

"What an attitude!" said the receptionist. "I noticed that her approach was guttery from the moment she walked in, so I was cautious after listening with every keen sense of understanding some of the things she said and the way she said them. Some I had treated like water under the bridge and some as a fast-passing squall."

Money now got even more scarce, so Nora started to think of selling her father's hovel to help raise the child, but in her moral consciousness, she said: “Who the hell on earth would want that curing old house to buy though?” And amid her discerning that the child’s doctor never came, she invited herself to the unit to look at her even though still boiling in anger.

There she saw the child sitting in the corner of the bed; and the fighting ill child was raised a little between two down pillows. She has been Nora’s chief concern for a long time. At seven months old and still in the hospital and unable to sit upright on her own, had given umpteenth causes for Nora’s concern. Left with no alternative, she took her with the promise of the social services assistant, but she went home the evening and placed the child in an improvised bassinet. And in the middle of her thoughts, she drifted off into slumber with the lamp still burning on the side table, its flame leaning away with the wind.

The same night she dreamt of seeing her mother and another woman who told her that she should be careful of the things she does or speaks about. “You should think before you leap,” the dream hinted. And as early as she got up in the morning, her first remark was, “the woman looks like my mother waving her hands but said nothing more.”

x It was only then that Nora got the message that it was either one of her dead sisters or that it could well be even her deceased mother warning her about her behavior. In any case, the result of the dream had only become visible in the years following.

The dream was her first warning and to which she took no heed. And she would not as much as be thinking of the possibility of something of an unpleasant nature that could be in the making.

“I have got more important things to think about than a dream, which in my opinion, was just a reflection of the day’s residue,” she grumbled. “Why should they dream me to tell me any negative things about their very own?” she queried, but her query found no satisfactory answer.

Several nights later, she had almost a similar dream; a man sitting at the barn gate dressed in flowing black, his hands resting against the wood gate. And with a look of penitence, he gazed at her as if to say young woman be careful; you must think before you act. She then jumped out of her slumber but waited until the following morning when she once more shared her dream with herself, and again treated it with triviality.

These dreams had her more wanted to find a way instead of hurting the child. "But again, to me, it seemed so stupid. What so important about the dreams that I should share with it anyone since I am not at the least worried!" she said, with an hear of indignance in her voice. "And more so, two nights now almost in succession, to dream about these people is something to think about; who are they and what for? "I want to put her out of my life and end my stress," she said. And I am not afraid to die, when you are dead you will stay dead, and for a mighty long, long time too, which will be good for me," she added. "I will not surrender under any circumstances. For what's the point of being a human if you easily surrender to those things?" she muttered. "They have already been dead---they have no life and therefore cannot do me any harm or bring me any message for me to obey. And the fact that I know that my mother was quite a religious person, she would not think of hurting me. And if she would do that, it would mean that she could not have been sinless at the time of her death," Nora said in the affirmation of her annoyance.

She remembered that she got up the night and had a light supper after feeding her sick niece, then they went back to bed. She ran into another state of torment after that, feeling as though the sheet was being pulled off the bed, but by the binding of her faith, she first declared herself the conqueror and pledged to sleep the night through regardless.

In any event, as the long tormenting hours of the night slowly rolled away, it was with a mixture of opaque

Darkness at times and that fading glow of the silvery moon playing its part in the atmosphere. And in those fading hours, it happened this time in reality. The white cotton sheet was pulled to the foot of the bed. And as expected, it got darker with the absence of the moon that slowly drifted behind the forming night clouds. When Nora finally awoke to check the fact, she felt her head as if it was swollen; her sweating was profuse. "Who is it?" she screamed.

"Me," whispered a faint voice in the shadowing Darkness in the wee hour of the night. So tormented, she could not get over the fact that she now got the autistic child home. "Home sweet home, you are home, my dear niece!" she said. It, however, seemed to her that the doctor had assured her that the child was well enough to be home apart from her being autistic. So, Nora got up to prepare another feed for the child and went back to bed. And in her slumber, she had yet another dream, as if she heard her bedroom door flung open. She screamed a scream that would have awakened an Arawak Zeami. And in the dream, there was a conversation she had with her mother, whom she asked: "What are you doing here and doing this to me?"

"I just came back to fetch my granddaughter."

"To fetch your granddaughter!"

"Yes, to fetch my grandchild. "What's that over there?"

"That's my niece, Amble."

"So, you got her out of the hospital!"

"If only I could stop thinking about what would become of us if…."

The child's voice was then heard---it was crying and yearning for love and a little tenderness. And all that she had to do was touch the child, who in her state of Darkness would have straight away felt the warmth and quieted down. Nora was too caught up in her dream and fretting over her situation

Chapter Nine

ANOTHER DREADED NIGHT

For the first time in just over two and a half years, while asleep, Nora declared that she heard sounds and voices echoing from outside through the window. She got up and went over to the window. "Who is it?" she asked. The dead silence made her admit: "Okay, maybe it's me. Perhaps I am hearing voices or thinking or dreaming too much about these people," she growled.

The voices faded, and a spate of utter silence recommenced. She returned to her bed, her eyes surveying the decrepit ceiling. She stressfully weathering the storm of her unsettled mind that filtered into her dreams. And in her restless poise, she wondered if it is a sound or good idea for her to continue thinking about killing the child. She, however, demonstrated a most graceful and elegant bearing with a let me see attitude.

"How, could anybody with any feelings for another, and with a clean conscience, do that to another person like all those promises I had made to myself?" Nora bemoaned. "In any case, after all, I think it would be best and much wiser if I wait and see what happens after this night before I carry out what is in in my mind," she said. "Or! I should try and sleep without dreaming or thinking about this child. I will not pretend, though, that I do not love her all that much; it was because of all the promises I had made. Therefore, I should not have been this worried about her. I have been trying to sleep, but I am either dreaming or talking with myself instead."

Another morning came, and a day that went almost in a swish then cometh another mother Night that perhaps gave Nora plenty of reasons for her to be of concerned. Her unblinking eyes remained unclosed, while her thoughts wondering about with grievous thinking, as deep in her were her wishes that things were otherwise. And these things she said chiefly after considering all of her misfortunes; and pulling her blanket over her face mainly was for her to fall asleep.

Nora, as customary, is a brawling woman. As a result, she found it hard to adapt to change. And by that, she would occasionally slip into her antagonistic and cantankerous behavior even with herself. "I am well aware that it is going to be quite a task for me, but let me see what can become of me if I try to tolerate this child any longer," she said.

Chapter Ten

NORA AND HER AUTISTIC NIECE

On what should have been a relaxing day, Nora casually walked in the hospital with her niece neatly wrapped in her arm in the comfort of her warm heart. In any event, she was at the same time pregnant with the idea that she may be forced to get rid of her one way or another as circumstances dictate. In her vision, there is no sign of help coming from anywhere. And according to her, she must go to Buffalo and make some changes. And driven by impulse, she severely chalked out a way to get rid of her autistic niece, for she had no intention or preparedness to cope any longer with her. With that in her troubled mind, she went onto the pediatric unit to swap her autistic niece for another child she felt was healthier and then hastened through the door. Failing that, she would be left with no alternative but to remain in Promise Land, taking care of her for life. And in her state of confusion and ambivalence, she thought of another way to rid herself of the problem by abandonment. Nora was fed up and angry about her situation, and in her anger, she began shaking and fretting if she would be without a man for the rest of her life. "What is going to happen?" she queried herself. She had thought about those things before, but through her doubts and troubled mind, she kept them under her pair of sealed lips. It was in the case of financial help that caused her to change her views about man, even though it was the assistance of a man that enabled her to get the child out of the hospital and then he disappeared.

It did not take her long before she named the child Amble. And once she did that, she remembered that her late sister Clara, had told her about the guy she was dating, name Lesley Lee. As a result, she registered and christened the child as Amble Lee. "Actually, I had initially thought of nicknaming her Calamity, but thought it over as it would have been too touching a reminder of the gruesome incident."

Nora recalled before walking through the door, that doctor Patrice reminded her that she must be aware of the child's form of illness before he said goodbye, and hand her two prescriptions, with a note for follow-ups. What happened next was over a three-year and six months period when it will determine if her threat to kill the child or abandoned her niece was carried out.

At the moment, she was still burning inside with anger, and to the extent that she had even contemplated leaving the child either in the lobby or a toilet before she got out of the restroom. In any case, at the instant of her barbaric thoughts, the goodwill of her heart rebuked her, and she changed her mind, at least for now.

Her feeling of pity prevented her from doing what her mind was telling her, so she adapted that part of her upbringing and abided thereto. She knew that regardless of the child's behavior, she firmly believed that she was a human being, and since so, there ought to be room in her that would one day change. Therefore, she had only side-looked, shook her head, pitifully swallowed her saliva by the second, and shook her head, again grounding her teeth in utter contempt. So, who knows what next.

Chapter Eleven

AMBER LEE ENTERS PUBERTY

It was a few years later, three and a half to be precise, a cold November morning; with a couple patches of dark weighed-downtown clouds moving slothfully across the azury. And as the time and years changed with the varying temperature, so did Amble Lee. In any event, as the element had promised there weren't any signs of early abatement of the threats of drenching showers, neither did Nora's intent. And it did not take long before the raindrops began pounding on the already changing colors of the sprawling grassland.

There was some early sprouting of buds from the swaying limbs above the half-scorched vegetation, even the worms were restless in their natural habitat. And there was that lingering chill that disrupted the promise of any early comfort.

It did not prevent the troubled Nora from giving her usual attention to her autistic niece, who start to show signs of growth and body development. Occasionally, she would make weak groans as if in pain and even, at times, utter words with more audibility. With this discovery, she had made it a little more comfortable for her aunt Nora who at one stage praised the idea of being in Buffalo. Amble Lee, would, anyhow, lapse into murmuring at times about her mere presence there.

This then posed another moment of disgust in Nora, and in her wavering thoughts, it so often provoked her inner mind whether she should kill the child. This is a decision she must make before it becomes too late. She woke up one morning, and the first thing she did, as if she slept with it on her mind, handed to her niece a unique piece of driftwood which was very strange, and strange because it had three colors: red, white, and silver. She thought it would be good for her as it serves three purposes, a perfect gift for her sweet 16th birthday. She also felt that since Amble Lee was having a visual problem and was now ambulating independently, she could use it to assist her in getting around, as she recalled being told by doctor Patrice that if her niece lived to walk, she would need a guide, considering that the daunting Darkness would constantly impede her sight. Amble Lee, however, dodged her focus from her gift by pushing her thoughts to greater heights. She imagined herself growing to be a woman and attempted to hasten her wishes when came some unexpected happenings. It was just another breath of her far-fetched thinking and desires that were less likely to come to maturity. With her unsteady gait and posture, she tossed her head from side to side, she rocked forward and backward in her stationary position until all broke from beneath her feet.

Life has been a challenge for Amble Lee from birth---living in Darkness from her inception until this early stage of her youthful days. She is a natural victim of unfortunate circumstances that will forever mar her life. First, she was squeezed from her mother's womb in the tragedy in Promised Land, where the mounds are still standing proud. And in the background, those patches of bare soil still stand with billions of grinning residuals of sandstone glistening in the red clay with the sunlight, not very far from the tragic sight.

The unfortunate infant has since been left to the care of her sole surviving aunt, Nora, who took upon herself the task of caring for her and secretly promised herself to toil for her all through her living years. And from that time on, her aunt has always been willing to treat her with love and tender care. It was not until at age three that she first witnessed what doctor Patrice told her. She is the first to realize that the child was not only autistic as the doctor told her, she discovered that apart from the child's mental condition, the child is also visually impaired. At that time, in Nora's tormented life, she wanted to rid herself of her either by swapping or carrying out the barbaric act of murder, or the brutal, inhumane act such as abandonment. She remembered that the doctor hinted to her the possibility, but at the time, she had no idea of the gravity of the child's illness. It was only later in the child's life that she noticed her sudden strange behavior, which she considered weird for a child her age. Nora also saw that the child would want to sit outside, chiefly in the Darkness by herself, and even in the coldest of times. And during those times, she would climb on top of the table, window sill and other places as well, and hide beneath her bed whenever the light came on.

Although not knowing how to differentiate between night and day, the child in her little wits with all the gifts of imaging things, would display some signs of preference for the ambiance-Darkness and mostly when it is in its ultra-opaque state. This behavior has caused her aunt to wonder how she knows it and how she knows the difference between the density of the Darkness, and even when it is in its translucent state. She shows more interest in the Darkness, which she cannot see apart from that which impedes her sight. And while there, she would rock to and from and occasionally bang her head on walls. It is here that her aunt could only imagine a few things, that in her personal view, Amble Lee's behavior is through the forces of her imagination and the unbelievable dedication she formed in her mind along with her bonded relationship with the Darkness, which no one to date has been able to separate.

"She is indeed a strange child," Nora concluded.

It's only now that it sinks in her, Nora, that she reconsiders what the doctor had told her. In remembering that, she figured the possibility will always be there that as the child grows, she will start showing some unfortunate mental bends. And this form of her illness was only realized when she claimed to be seeing things in her behavior and became an ultra-curious observer of Nature behind her darkened vision as she rocks.

It then became more evident that behind the dark screen of her sight, she developed a penchant for the Darkness and began to imagine things more as time changed. Those are among the only things she knows, as far as Nora observed. And as time went on, there were other things that she had formed in her youthful mind. Her firm belief is that the Darkness was her mother, which she found within the border of her own darkened world. She, should, however, be forgiven, for she knows nothing else but that which stands continually in her path and the way of her darkened vision.

Suddenly one day, she developed and voiced her burning desire with her limited scope of rational reasoning to know the truth and hidden secrecy in the world of the Light she heard her aunt talks about. She started to show signs of resentment at any glare. She did not wish to know the world that is with both Light and the Darkness, as told to her by her aunt, who considered it strange.

Of course, this had made it a most staggering concern for Nora. "It is unfortunate that the only man who I had any interest in disappeared after showing, at least, a little interest in her. I do not think though, that he would have had any feelings or care a biscuit regarding her likes or dislikes. So, everything happened for a wise purpose," Nora said in her self-consolation.

Amble Lee seemed to be a special soul, and who already knows the wisdom of man, and the regulation of life. Whatever her reason for wanting to know those things, nobody knows. She would constantly cast her eyes in a shift of make-believe to the heavens, tossing her head from side to side.

"Most certainly, I will not be able to deal with those things for any long time," Nora said. And she went on to say: "in Amble Lee's act of torment, what made provoked me more was her steadfast gazing at nothing in the open atmosphere. Seeing those things did not only scare me, it infuriated me even more," she added.

There was one thing that Nora had in her secret quest, and that is why Amble Lee is constantly asking about the Darkness and where it goes when the Light comes on, which is the outermost part of her niece's autism. As a result of those questions, Nora valiantly tried to steer her niece away from her belief about the Darkness, but all to no avail. She could only voice her wishes and with all her hopes that the Darkness would disappear from her niece's sight, or even just enough for her to see or get a glimpse of the natural world.

It was not until Amble Lee's seventeenth birthday that Nora noticed that her niece was at the extreme of her anxiety when she realized the degree of the child's problem. For one thing, it was the child's interest to know more about the Darkness that obscures her vision and why it will not leave her. And if it does not, then she may one day commit suicide. Amble Lee has been questioning her aunt about it since she was able to speak, and want to know why it has been with her for all these times, seventeen and a half years of her life.

"She had before made this kind of utterance---wanting to hurt herself when she was less than ten, but it was never to this degree. And so much now that she has found things in her vision of Darkness and her harbored beliefs that I could never think of," Nora said. "Because she has not so far seen Light, and although she is not so fond of the very word, and according to her, she hopes that one day she will be able to see anything apart from Light and what are the missing things in her life."

With all these feelings, there came a sense of deep disquiet about life and the Darkness. In her imagination, she challenged every semblance or any glaring garish of Light. And as her confidence grew, all in her mind's eye, she believed she can see. And as a result, all her hopes are built on the increasing effect of several wakeful hours, which have now stirred her wishes. And so, in her wishes and Nora's hope, she will one day be able to see all the splendors of life, let alone that which obscure her sight, and what she so-called her mother removed from her eyes.

Amble Lee, now speaking with much more audibility and clarity, one night, after spending hours on the terrace where she had gone to gaze into the unknown, she called her aunt to escort her back to her room. And in her room, she sat in a corner where she spent the rest of her time. Nora, acting out of curiosity, unannounced, barged in. "What are you doing in here?" she asked.

"I am thinking about life and what it is all about. And I am also thinking beyond your scope of knowing," she replied. Listening keenly for her aunt's reply, which it had only come in retreating footsteps. "Thank you," she said sarcastically.

Nora was conscious of the child's sarcasm, stopped, turned around, and as usual, escorted her into her room. And soon, a soft shade of brightness came across her face.

"Thanks," she said, "thank you for bringing me in here."

And before any extended time, the incredible strength of her longing and that need to see the other world she kept it in her wishes, and with all hopes that such a day will eventually come when she would be able to see visibly the world around her.

"Amble, you need to sleep now, sweetheart," said her aunt. "I will have to take you back outside of your room if you will not."

"I am waiting to see what I hear you talk so much about, even though I am having a problem thinking whether they are something that I would care that much about. So, I'm waiting until the time comes around, and hope that you will be able to tell me," Amble Lee said.

"Amble, you would be waiting forever or for some miracle to happen before you will be able to."

While Amble Lee's undying wishes operated by the unwitting faith that contained her, her positive restrictions, which should have brought her more than what she believes, did not produce any promising outcome. And as a result, in her confusion, she said all manner of things that infuriated her aunt.

Her infrequent and edgy consciousness of her state of affairs, with uncertain hope, worked anxiously through her impetus. Her thoughts, in the meantime, innocently spun and swayed inside her stupendous behavior as well as what is in her thinking pool. Her freckled mind changed courses like the wayward wind, as her autism dominated and controlled her every action, which further infuriated her aunt Nora.

Then occupied by the confusion, her blindness along with her mental inadequacy, Amble Lee created a host of frustration and concern for her aunt. And there was every practical reason for her aunt to be concerned, realizing that she and her niece are the only two with the same bloodline left in the world that she is aware of, for as far as she knows, all other members of the family are now deceased.

"Why me Lord?" Nora indignantly asked. "Enough of this," she said, throwing her hands in the air. She then rolled balls of her teary eyes down on the dainty and confused autistic Amble Lee, who wrapped herself in one clumsy bundle of withering flesh and bones on the floor. And in Nora every degree of her sadness, there followed drips of tears while she laid bare her hope that Amble Lee will be one day better. Then she again flung her hands in the air and again uttered the question: "Why me Lord?"

All these times, in her teary eyes, there were several small streaks of redness. Her choosing to take a snooze was vital. Without a timepiece, she imagined the time along with her feeling and threw herself at the foot of the bed, her hands across her forehead as she pondered. And as she does so, she placed the blame upon herself that it was because of her non-religious belief that fate has barred her from all avenues of success; and with that, she can only make the best use of that which had given her, which is high hope.

Then her mind further turned to her accustomed round of trouble; and then asked herself, "what if I fall asleep and the child in her state of confusion, walks through the door in the bitter cold that reached subzero at times?" This thought touched the very core of her concern, and arrested the path of reconciling with herself about her non-belief and her conscience.

The striking identity in her conscience was easily found, and all within her care and consideration. And drained now from all the nights of sleeplessness, she soon succumbs to the call of one act of Nature she could not have resisted or ignored for too long; and by then she drifted off into a fast state of slumber.

It, however, was not for very long. She got up to the annoying and loud sounds and a set of pounding footsteps. Nevertheless, she remained quiet and listened as if to identify them. Then while half immersed in her state of slumber, she turned and wittingly patted the comforter feeling for Amble Lee. And as she feels along, there came a faint thud that sounded as if against the outer wall of the house. She sprang to her feet, and in a loud and uncontrolled voice, she shouted: "Amble! Amble! Amble! Where are you?" There was a spate of utter silence that had followed her frightful calls. "Where the hell is this child? I hope that she did not go through the door!"

Now out of her slumber, she was faced with the raw reality that Amble Lee might well have gone through the door. She has not been seen; lost in the Darkness it would appear. Nora called the first, second, and third time, and in her scared voice she, yelled, "Amble Lee! Amble Lee! Where are you?" Then in her state of panic, she fought the dense Darkness of the clustered quarters where she delved in her vain less hope that nothing happens to the child.

In keeping with the law, a tradition in the system, she must endeavor to find her, for Amble Lee is underage, and more so, she is plagued by mental inadequacy. The slightest neglect in finding her will be deemed an act in contravention of the law. In addition, her earlier professed interest would be defeated. Amble Lee's missing must be reported to the police within twenty-four hours from the time she was discovered missing. The force of Nora's hunger for sleep created disobedience to the rules of law, her responsibility, her concern, and her love for her niece. And with the spread of ice and impeding snow still on the ground, she could only search within confined limits. And outside on the ice, Amble Lee's footsteps could not be heard, seen, or traced, for there would be no visible impression of footprints to trace in the densely pitched opaque Darkness. Not finding her on time, Amble Leigh could end up at the edge of the deadly frozen lake of thin layers of fragile ice and fell in.

Preoccupied with the possibility of the danger facing Amble Lee, Nora twirls half happily. And with her eyes half closed, she lowered her head and offered a short spell of unvoiced prayer, hoping Amble Lee did not go through the door. And with sleep having the upper hand, Nora went back inside and into her bed, where she laid herself down. It did not take long before she bowed to her mind and her thoughts before she came to the realization, got up, and fumbled about for the knob of the front door she found unlocked. Then in her delayed reckoning, she went for the shaded lamp. This she used as a guide to her path along as she rummaged around within the limited scope of the lamp's offered flare, but little autistic Amble Lee, was nowhere to be found. In the meantime, there was thunder rolling as if breaking loose. Then came a lull and another brief spate that lasted for another minute. "Where the hell is this child?" Nora again asked. And in her now confused state of mind and half wakefulness, there was one question she kept asking, which was: "Where is this child." She was confused, fretting that the child may have drowned in the icy lake.

It was a tense moment that lasted for some uncalculated time. She went back into the house where the sound of another faint groan had carried, was heard coming through the window, but Nora had yet to determine the specific location. She listened and listened as the groan faded in the stillness of the opaque Darkness. She then stood speechless in the sprawling backyard---contemplating what to do next. And amid her troubled mine, she continued to fret and went back inside. And as she worried, she unwittingly created more confusion that her mind misdirected her to do odd things if Amble Lee did not show herself up. "Amble! Amble! Where are you?" she asked in a more solemn voice. In the pitch of the Darkness, there came another faint groan that suddenly awakened her to full awareness. She then thought of walking again to the back door leading to the edge of the icy lake. And in the Darkness for the second time, she fumbled with the doorknob, she now found it unlocked. "Oh heavens!" she shouted.

She had no one to call upon, and with no one to call made it quite an arduous task for her, and not even as much as from the sky cometh any help. The pervading thick clouds and densely opaque Darkness shielded the entire element. And the only light, which was that of the crescent moon, had long disappeared in its temporary retirement for the rest of the month.

Several nervous hours came and went with the changing mood of the Darkness. Burdened with all the problems that brought her anxiety, she gave up and employed that I don't care attitude: "What more can I do? she said, "I have tried my best up to this stage," she muttered. Nobody knows where this damn child is. She could be prowling the Dark valley to her death, although it would have been only if she had walked by the edge of the deadly waiting icy lake," Nora pondered.

While waiting for an answer, she walked back to the bedroom and said in an angry voice: "Child, you are creating problems for me. I know that you are somewhere here. Just tell me where you are. I want you to listen to me, and I want you to understand that you may not be with all your faculties, but for heaven's sake, listen to me and show yourself up. Please tell me where you are by simply knocking or making another sound. Next thing, you might be frozen to death, as all you have on is that flimsy nightgown," Nora beseeched.

Nora in her troubled state hauled her coat over her nighty; and in her unwitting mind she went back outside in a simple old pair of toeless slippers. And as she headed for the lake, a faint groan came again: "Mm, Mem."

"Where are you?" she frantically asked. Her search of the yard yielded nothing. She then walked to the western side of the house, where she heard yet another faint sound, but found only a stray undomesticated cat and her kittens shivering in the cold. And from the other side of the house--- there came another fainting cry--- the sound of mew.

Nora's feet and fingers begin to numb if not frozen, her temples cracking in the cold wind. Now fully awakened, it sunk more profoundly in her the importance of finding her autistic niece. So, she intensified her search that revealed nothing, and not even at this stage when the numbness of her fingers and lips made her think of rushing back into the house.

"What else can I do!" she cried out. "I am not sure if she went by the lake!" she said. "I think I better go back inside and warm myself up a little, then go and search other places." She headed back inside the house, and on returning, she heard yet another faint mew. She trailed the sound to the back room adjoining the kitchen, but the sound had ceased by the time she got there.

"Where the hell on earth this cussed child could be?" she asked in apparent distress influenced by the vacuum of emptiness. She tiptoed, while with craning neck, stop asking before setting her ears for any possible slightest sound. Then, "Oh my God!" she shouted.

"I can't believe this! Child, what the hell are you doing here?" she asked, "give me your cussed hand."

Amble Lee sluggishly reached forward and held her hand. Nora pulled her from inside the kitchen cupboard behind cardboard boxes. "Why did you do this?" she asked.

Amble Lee was shivering and was as mute as a tomb. Her head down, her right thumb seemed stuck between her lower and upper jaws; her teeth clamped into her flesh as she slumped into another stupor and another of her state of infant-like behavior. With no response or attempt to, it had further infuriated Nora and appeared as though she had almost lost control of her temper. However, she quickly arrested it, which she held fast for some considerable time. She had rebuked herself at the instant; then, she turned that awful moment of negative thoughts into some of the noblest actions after reexamining what doctor Patrice told her. It was then that it came to her that little autistic Amble Lee does not have all her wits carefully wrapped in a coherent parcel. This was an agonizing period of concern for her, an endless activity that brought on her second phase of elevated stress and the resumption of her homicidal ideation.

However, her bleeding heart was strengthened when she considered that it could have been her in such a situation after thinking that Amble Lee's illness could be of a genetic cause, and it had nothing to do with the time of her untimely entry into the world.

"Then again, I think I heard it, by the way, that some great grand relative of her father, perhaps her great grandmother, was not altogether of sober mind either," she said. "It is unfortunate that it happened to this poor little child?" she said. "Well, for what it is, I supposed I'll have to live with it until eternity. I have already committed myself, and there is nothing else that I can do except abandoning her," she added. "But if there ever comes a time that any cause or reason dictated by circumstances, I will be left with no alternative but to pursue my mission."

Soon Nora formed her consolation and adapted such in-conceited reasoning with herself. She did not only comfort herself about the possibility that it could have been her, so she thought for a while, and used such a prospect to cherish her niece's existence. And within this feeling of forgiveness, she reshaped her mind and created a new standard of understanding, which she brought about to employ a little more tolerance, even though it may last just for a short time.

The task though was utterly unhearing; there was that influencing feeling of herself that came into her when the hardcore feelings of coping with the condition that seems to be getting worse by the hour, and is growing with Amble Lee's age and time. And there was no known organized group to discuss the issue with. And even if there had been, it would have been another issue of understanding the autistic Amble Lee's odd behavior with the Darkness and her occasional catatonic exhibition.

One night in her slumber, it came home to the frazzled brain of Nora quite vividly that it would have been best if she had considered staying where she was. She may, in the end, have to abandon her niece some place or the other if her condition doesn't improve. So, engrossed in her concern, it reflected along these lines in her nightmare, which is how she thinks when life's task soaks into her. "The pain it has caused me to deal with this child over her years of Darkness is taking its toll on me," she grumbled. "Everything seems to be changing in me as the stress is becoming more and more unbearable. There was never anyone around to help, not even the government. After all, I believe I have the right thinking and care not what anybody may say this time. For I do not know how worst can it get before I get any help?" she bemoaned.

Chapter Twelve

AS AMBLE LEE GROWS

Through the depth of Nora's frustration, she had mustered the courage to return to Promised Land, where she first promoted the impetus to make all the adjustments in her preparation before heading back. One thing she seriously thought of this time and without any qualms, was abandoning her autistic niece before she was ready to leave Buffalo. She believes she would be better off returning to Promise Land without her and the constant headache and adversarial confrontation she is having with her. She also thought that it would be best for her to, particularly, when dealing with a child who has shown no promise of any sign of improvement in her mental situation. Her thought of such resulted from her lacking wisdom about autism and how to deal with an autistic child, especially one such as Amble Lee. In any case, on the same day preceding the discussion she had with her neighbor before packing up to leave Buffalo, with the ambiance still in Darkness, because of her distress, she thought of several alternatives. And bending under the pressure of her own will, though slothfully, she finished packing their earthly belongings and again took to the challenge and headed to the road. She did not care how Amble Lee would react since it would not have made any difference to her what color of the day or time it was. She had just decided to leave as she figured it would not have made any difference.

Amble Lee did not know the difference, and Nora, whose understanding of the condition was less important than being aware of the zone of her dwelling place, made no difference. Several days of bitter cold had made it more problematic for her to stay longer than planned. All she wanted was to get her aunt to understand her situation and to admit that she, Amble Lee, was there for a purpose.

Although she has become acquainted with the fact that during those periods of dense Darkness and bitter cold, without any semblance of daylight, Shadows and Shades were fewer, it didn't matter to her. These were just some of the excuses that Nora put forward as her reason for leaving, all of which were hidden within her.

"For what reason do I have to tolerate this?" Nora angrily questioned herself. "I must do something about it, even though I have no obligation to tell anyone that I am leaving. The child has been in Darkness for all her years until she is now taking it to be her damn mother. And if I even complain aloud, nobody will understand that because the child is not with them, and more so, what the curse anyone, including me knows about autism and blindness anyhow?" she muttered. "And even if I gave any credence to that which anybody might know, I hardly believe it is as much as I know."

Nora contemplated the whole thing about Amble Lee if she will still be around. But she soon gathered her thoughts and began packing some of the things she hid under her bed. And deep in her were those feelings that were more oppressive to whatever little sentiment or feelings she may have had. And as she thinks about her autistic niece, she was unwittingly taxing herself by challenging her thoughts concerning the whereabouts of the Shades, Shadows, and the Silhouettes.

She had long nurtured in her mind all the displeasures of the extended spell of bone-cracking cold she had experienced.

With the process of the passing of time, Amble Lee is growing, and with puberty stepping in, all her authority and her world of Darkness have taken on another dimension. Then, things worsened with the inevitable doings of Nature and time and Nora getting older. She followed the influence of her dream and began thinking about the move she made in leaving. She is now worried about what effect it will later have on her without any help and facing continually all the troubles and worries. She is tortured and remained in a state of mystery as her guilty conscience is crawling about her and gnawing away at her soul. Every now and then she would reflect on her action, and the many things she has done are now standing vividly in front of her.

In her view, the sun Light should be seen for as long as a day, which is to her selfish preference, not thinking that her niece has a phobia for any form of Light, and tries to communicate her dream and her thoughts to the autistic Amble Lee. Still, the child's limited ability to reason, it only leaves Nora to make her assessment of her personal and final take on any decision she already made.

"With man now out of the picture, I know that after twelve years, it would have been a sure no, even if I were to one day run into one," she said. She cannot at this stage accept the fact that life is not finished with her.

And as she and Amble Lee hit the road, they found themselves in the half-dark path of time and the valley of lonesomeness. During this time, Amble Lee already saw in her vision a couple of grievous things that amazingly existed. In her are things that further invigorated her autistic mind, heart, body, and soul. Amazingly during those periods of her fluctuating coherences and incoherencies, she surprisingly appropriately questioned herself concerning her hope, which is a question that not even the ultra-sane had ever asked: "where does the Darkness go when Light comes on?"

Why it took Nora such a long time to fathom Amble Lee's views since she has been with her most of the time and could see all her antics? Nobody knows. Before this occasion, it had taken her hours, if not days, to realize that Amble Lee has no control over her behavior and particularly those moments when she would occasionally lapse into her immature antics. And worse, when in-and-out of her coherency, along with the voices she has been hearing from the wilderness she so loved to listen, makes it more difficult for her aunt to have any worthwhile discussion with her. This then set the stage for her aunt's added formidable task to cope.

And worse, now, with the total disappearance of the last glow of the crescent moon, Amble Lee rejoiced and wandered about it in the double passage of mother Darkness. At this stage, she advanced her wisdom and let it known. And as if Nora had caught up with her knowledge about the mother of Darkness, she became consoled. To Amble Lee, though, Nora's vision is different. Its closeness explained to her that her aunt had no idea of what she was going to do with mother Darkness. And all this time, she knew not that Amble Lee had disappeared and delved into the core of the opaque Darkness, which she declared to be her mother.

It was an opportunity that Nora would have loved to use even if she had known to permanently sever all communication with her, as it would relieve her of all the mental strain regardless of what may happen to her.

"With bugaboo men and rapists around, anything can happen to her. But what would I now care?" she said, with frustration taking its toll on her.

As the Darkness slowly transformed from its firmness and the eventful night passed, there was a glimmer of hope that the bright orange glow would soon come again into the eastern sky. Amble Lee has yet been seen. And with the low floating fog motionlessly capturing the ambiance, its obscured Nora's view of anything in the distance. And with her thumb pointing at the translucent Darkness indicating the break of a new dawn, she tried to hitchhike from a lone motor vehicle approaching. Its bright beam pierced the fog and the translucent mother of Darkness across the vale. The vehicle failed to stop.

Nora reflected on how, when she was young, she traveled around with her first love, the man that caused her to be so skeptical about men. She also reflected on how she had loved sitting on her deck in the periodic state of Darkness much before November 1936 and much before

7: O'clock the evening. "Yes, I even recalled gawking into the region of the heavens without any specific reason, although I would sometimes recognize the stars changing places," she said. It is obvious that she had only use those nostalgias to appease herself. "And I also remember when by some fading hours of the nights, there came a gradual transformation of the heavens; and the horizon seemed to me darker after that color-painted orange sky with a phasing edge of the blue lasting away, far beyond the scope of my comprehension. So now, seeing Amble Lee with some semblance of those behaviors makes me wonder."

In the midst of all her reflections, she wondered if the driver had offered Amble Lee a ride, and with whom she went because the driver did not stop for her. Or, maybe, in her state of confusion she may have walked off the road and got lost into the bushes. Nora pondered. "It would have been fewer headaches for me anyhow, what else I can say."

Now driven by her frustration, she had abandoned the promise and commitment she made to herself to care for Amble Lee for life. Among her new thoughts, too, was the man she spoke about and his promises, a future she might have blown herself of enjoying a brighter tomorrow. In consideration of these, she debunked that strong feeling she had for Amble Lee and hope she will never show up. And all this time, she hopes and wished Amble Lee is left behind and engulfed by the thick Darkness and fog for life.

There were moments when Nora felt that Amble Lee knew what she was doing, and that's why in the beginning she had refused to hold her hand. Then again, it would be only she who knows, even if she did not understand the possible danger ahead of her.

Several hours passed with the morning star moving closer to the edge of the sky. And as Nora trod the foggy road, she thought for a while, stopped, and then retracted the several feet she had before walked. And around the bend, she craned her neck, and in her roaming eyes, she saw in the yonder, a fainted image caught in the beam of the rising sun, which was akin to that of a little young lady. It was here that she then felt the voice of her conscience speaking to her, so she waited until the image became more pronounced. She postponed her anxiety but temporarily, as the image gradually got closer it revealed no resemblance to Amble Lee. She then waited and waited to see and to ensure her wishes come through.

With the sun slowly climbing the steep of the heavens, several anxious moments had elapsed. Nora, however, kept a wise head and questioned herself, soberly thinking about how Amble Lee will manage to find her way, which has yet to be determined.

It was only then that she realized Amble Lee had with her the piece of driftwood she gave her on her sweet sixteenth birthday. The fickle-mind Nora would once again adopt that sense of strong feeling and pity for her the moment, but only if in the end Amble Lee finally caught up with her. And fate had it that with a little extra patience, she waited at the next crossroads, the junction where the two again got back together in the long spell of Darkness. It was a joyous moment for Amble Lee, after spending those long hours in the dense Darkness and mist. Now the two holding hands and again engaged themselves in a conversation that did not last for any time.

Due to Amble Lee's mental inadequacy, she was trying to explain to her aunt the pleasure she had with the mother of Darkness, which she declared as her mother. They, however, in their silence, together they trod the lone and rugged path of the carriageway until they caught sight of a bus shelter. Amble Lee, however, refused to board the bus, reacting in accordance with another episode of her phobia. If there were anything that came out of Amble Lee walking in the double-fold mother of Darkness, it must have been the question she conjured about it and asked her aunt: "Where does it go whenever the Lights come on."

It took the autistic and partially visual impaired Amble Lee to collect her thoughts and put them in her question just for her aunt to begin thinking about Nature. It was here that the reality of things began to dawn upon Nora. And it was only then that she finally got the understanding and the occasional feeling of concern about Amble Lee's behavior and her question. Now she regards Amble Lee's question as being amazing. "You know, to think of it, where does the mother of Darkness really go the moment, the light comes?" she asked. "It is really Something to think about!" she said.

That's all she had ever asked about Nature up to this time. It was however hard for Amble Lee to understand that, and it was too difficult for her to understand her aunt's utterance, which was the result of she Amble Lee's startling question. For within Nora herself, she could only recall how lazily her unwitting gaze had set upon her personal thoughts at those times, although within them she had harbored no feeling or interest in nature, for to her, Amble Lee is stupid.

Amble Lee begins to think why she hasn't a mother if the Darkness was not her mother as she has been so often told by her aunt. Engrossed about not having a fleshly mother, Amble Lee adopted and anchored the feeling that her mother is the Darkness, and what her aunt Nora told her is not true. According to her belief, if her mother is not the Darkness, then she Amble Lee, must have been otherwise live therein. There was nothing that Nora could tell her that she accepts, except for that which is of her own personal belief.

Amble Lee's concept of mother Darkness has made it extraordinarily challenging for Nora to consider trying to convince her, or suggest anything further that would be acceptable to her. Amble Lee determine to continue in her view, and holds firm to her fantasy and her relationship with the Darkness.

The mistake Nora made was, she should not have let loose of her views and openly denounced her personal brutal experience in Amble Lee's hearing. For with Amble Lee's autism, she adopted the Darkness idea, and in her opinion the Darkness is more than what her aunt told her. This leaves Nora with the burdensome task of convincing her that the Darkness could not possible be her mother who she was told died before she was born.

Nora was wrong when she told Amble Lee that she was not of normal birth, and that the Darkness is no friend of hers because it is not of any solid body or substance, nor is it with flesh or blood. For with Amble Lee who is lacking the competence to grasp these in the proper context made things even worst for both of them.

As a result, it's now quite a growing task for Nora to convince her that it is all in her thinking; and that it is a simple act of her imagination, which is foreign to reality. And although Amble Lee occasionally listens with unvarying attention, her understanding is yet unclear. At least, not until after she heard her aunt Nora say they are now out of the town of Buffalo. And at which stage she wordlessly expressed her feeling with a visible expression of joy.

It was clear how much Amble Lee had cherished this idea that she will again be going to some warm places, a place where she will be warmer; and she will be able to sit as long as she would like to gaze in the Darkened vacuum in her sight. She was extremely gleeful when she heard she will be at a palace where she will be in the company of the external mother of Darkness, which she called her mother. From all appearances, only that could bring her some form of happiness that brings on the expression that came upon her face. This level of joy is indicative of the degree of her autism.

"I now see that you are very happy Amble," Nora said. "You are as happy as a bee around a honey tree now that you have left that place, eh?"

And as Nora spoke those words, she herself called to mind how the mustard color and purple leaves were so beautiful, especially when they would visibly tremble and shed themselves from their stems and branches even the day before they went to Buffalo. And now she is anxious to go back to see again those leaves in repeated fashion when the time again came for them to. Nora reminisces how within the falling gestures of the leaves how they use to dance with the cool evening breeze before hitting the ground upon their soundless impact. Those, though, were only Nature's displaying its splendor and virtues.

"Oh, it was beautiful to watch Nature in action. Where were all those in Buffalo? I never saw much, if there were any."

In the meantime, as Nora reminisces, Amble Lee could only gaze into the imaginary world of wonderland by nights, and listened to her aunt's vainness utterances. And as the Darkness stood continuously still, it was all in the continued path of Amble Lee's sight.

Amble Lee, by misadventure, found herself locked horn with this unfortunate state of her condition. And as a result of her unfortunate situation, she unwittingly denied her herself the ability to behold the splendor of Nature in reality, such as earth, the trees and other things such as the transferring of Shades, Shadows, Silhouettes and the stealthy changing of the atmosphere her aunt talked so much about.

It's a pity that Nora has never been blessed with the wits that she had reiterated. Had she been blessed with the wits; she no doubt would have ceased from her continuously playing those unseating roles that are not good for Amble Lee. All they are offering is the displeasures and discomfort to a child whose prospect has been blighted and denied by the unfortunate and unbiased act of Nature.

Deep within, Amble Lee relaxed her belief that the Darkness is with her as a mother to a child as well as a companion of Nights. It's a thought she harbored long before it would gradually seep its giant body of still blackness in. She took her impaired vision with valor at times, but has failed to come to the realization of her other form of illness; the deprivation of a sound mental and physical health. She saw her illness only as her varying temperaments; nothing was wrong with her. And it never came home to her that the chances of growing up to become a wife and a mother may never be, and how a high improbability it is. And although too young to tell, the prospect from a radical like her aunts Nora's point of view, it is utterly impractical.

"Poor little Amble Lee. She is not only blind and mentally disfranchised, she is also "sloppy," Nora said. "She cannot do anything for herself, not even to comb her own hair. Yes, to do other things such as going to the bathroom is fine, but not until she was about thirteen. And even to this day there are certain things such as her personal hygiene she is not able to do on her own. How can I tolerate these, and for how long?" Nora lamented

Chapter Thirteen

THINGS THAT HAPPENED LATER

Not long after reaching Albany, they again stopped briefly to refresh themselves. Amble Lee seemed to have got another glimpse of things and gleam. She tried to make up for her occasional annoying and naughty behavior she displayed along the way. And there were those occasional moments that she changed from her sane state to her state of irritating misapprehension. She seeks to be forgiven, and not to be seen or construed as being rude, or crudely ungrateful. Then penitently, she asked her aunt to forgive her and tell her a few things about the world around her. She asked to be told about things such as the makeup of her body and other things about herself; what the house looks like, what the roads and a number of other things are like. She went to the extent of questioning her aunt, why she can only hear her voice and cannot see her, and if she is as dark as her mother.

Nora tried to explain to her just enough of what she thought she had the ability to understand, but the moment Nora hesitates or attempts to hold back anything, Amble Lee got upset. According to her, "there must be much more for me to know," she said. And in her displayed annoyance she barked at her aunt. Her facial expression invoked several deep contours across her brow.

"I see that you are angry Amble Lee, but what can I say."

Amble Lee at this stage once more expressed her desire to be forgiven for her recently displayed rude behavior. Yet she was resentful to anyone's belief that she is to be blamed for her action. Based on what her aunt told her, she acknowledged that it might be very painful to her aunt Nora to tolerate her, even though it has not been her fault, it is a result of her deprivations of some of the amenities of life and when the other side of sanity comes around.

Amble Lee in her own peaceful and sometime restless world, imagined what the element does and sometimes coherently tells how the firmament changes in its gradual form. Yet it's all in her imagination, and chiefly at these times when she would drum up various ideas; and ideas that carry the hallmark of someone who has all the faculties of a sane and reasonable person. It would be interesting to know what else to expect from an autistic child with multiple disabilities, and who is so disfranchised of her equal share of life.

During these times, Nora was having countless difficulties purging herself of the several mistakes she had made in her personal life. All along the way she murmured when in all her reflections, she had talked about the dreams and all the promises that were in the budding state of her financial development. Yet she did not forget the many things that are related to Nature. She thought along about the falling autumn leaves and the intermittently changing of the weather in the zone of standard four seasons. Sometimes her thoughts are as swift as lighting and as cheering as her spongy memory that broke open to her as she ruminated on the bad and of some of her pleasant pasts.

And so, she continued to labor in her thinking. And by then, in a peaceful transition, how the orange and crimson color that had long painted the half-lit sky. And all in her constant imagination, she thought of the pinnacle of a fusing red and amber arc shape object she saw delicately glowing, and there was a gleaming in the sky until it gradually disappeared. In reflecting on what the autistic Amble Lee told her about Nature, she now remembers vividly how the color-changing firmament formed an amazing spectacle to behold; and how slothfully it transformed the ambiance into a setting of its non-facial appearance to an appearance that will always be desired to be seen tomorrow. But it is to be realized that all this came in the quest of her consolation as she increased her effort to soothe her sorrows.

"I am so sorry that Amble Lee cannot see all the beauties of Nature in reality, and I would hope that one day God will help her that she will live and become sane that she can behold and acknowledge his handy works in trueness."

Then, because of Amble Lee's autism, the same is true to her as the beauty of Nature caught in the vision of her darkened eyes; the brilliant and most colorful glow that had followed a pattern peering from behind the foliage, setting on the hills far in the distant, she imagined. It was only then that she realized that she is sitting in the midst of the Darkness, that immense sheet of blackness; and that it will be years before it will ever get behind her. And only then that she will know the difference between the constant Darkness in her sight and the Darkness of the atmospheric ambiance.

And Amble Lee carries with her yet that perpetual feeling of an emerging sight.

And as the Days rolled and followed by the inevitable Nights, they were dropped off the bus they took at the next rest area. It was here that they realized they had unnoticeably crossed several state lines, until they finally reached Promise Land. Many Days went in a flash, and were barely observed by passing motorists. But now they are resting under the cool arch of their hovel.

Amble Lee in her curiosity, craned her neck from the half old wooden armchair to get another imaginary glimpse at the pleasing but phasing mother of Darkness in which, according to her, is her mother. It was, though, in her wishful thinking that still lags in the constant Darkness all in the sight of her mind as well as her vision.

It was the other side of Amble Lee's illness that brought on the illusions that her mother is the Darkness. To her, everything in her mind is real. And she wished that no one would bear any false information that she is being confused. She became unusually receptive, with all the uniqueness of her mind's eye, which is remarkably dissimilar to anything, or persons that lives. And even in her split minutes of coherency, to her, all that she talks about are factually real.

"Amble Lee's ability to know the difference in time and to reason rationally is infrequently present. But whatever her misfortune may be, she remains the choice in God's creation. She is an unfortunate young girl who with God's blessings, her situation will be reversed; and one day she will gain all her faculties, will have no counterparts who will be like her and in her present situation. I wish they will not encounter similar faith through the unfortunate gifts of the unbiased and unselfish acts of Nature," said crampy.

"Mr. Crampy, I told you before that I need no pity, but I thank you for those kind words."

When in her state of lucidity, Amble Lee would ponder about various things like the sane themselves often do. And the moment she slumps into the other phase of her illness, she engages herself in her bizarre thinking and wonder if her aunt, too has with her that massive sheet of blackness that sets itself before her. As if her aunt were able to read her mind, she occasionally responds before to Amble Lee's silent query.

"No, Amble Lee, I do not have that constant sheet of Darkness in front of me as you do. There are those occasions when I am confronted with it, and chiefly when it is cast in my path. And it happened Amble Lee, by the changing of time such as when day turns to night, which is invariably accompanied by its presence."

"What was in you aunt Nora case? For as for me Amble Lee, it is different."

"You have an apparent fixed spate of the Darkness with you, Amble Lee, and that is why you cannot see me or anything else but that which you have declared your mother."

"How do you know that?"

"I mean to tell you that the Darkness you have been seeing all along is a result of your blindness which probably will be with you for the rest of your life."

"So, what do you have there now before you?"

"It is presently with me, and is all about the place but not to preeminently impair my vision as in your case."

"You are still referring to my mother as 'it!' aunt Nora, which I hope you will stop."

Chapter Fourteen

A MIRACLE IN SOHO

Some years later came a startling revelation. Amble's action gave the impression that she was having a glimpse of things. The passage to the terrace showed traces of the presence of a dim light, and to her there was a semi dark glare moving noiselessly in the sky. This brought on a frightening spell that induced glad tidings mingling with tears of joy for Nora that something good is happening in Promised Land. The bearing tears in Amble Lee's eyes caused by her whispering hope were trickling, and her swollen hope brought on a rash of ecstasy when she asked about the fluttering towel flirting on the clothesline next door with the wind. Something of a miracle about to happen as it would appear. And too, where the tears of joy came down Nora's face.

Nora cast her eyes across the neighbor's backyard on their clothesline and there was in fact, several multicolored towels fluttering violently in the stirring wind. To Nora it was not entirely clear if Amble Lee had really seen the movement of the towels or it was a result of her imagination born out of wits through her autism. Whatever it was, it had sent off an alarm. Nora's antenna rose, marrying a euphoria that Amble Lee can now see.

"Could this be real?" she asked, elation taking the better of her lot. She then stood silently awaiting the other segment of Amble Lee's remarks and perhaps another stupor or an episode of her autism.

"Mother Night had not long gone, so my mother may have followed her," Amble Lee said, while swallowing her salvia with regularity. And soon she drifted into her other state of confusion. And in her utterance came the question: "where is that blackness in which company is my mother?" she asked. "When I first sat here some hours ago, I saw her moving about, where is she now?"

"There it is, her mind remained cloaked in a box of halter- shelter, her views, her behavior, and her fondness were all distinctly her own and came out of the influence of her autism" said Crampy. "As it would appear, Amble Lee's world of fantasy caught up in her staunchest imagination, continue to torment her aunt," added Crampy.

It was her pondering mind that led the way to her imagination, which was the way to her half-diluted coherency at times tells her that the sheet of blackness has disappeared. And it remained with her in the fixed belief of her expectancy that she will one day see other things outside of the perpetual sheet of Darkness she is seeing.

It is Nora's high hope that Amble Lee will see, and see enough that she will know that there is that other form of Darkness beyond her impeded vision, which it is an act of Nature, and it often spend some of its time, and particularly in visible assortment when encountering Light, but in total obscurity in the absence of Light.

Nora had before told her niece about the rising of the sun and passed on bits and pieces of information concerning the movement of the appeared to be physical mother of Darkness, as well as the occasional intrusion of Lights to her. And she also often tried to explain to her more, but she must catch her when she comes into her receptive state of understanding even when it is just for a moment. And it would have been only then that it would have perhaps come home to Amble Lee that every living soul on earth faces the periodic presence of this great mass of blackness that encompasses both the habitat of man and that of beast and all other living things when all Lights disappeared.

In Amble Lee's case, since she is deprived of Light in her vision, she will have to live within the perpetual presence of the mother of Darkness, and that which is in her sight until some miracle takes place. And so, she prepares to accept it that there is no quick or permanent escape for her, therefore, it would be wise for her to make the most of its presence and her situation.

As she grows, she comes to acknowledge her situation further that her sanity and her lacking permanent coherence will continue to fluctuate, and the chance of her seeing all things is perhaps a daring impossibility. Her courage comes and goes, as does her coherency. For some moment, she came to accept it that her aunt's decision to leave Buffalo was an excellent idea and would perhaps be helpful to her in some sense of the way, which time was to reveal, but how much she understood is yet to be determined.

Listening to her aunt's regular talk about the Sunny Light, Amble Lee wondered what happens when her aunt's darlin Sunny Light comes around. But soon she resolved that her tolerance for living with the mother Darkness was easy enough because her mother is living therein, and gave her all the comfort she needed. Unfortunately, though, knowing where her mother goes whenever Light appears poised another problem; the mysteries that set themselves into the frame of her non-acceptance of Sunny Light.

Amble Lee then conferred with her confused, imaginative and inquisitive mind about her mother of Darkness who comes in for scrutiny, and how the light her aunt talks about comes into view; and from no given distance from which her mother of Darkness appears and disappears.

"I have never heard my aunt talks about where she comes from and where she goes," Amble Lee said briefly in her state of coherence. "I heard her talk about her darlin Light, and that it comes on and goes off, but I never heard her say where my mother goes when he comes around. It is not that I care anyhow; I am only asking out of curiosity as I know my mother of Darkness is a very secretive mother, and perhaps that is why aunt Nora never said anything about where she comes from or where she goes when her friend Light comes around."

As Amble Lee's wisdom grows, she becomes more concerned about the coming and the going of the Darkness, both in her sight and the ambience. After all, her ask was only out of her curiosity and not of her anxiety as it was observed that all her preference, if she had a choice, outside of her illness, it would have been the mother of Darkness. She was concerned to the extent that she asked about it, but chiefly when she heard her aunt talks about them, Light and the Darkness, and that the two together formed or caused the Shades, Shadows, and for even the Silhouettes to exist.

Nora has before tiered herself out in explaining to Amble Lee the behavior of the Shades and Shadows, their formation, and how they are generated by the presence of Lights when mingling with mother Darkness.

Your mother of Darkness grows minute- by-minute my dear, just as we do, and is in our presence before it disappears," she explained. "And while it is with us, everything in its path apart from what you refer to as my friend, Light, gradually adopts its color. And it even sometimes it unhurriedly transformed itself every evening and morning before it slowly disappears from our unsuspecting sight," Nora added.

"Then how come I have never seen those that you said are Shadows, Shades, and Silhouettes?"

"Amble Lee, don't try to confuse me. You said on humorous occasions, that you have seen them and refers to them as your siblings."

"I did!"

"Yes, my dear niece, as I have told you before, because of the Darkness, what you are seeing is constant in your eyes but without any form of light to enter your eyes in any open ambiance, you will not be able to see the others."

In the meantime, Nora looks in retrospect, and what she saw made her muttered: "How the days before were sometimes coated with brightness and how it had deceitfully change into that gradual form of an opaque Darkness and again changed into still and transparent Darkness. She had even mirrored at the specks of Darkness that were before her the evenings prior, and how well things and all bits and pieces that were adorned by it and often either chased or trailed by lanky Shadows who mimicked every action of all temporarily active and latent objects.

The moment Amble Lee heard these she relapsed into one of her other states of stupor: "it must have been my mother and my siblings and no one can fool me!"

"Once more Amble Lee, there is no need for anybody to fool you. You have already fooled yourself by saying the Darkness is not your mother. And I am appealing to you to drop the idea. It's annoying the soul out of me, and I hope that you will understand that," said Nora.

Then in Amber Lee's current state of incoherency, she tried to console herself. And in her own world of make belief, she mock-watched how often the Darkness returns and flirts around her at times, and how at Nights, it presents itself in dense thickness and well in galore. Amble Lee, then in her own words, trumped up this short tale like the one she had trumped up about the flagging towels on the neighbor's clothes line that later proven to be false.

"Yes, that shows that I am a special person and a person with special gifts," she said with confidence.

Nora became spellbound as she listened to Amble Lee's voicing what sounded as if real. She listened to her retorts on how she watched the Darkness as it goes and comes with the Light of Luna Moon, and how it gradually returns at times as it would appear.

This had caused Nora to again wonder if Amble Lee is really seeing things, or is it that she is actually caught up in her world of her illusionary port that made it so often sounds so real. And it was even when the mother of Darkness sometimes comes in as a skimpy sheet of blackness with often-giant clusters that hangs about intermittingly. Then, Nora, she too in reality, often watches how it waves with frightening specks as it hovers with bordering lines as so often stated by Amble Lee.

Amble Lee got fidgety the second of any glimpse of Shadow. Nora would right away accept it as a slow improvement of her sight, but wonder how come she would refer to it as her sibling. And it went to the extreme that in a single act and mystifying behavior of the Shadow, it amplified her anxiety that caused her to feel sorry for herself over and over, and at other times when it was in fragmented form while in mixture balance with fragments of Lights and other things. Again, this made it more mystifying for Nora, since Amble Lee has that way of saying things that sound real. It is within this line of Nora's concern that often stirred her fears, along with some people; and the moment the Darkness sets itself boundlessly about. She discovered that the daughter of Darkness lingered with her both in her rooms and bordered quarters. And while this was happening, in the huddled of the wilderness there present the mother of Darkness. And within and around her wherever she is, whether at home, on the road, or even in any one-bedroom cottage, the daughter of Darkness often stilled herself as in the wilderness where her mother inhibited the gifts of evildoers and created a virtual heaven for them to perpetrate their evil deeds.

"These are some of the things Amble Lee imagined whenever she is out on the terrace in the company of what she called the mother of Darkness," her aunt explained.

As Amble Lee's state of mental dysfunction, coherency, and incoherence come and goes, she was carried her to the bewildering end where in her view: "My mother Darkness is one mysteriously amazing arrangement with her non-blistering activities, and with her full inundation of the life of human such as myself, which lays abundantly in an immeasurable portion of our domain," Amble Lee expounded. "I hardly think my aunt knows this," she added.

"It is quite baffling to know how an eighteen-year-old mentally disfranchised girl arrived at these ideas about Nature!" Nora said. She also wondered how come it did not present itself to her in her world of Darkness, and the indifferent features that do not make her believe or considered it the way Amble Lee does. "To me, it is scary," she said.

Amble Lee's selective memory allowed her to expound on what she heard her aunt labored on daily in explaining to her the action of the ambiance of the mother of Darkness that is separate and apart from that which she sees in her screened dark world of vision. As a result of the constant problem with Amble Lee and the mother of Darkness, Nora had for a moment wished it were possible for it to be condemned, if not abandoned, its ever-frightful appearances just enough for her to be relieved of the ongoing agonizing pain brought on by Amble Lee's passion for it for to her, all is well. She has never felt frightful about the ambiance of the mother of Darkness since she knows nothing of it except for the illusionary view she holds about it. Her strongest belief is that her mother lays herself within its fold, even though it is by some unnatural and unfavorable act of Nature with its groups.

Like the mother of Darkness, Amble Lee slipped in and out of her illusionary pit of insane behavior, curiosity about their going and coming remained the same. She has that fixation on the Darkness, which she believed is her mother.

Amble Lee has no knowledge of her biological mother, her doings or anything about her life, or any knowledge of her characteristics. She is fixed on learning where does the Darkness, which she called her mother goes the moment the light comes on. And all her beliefs are resting purely on the strength of her illusion; thus, she accepts nothing as an answer.

Chapter Fifteen

AMBLE LEE WENT BERSERK

Her already half pale skin quality seemed to be slowly adopting a permanent tone of ultra-paleness that was already starved and was deficient of sunlight; and her to-the-bone meagerness is the result of her refusal to eat, while her already fragile body began to show signs of declining health. On top of her autism, she is carrying around a virtual facsimile of an ailing person with anorexia nervosa disorder. This added state of her condition is what rips the heart of her aunt apart. Her disgust with Amble Lee cannot be worst.

"Look at you! You have made my life so miserable that it's unbelievable. You are as pale as milk and as skinny as a needle. You will not eat and will not do anything. You will not even go into the sunlight when the sun is here. I have made serious sacrifices to bring you back here to get some harsh sunlight on your skin, but you refuse to sit out in the daylight. You are already in Darkness all in your eyes, so please let the sun shine a little on you. I'll give my heart just for you to do that," Nora beseeched.

"I agree with you, Nora, for, at last, you only now muster the courage to mention the use of sunlight to her again," said a voice from the wilderness.

It was at this instant she remembered that in the beginning, there was no light or any indication of the presence of humans, and now since mother Days and the mother of Darkness are both here, they should be equally enjoyed and treated with some or the same degree of reverence. "In and out of their transposable presence, we should offer our admiration for both and not only the mother of Darkness, but Sunny Light as well," Nora said.

Nora, who spoke with all the evidence of sanity, tore her heart to bring in all her experience with reasonableness. Amble Lee who already been so crudely enchanted by mother Darkness, could only see one way; and that was through her darkened eyes and her already deep-seated affection for mother Nights that are caught in her personal vision and mind.

The task for her aunt Nora to transform her became more difficult as time went on. She had even tried another form of their environment as far as her imagination took her, and thought of removing again from one region to another as she quests the early gaze of freedom; and in a pleasant region where she could commune with the creatures of Amble Lee's fantasy. But soon she reckoned that there was no bearer of the mind, and there was no bearer of any eyes that could behold the vast nothingness, how it slothfully cloaked by mother Darkness when Sunny Light disappears. Therefore, it would have been pointless. And what would it profit her to lock herself in the more profound wilderness and to face the sound that will come from the darkest Night of timber, which would do more harm than good, by feeding into Amble Lee's fantasies.

The mother of Darkness is everywhere, although sometimes, temporarily. And at those times she tarries, occupying all the spaces vacated by Lights. And wherever Nora may consider taking Amble Lee there, it would have to be that fleeting moment when Light again disappears. And even at those times, if any other person were to be present anywhere near, there would be no one informed enough about her life and her condition, and no one to convince her that she is sitting in her world of delusion. Moreover, that person would not have had the blessings of seeing any pleasing facial landscape about her, more so the petrifying state of affairs of the autistic eighteen-year-old.

For now, she is only bloating in her glimmer of falling hope, as in her illness, there is mother Darkness that fills her mind and surrounds her whole. She is so set in her world illusions that all Nora could do was to pray ceaselessly and hope for her vision to come, that her illusions of the world of mother Darkness will soon banished.

Amble Lee felt more and more assured within--that her mother was caught in the midst of the Darkness, and that there is life within. Nora meanwhile can only continue to sit on the imperceptible pedestal of hope that Amble Lee will one day get better.

"Amble!" Nora called, invoking every conscious spirit that dwelled in her. She was with all the goodwill and intent to bring her to the realization that her belief is of pure false impression and illusion. And Amble Lee who knows not a father or any other person with flesh and blood but Nora, who has been left alone with the heavy burden of transforming her pitiful depth of false belief into reality is like a fixed thorn in her life.

All this time Amble Lee curled her bantam self almost into a ball on the floor; her brown eyes barely glowing in the Darkness that enfolds her. She cried and sobbed uncontrollable, and in her anguish, she screamed and bang her head against the wall and yelled: "Oh God let me see my real mother then since my aunt is telling me that the mother, I am seeing is not real. For I know that she is within this Darkness, both she and my siblings. Let them not play anymore hide and seek with me," she cried.

When Nora saw the painful state of her pitiful condition, she too cried--- rivulets of tears rolled down her cheek. She already knew that Amble Lee's teary utterances were a reflection of the degree of her deep-rooted pain and fantasy---something she will have to live with as long as there is life.

"We are here as a set of true human Amble Lee, and now with the Darkness we presently stand," said Nora. "When will this pitiful situation of my only blood be abated, I do not know?" tearfully, she queries. And it was only for about the third time that she invoked the realization of the existence of God. It was within her knowledge that the Darkness is just the form of a mysterious mass of nothingness, will she be able to survive its presence when it is in its most opaque stage? The fact that it is at these stages that Amble Lee acts out more, and with all the confusion she caused and the agonizing task of reforming her, will it ever be possible for Nora.?

Amble Lee, however, sees things completely different. As a result, it gave Nora every reason to wonder how and when she will be freed from such state of torment. To Nora, it is an infinitely strange behavioral practice, but to Amble Lee it's natural, a phenomenon that comes within the awe-inspiring acts of her illness.

Contrary to each other's belief, Nora became extremely tormented. She was more concern about the Darkness the moment it presented itself in such less magnitude, with the presence of the sun sharing their duties. There are often the presences of dark portable spots with her both on her right and on her left, behind and in front of her, as well as time when they are at her feet and over and above her. She is even more concern when with much frequency, they magnify and present themselves as the curtains in the heavens, especially during those moments when Sunny Light and Lunar moon vacated the sphere. Then with the opaque density of the mother of Darkness with any glare of the phasing Lights, that's when Amble Lee become more belligerent.

"Now, if I can feel this way in my sane state and sober mind, it makes me wonder sometimes myself, and imagine how Amble Lee feels about Lights with which she bears no part. I Can imagine that I am in my sane state, but yet at times I am afraid of the pure Darkness! So, in considering her illness and her phobia, I can well understand how she feels constantly seeing gleam of sunlight," said Nora.

Amble Lee's love and her view of the mother and daughter of Darkness are less transparent to all sober human beings. They will not see her situation the way she sees it, and they will at no time understand why she took on such preference for the Darkness as against her fear of the slightest gleam, even though she has yet to behold anything in the true sense of seeing.

Taking it from her approach, it affects her, even at the slightest glare as if she is seeing things. She at times acts in a manner that shows up the degree of her illusion, a behavior she displayed when caught with any formed specks of the daughter of Darkness, whether it's Shades, Shadows and Silhouettes, her siblings, according to her. And what is strange, her strange behavior is generally when they dilate themselves while standing in her midst and objects against the teasing wind.

During the acts of the fusing of the mother and daughter of Darkness with Lights, their fusing amazingly further provoked every figment of Amber Lee's imagination about the Darkness. And at such time, it engulfed her presence as well as that of her mind. It then disrupts and promotes her frightful behavior, which usually rob her of her tranquil spirit, which is contrary to those times when she is in the company of the sole composed mother of Darkness.

"It must have been extremely difficult for a person to be caught in a world of stationary Darkness, and for years while at the same time, encountering the Darkness of the ambiance. Within the frame of Amble Lee's unmoving Darkness, there seemed to be those occasional disruptions that brought on another spell of promising indication that she is seeing things. And this behavior gives Nora some glimmer of hope that she will soon be relieved, at least, to some extent from her day-to-day problem," said Crampy.

Outside of this placid moment of the mother of Darkness, and at the time of the presence of the daughter of Darkness, when they are fusing with Lights, it is noticeable that even Nora herself becomes unwaveringly troubled by their action. And worse, if they exhibit themselves at no specific place or is on no set foundation.

"You are so right, for they roam about and often in groups of unspecified specters," said Nora. And what bothers me most is, during those time, in most cases it is where the daughter of Darkness is always present; leaving no unoccupied visible tracks although present when the morn of Light comes in with its smooth and glittering beams. This I hate hates to see as it invariably sends Amble Lee on temper tantrum."

"I can imagine that those times are when you are more troubled!" said Crampy.

"Oh yes, I am concern about the low and draping patches of dark clouds appearing and disappearing at will, and often considered if I am in my sane frame of mind and can be so provoked by the presence of the those hinging clouds with their edges of Lights and darkness and get such scary feelings, I could imagine how Amble Lee feels."

Lights, whether it is that of the moon or not, how difficult it must have been for your autistic niece Amble Lee. Nora is well aware that her niece cannot understand that these movable specks are created by the faintest presence of Lights that shows up anywhere.

Nora then called to mind years back on a morning in June in Promise Land, while she was at home gazing through the half open window at the fused red, orange, glow of Sunny Light, when suddenly an admirable arch image peered from behind the hills how she felt as the Darkness cunningly disappeared. This now gives her every reason to think more about it along with all the hassles with Amble Lee. For she also remembers, and remembers well enough how she, Nora, acting out of her curiosity once searched where the Darkness could have disappeared to but found nothing. She also wondered if it was because she had used her tin lamp why she did not.

"In fact, I also remember those evenings while lighting the lamp before my parents died, when with my swift glances through the window, I saw how the Darkness slowly thickened as the sun slothfully disappears behind the narrow uninterrupted line of the ocean and the sky. And as the works of Nature filters through the night, the snail crawl Darkness robotically continues to pervade the ambiance, which was much not to my delight. Then little Amble Lee, who has yet to see anything but that which has been fixed in her imaginary sighted eyes, is deprived of beholding this aspect of Nature."

Amble Lee went to bed late the night after listening to her aunt talking about the Darkness which further invigorated her personal interest. And at last, in her condition that was mauled by several misfortunes, she surprisingly humbled herself to the mission of her creator and resolved that it's all a part of Nature, and that's life.

* * *

Several nights later while in her slumber, came a frightening moment. Amble Lee leaped from her semi slumber by a dream. And in her state of half wakefulness, she heard a loud bang against her window. She sprang from her bed and rushed headlong to the window, accidentally hitting her head against the sill. And in her blistering state of derealization, she shouted in a loud and terrifying voice: "My head! my head!" Dazed and temporarily disoriented, she staggered to the opposite side of the room--- repeating her cry to her aunt, the unwittingly self-inflicted wound to her temple that drew just a few specks of blood. Nora now arose to the screaming of the frightened and confused Amble Lee, she slothfully got up, turned the flame of the lamp up before throwing a quick glance across the hall way to the room. And because of Amble Lee's customary strange antics and bizarre behavior, Nora was more adamant in finding out the gravity of her cry. She went back into her room and threw herself across the bed, pulled the comforter covering her head. Amble Lee's unceasing nagging cries got the better of her. She sprang to her feet, hissed in annoyance before she shouted: "What the hell wrong with you child?" she asked, the tone of her voice evidenced the rising of her temper, as the child's constant plaintive cries aroused her conscience, and in a more somber tone she asked: "Amble! Amble! What's wrong with you?"

All that time the opaque daughter of Darkness had dominated the limited glow of the shade lamp.

"Oh, my head, my head hurts."

"What's wrong with your head?" asked Nora.

"My head!" she cried, touching her temple.

"You hit your head?"

"Yes."

"Let me see."

"My head, my head hurts."

"My goodness what happen!" shouted Nora, after a crisp look at the gash to the child's temple.

"My head hurts."

"You have to go to the hospital! What the hell must I do now?" Nora pondered behind the fright that brought on an anxious moment. I would not have been in the spot, had I not taken on this responsibility."

Nora not knowing the severity of the pain Amble Lee was feeling, she looked on as the bleeding was limited to occasional drips. And applying a quick sense of thinking, she placed her thumb upon the wound with all her pressure and thwarted any possibility of profuse flow. She then muted Amble Lee's bawl and ushered her back to her room.

There were still some hours to pass before the crack of dawn; the stars were still shining in their bright and spectacular fashion. And minutes by minutes the hours came and went. And in the remaining sheet of the daughter of Darkness, the silent hours broke to the sound of someone counting; 'one, two three…'

Nora listened and, with much concern, when another silence came. She laid her head upon her pillow as she pondered the recommencement of the counting sound: 'four, five, and six.' She ignored the sounds and went back to her bed, where she hopes to slept the sleep of the just, until the night turns day as it must. All these time,

Amble Lee was still awake, but as usual, she slumped into one of her silent spells while gazing into the unknow. She counted until she finally fell into another of her short spells of stupor.

At the dawn of another day, she got up before her aunt, who knew so well of her mysterious climbing habits. She likes climbing upon high places, the countertop, stools, chairs, and shelves. Wherever she goes, because of her bizarre behavior marred by her blindness, there is always that danger as she believes she sees things and places. This behavior has always been a part of Nora's concern.

Many hours had passed that night while Nora was still half awake. She got up, though a little late, she tiptoed into Amble Lee's room. And in the act of showing her concern, she leaned over at the side of her bed. And acting on her impulse, she reached beneath the comforter to touch Amble Lee, and with every assurance that she was firm in her slumber: "what are you doing my dear?" she asked, "you are so quiet now!" she said.

There was a stunning surprise when she got no reply. Nora repeated her question and extended her hand to feel Amble Lee's temple. Only then Nora realized that she was speaking to linen of emptiness. The sheet and comforter rolled in the shape of a person, and a sound from the adjacent room that told a different tale. Still in her half slumber, Nora frantically walked to the direction where she found Amble Lee rocking to-and-from, leaning against the unlock old window. "What are you doing here?" she asked.

"I'm looking at the colorful clouds in their splendor parading in the glare of your darling Sun," replied Amble Lee.

"Come, poor little soul," Nora said mildly, signs and sounds of pity made their presence upon her face as in her voice.

As a result of the illness of the autistic Amble Lee, her off utterance instantly whipped all concerns and urgent attention from Nora who already knew that Amble Lee always doing things that pose danger to herself, and saying things that are in most cases are not fitting to reality. So, in her quick thinking and short reflection, Nora advanced three steps towards the window, sat her autistic niece down, and took a keen look at her before she slowly waved her hand across her eyes. On doing that, she noticed that Amble Lee's head slowly turned---following her hand in every way. Nora in her glee, hastily rose from her bending position and gave a frightening breathless sigh. She then glanced through the window to satisfy her curiosity just to catch a glimpse at what Amble Lee said she was watching.

Then out of her curiosity, she again passed her fingers in the opposite direction, but with dissimilar pattern. Seeing this, Nora sat at the side of the bench with further raised interest. And there she again twiddled her fingers in front of Amble Lee's eyes, which brought on to her amazement, a house of gleeful smile upon her face. Then, with this unbelievable discovery that fell beyond Nora's imagination, it has incited a wafting sound of uncontrollable screams that echoed outside and across the vale.

"Oh my God, she is seeing!" she said in added sounds of acclamation. "I cannot believe this! I just cannot believe that at almost nineteen years of age, Amble Lee is now seeing! What such relief. It's a miracle!" she further exclaimed. "And is it true!"

Nora was now left with the incredible task of proving further that Amble Lee has really gained her full sight. Nora's sounds of joy would have been enough to awaken every member of the neighborhoods if they were in proximity. In the meantime, Amble Lee did not display any sign of excitement, perhaps she was afraid of the appearance of what believed to be glaring light. It was impossible to tell what she was thinking at that time.

Clarity now needs to be gained regarding her vision; for if there were any truth that she gained her sight and is seeing things, it surely would have had her aunt awestruck since to her, all that Amble Lee maybe now seeing are the things she has been seeing from as far back in the years that had long gone. And those were things that were in her imaginary mind from she was an infant unto this day, and they had all remained in her world of darkened vision. Nora's added job now was to ascertain whether Amble Lee's sight is now really there, or should she believe that what Amble Lee said she is seeing is factual. Nora knew that whatever Amble Lee said could well be a result of her autism.

Because of Amber Lee's autism, Nora feels that all governed authority set by her feelings, all events took place that morning, were the strength of her belief. And it was in reminiscence of the act of the Darkness she had encountered some years ago when it had disappeared without her noticing. And whatever she may have said happened, whether it was yesterday, today or in the future, false or factual, it is nature that made her that way.

Lacking any absolute intellectual ability, Amble Lee at times could not, even as much as drawing her dress over her own body. She cannot close or lock the door of her little unpainted cabinet. Her more stabled minded aunt has been doing it all for her, while she, Amble Lee, frolic with the daughter of Darkness left in all its mystic forms; the Shadows appeared as if they had pasted themselves on the frame of doors, beneath the ceiling, and around the curved woodworks of the cabin stilts as they lingered still.

Chapter Sixteen

AMBLE LEE GAINED HER SIGHT

With what seemed to be at last the eventual gaining of her vision, she saw how Light and the mother and daughter of Darkness, using their clever ability have often leveled themselves at the base of things. They enfold themselves behind things and Light perched on top, and in its most visible poise. And they did so at the various places such as on the road ways, beneath branches while the clouds clothed the naked ground. And in an immeasurable depth, deep below earth surface they allow their formation to be at all times referred to by Amble Lee as her relatives.

Amble Lee needs to know that the Darkness she considered her mother, shines not or reflects upon nothing. And it is only at these times, in a peaceable act that it may lift itself and give the appearance as if to flourish among all the invisible objects around with the unaided task of lights. There were no objects then, but now. Therefore, it had caused Nora to wonder how Amble Lee was able to see these is not quite clear.

"It is now her firm belief that she is seeing things and humans; the sun and even flowers everywhere. And in her opinion, she can see a host of other things as the daughter of Darkness seemingly ceased from dwelling in her, and no longer obscuring her vision.

A new dawn now presented itself with all the shining lights. And only the varying speck of darkness leisurely dodging here and there about at will. It's no wonder that during the time Amble Lee is in her state of illusionary bombardments, she has been so gleefully compassionate with the Darkness, adores it appearances and disappearances. She loves that beautiful placement or portion of its presence against the wall. For to her, it will eventually grow up but gradually; and like her siblings, it is playing game with her on the wall which is most noticeable, but only after the light moves away. In any case, it's only her personal heart that knows its own fulfilling. For she has been filled with that inborn tendency from she was in her state of infancy and even to the present moment that she is able to see. It was observed by her aunt that Amble Lee has a gleaming passion for the Darkness… something she will maintain for the rest of her life.

And there is that shocking fact that sometimes the Darkness hangs in and on the ridges of the floating the drifters. And at their lofty height they hurry to no specific place. Such action made not only Nora shiver, but also the very angel scared.

With all this, Amble Lee continued to admire both the mother and daughter of Darkness, and even in their flimsiest appearances when as usual, they would sometimes loaf transparently in her presence. And when in the frequency of their simulates the disguise of Shadows and Shades bring about their illusion- causing Silhouettes. These she referred to as her siblings.

It was during these periods that it invoked concern and fear in her aunt and others as they traverse from place to place. Amble Lee, however has no fear. Nora's hope now that she is able to glimpse at things a little, and understand this other form of Darkness, maybe she will better understand that it is unlike that which she had lived with for years.

With her now is that visible but skimpy view of the ambiance Darkness she will soon come to grip with that it actually roams with the movement of all Lights, which might well be poising some additional difficulties for her aunt. Amble Lee does not know this and would not give up on her fixed belief.

After watching the wayward gestures and some of the behavior of the daughter of Darkness spreading herself on the ground and beneath the limb of trees. Her view of her as the daughter of Darkness, had caused her to worry as her sister emasculates herself on the ground, leaps to expand herself in buildi1ngs and beneath bridges. And whenever she gazed in the yonder at her slow amalgamation, she did so with whispering hope that the lingering sparkles of Light about will not tarry any longer.

Amber Lee definitely has a grouse against Lights and still missing the ability to accept Light for all its worth, regardless of her aunt's explanation. She was unsure of the occasional coming of this vast sheet of blackness with its occasional dark patches. She gradually became familiar with not only their names, but also their mystifying acts they perform with Lights. She found in her mother of Darkness all the solace she needed when she was totally blind. Now came the other moment when the ambient Darkness piled in without its breakaways, and made those intermittent changes that brough on her sister more difficult for her to fathom.

"What now are you going to do?" Nora asked.

Nora, too, was still without the full ability to understand a number of things about the Darkness as much as she took this unchanging mutual acceptance of it. The little understanding, she had, she threw the argument to Amble Lee.

"Amble Lee you are still less than advanced with the full knowledge of the Darkness, and especially how it has often mass -placed itself and establishing its presence in various forms; from deep spell of blackness to that gauzy like brilliance it spreads across the sphere at intervals," Nora said. She now acknowledged the fact and added: "how could Amble Lee with her autism understand this unnoticeable wonderer in its sometimes-rusty formation that often tilts the beam of lights, and especially, with its eminent appearance that sometimes appeared with the emerging mixture of Light."

Amble Lee in her state of illusion stood at times and rock to and from; and even when she at the end, gained the full complement of her sight she showed no marketable difference. And even when she beholds the billowing black smoke, she swore further that her mother is showing her the many things she is able to do. This really rest in her as a portion of her delayed illusion about her mother and the Darkness, and it does not appear that anyone will be able to change her belief any time soon.

And so, came another night of torment for Nora following another.

* * *

The half Luna Moonlit night was extraordinarily brilliant, the several billowing pillars of clouds mixed with the dim glow of Luna Moon pulling on high in the distant far. The moment Amble Lee saw this, in her rapture she annoyingly gave praise to her mother for her beauty. And in her jubilation, she raised her hands to the heavens, calling upon her what she perceived to be her siblings to visit her here a little more below.

To that stage, the autistic Amble Lee, had not possessed the ability to realize she was appealing to the patches of the daughter of Darkness gathered with the cloud in condensed form. All things that are dark and even now, all seemed to offer added comfort to her. She gazed steadfastly at the speck of the daughter of Darkness lining the edges of the floating drifters and will occasionally gave praise to them for their ability to hang on. She constantly refers to the slow developing daughter of Darkness formed in the floating drifters as the mystic appearance of her siblings therein.

"My mother dresses well," she said in a tone that flavored with happiness.

In the absence of these dark floating drifters---there comes the lone discomfort to her when the day falls in that prudish state and is full of Light. She gladly cherished the vanishing of days the moment they are transformed into twilight and slowly seeped into the darkest of Nights. And she had definitely demonstrated her homely preference not to have anything to do with any portion of Light, which proved the blatant dislike she has for the slightest glare or any form of Light.

Whenever the mother of Darkness is in her half-darkened twilight frame, if in Amble Lee's presence, she plainly leaped in the air displaying her gleeful manner with triumphant sound of praises for the guaranteed change that was soon to come in full. To her another Night is in the making, and is sure to be cloaking everything when comes her mother of Darkness.

In the midst of all he glee, there is that misfortune moment when the cycle of time sets the mother of Darkness into motion. Then she would cloak the Night until she brings on the inevitable merging of another daylight that sets Amble Lee off on a tantrum.

Amble Lee now blighted by her fear and arrested curiosity, would press home for an answer to her question where does her mother or any of her siblings Darkness goes when any member or believed to be dissidents of the father of Lights comes on. She maintained her strongest disdain for any members of Lights, whether it is during the course of a day or not. She is never anxious to see any of them. And that is why she never questioned their whereabouts. It is noticeable that she is wholly confused mostly during the daytime hours wherever the glary presence of the youngest or the smallest member of Light may seep in.

She has exhibited ever reason why people should believe that without the taking of any precautionary measures, she will one day out of her fear, mutilate herself or even carry out an act of suicide--- an ideation she had previously voiced to her aunt if Light sticks around for too long a time. Amble Lee voicing of being suicidal, further brings on a mountain of quandary for Nora, who seems to fast becoming over burdened by her no- way- out- state of affairs. Nora now knew that she must clip the bud on time.

So, she tried, and tried to nurse her built up burden that has arisen above her ability to withstand Amble Lee's threat. How long will she be able to live with such, the fact that her heart got weaker and weaker after eighteen and half grueling years of misery with Amble Lee is not well known? She had long ago and again sought about making another drastic change of her place of abode to a place where the sun shines less constantly and the Darkness presents itself more frequently. But soon she reckoned that she would be only feeding into Amble Lee's fantasy.

She begins to think of Alaska again, but with such wish that offered no promise, it would have to be a case of going to Anchorage, a place she profoundly detested.

"What the hell is this am I thinking," she queried herself.

And she knows all too well that the prospect of such is as remotely impossible as finding any clarity in a utopian dream. And again, if she were to be again relocated, it would have to be--- Nora was also too well aware of her predicament in another form; the fact that with the frequent presence of the sunlight, it will further cause a severe state of nervousness where Amble Lee is concern.

"And in fact, I don't think it longer necessary," she said. "I must now come to the realization that I must stay where I am that it is already a four-season zone," she said. It is good that she examined the idea of moving to another region where it would probably be more conducive to the betterment of Amble Lee; it was an indication that she would never find a resting place; she needed the type of comfort for which she is in the quest. She must realize that everywhere on earth; it must either be Night or Day, even where time is of wide and varying spells.

Nora must live for herself and Amble Lee, and that's where her problem comes in. She knew it must be in a region where the Darkness comes and goes periodically. For example, in her current four-season she used as a rebreather, she will always be presented with the grand task of regulating the short spans of going and coming of Light and Darkness when interacting with each other.

The fact that with these short periodic spells of Lights around, there will be shorter presence of Darkness that will trigger off another blighted prospect of her finding any comfort because of Amble Lee's phobia for any relative of Light. And to the contrary, her distinct fondness of the mother of Darkness, sets in another stage of perplexities.

Amble Lee had no participation in Nora's plan; all was left to her well thinking. And if she were really to do anything to her own betterment, she must think wisely, and within all that she had planned or had organized. She must take into consideration that without a husband, and there is not a father for Amble Lee, physical and financial help will be needed.

Caught in her web of confusion, she acknowledged that she made several grievous mistakes, that will not be corrected without encountering some hardship. As a result, she is absorbing a tremendous throbbing headache in trying to unravel the puzzle she has tied herself into and how well will she be able to cope in another environment if all her efforts fell on barren ground. Had she been known around, and among whom would have been another portion to be considered.

And, because of the stigmatic nature of Amble Lee's illness, little was known about their existence. Nora felt ashamed as if she were the cause of her niece's illness, and for most of the time she, too, excused herself, although not quite clear from whom. She therefore believed that she got the worst of all the gifts of life, and in her doleful state and frustration she groused: "I wonder at times why me with a sick niece whose mother died before she was even born. In fact, I don't quite know if she was truly meant to live. All I know is that I am here with her and with all the trouble that came with her. It is a cursing good thing that she is now seeing, and that's the only savor to my dilemma."

All this time Nora in her thinking and in her planning, she sat silently with her palms covering her chin. Amble Lee briefly, in the meantime, came around and within the frame of sanity she walked to the half-opened door that allowed the stingiest of glares through.

"Do you wish to listen for a while?" she asked, but hurriedly closed the door to close out every speck and peering of any member of Light.

"Peepers eyes," she shouted in anger.

"You have something to say Amble Lee?"

"Nope."

"There are a lot for anyone to understand about you. Open the cursing door I need some fresh air."

"Nope."

"I demand you to open the cursing door!"

"Why?"

"I need to breath some fresh air in the place."

"I don't."

"Just stop your damn nonsense and open the cursing door I said!" Nora bellowed in an extra loud and uncontrolled voice.

"Then you open it." Amble Lee replied angrily, and in a jiffy, she relapsed into the other side of her illness.

Nora opened her eyes in amazement, forming several contours across her face.

"You are turning into a woman eh! After all its senseless worrying myself," she said, then employed a temporary still tongue. The correlation formed by the fading of the father of Light of an evening with the mother of Darkness and the mixture of mist gained them some moment of attention. It was drawing near to December and with the slow replacement of another Day presented Amber Lee some added comfort. She soon again got passionately involved with the mother of Darkness, sending a stronger message across. Nora hissed at her action; another dull frown masked her face.

"Cut your damn baloney out and open the door I said," yelled Nora.

Chapter Seventeen

THE AUTISTIC AMBLE LEE AND THE FULL MOON

The full moon was glowing everywhere with the blueish tinge of a four-season flavor, staged the tropical feeling and set the ambience for a comfortable evening. And whatever decision was to be made regarding leaving where they were must be done at the earliest date. So, although Nora was frustrated by Ambler Lee's behavior, rather than staying for the rest of time, she and Amble Lee once again pulled up their temporary roots and commence their journeying to the zone that would offer better comfort for both according to her.

As they trek along the lone foggy and rugged unpaved road the evening, they came upon yet another troubling task. With all their earthly belongings burdening their backs and shoulders, they had before them another five weeks of miserable weather wherever they were heading with constant drizzling, dense fog and annoying overcast.

Tired and weary, they stopped at the sole shed they came upon, which was all to Amble Lee's delight. And while she adored the fast-coming grandmother of Darkness and the visually penetrable fog, they were to Nora's displeasure in one sense, and a pleasure in the other. In one sense it made Amble Lee comparatively quieter while making it more difficult for Nora to cope. Nora knew that she must reach the state she so- called better Four Season before the cloaking moonlights appears. And Amble Lee, in the meantime, enjoying the half-concentrated grandmother of Darkness she believes is her mother. This brought on yet another aching problem on Nora who thought that since Amble Lee is now able to see things and comparatively well enough, she would have divorced herself from the illusion she has with the

Darkness. This idea though, was only in Nora's wish that was all in vain. She became angry at Amble Lee's annoyance and shouted: "c'mon, stop your foolishness and walk up. As a matter of fact, give me your hand. We still have another couple hour to get there, and I do not know what train and what time it is coming, which I will find out on time."

"Why can't we stay here?" Amble Lee asked.

"Of course, we could stay here yes, but you are the problem."

"I am the problem?" she asked in a raised voce.

"Yes."

"What am I doing?"

Amble Lee was sill fixed in her belief; and yet to come to grip with the reality of the other side of her illness. To Amble Lee, everything was well while her aunt remained the problem. She believed that because her aunt refused to accept it that the Darkness to her means a lot, she developed a hate for her. Nora, though, always been more coherent, weathered the gritty storm of her niece's figment of imagination and finally got her to continue their trek.

"Things would have been much less difficult with me had it not been for your preoccupation with the damn Darkness. I wish it could change; at least for a while." Nora said, as her burnt out spirit acting upon her will while they trod the unpaved road with her hope fixed on getting an early idea of what train will take them there. She had yet to say what other state or place she so called Four Seasons.

It would seem like there is no end to their task, but their hope of reaching before the change of time remain strong therein. There was still no sign of any comforting promise of the father of Light but those of the slight brightness in the sky, which were purely the poorest reflection of the stars and the fading glow of Lunar Moon. In any case, as faint as her glows appeared, they managed to create a state of disordered thinking in Amble Lee's mind. The regular fluctuation of her disconnected thoughts sustained by whatever little intelligence she had, allowed her to say the things she had occasionally said. Nora had a bitter time understanding the degree of her incoherency that lasted for the duration of the four hours journey and beyond.

Now running low on money, Nora soon has to continue to hitch hiking with her thumb gesticulating; a dangerous practice she knew.

They were bewildered and with nothing definite or concrete. One holding on to her personal belief, the other was indecisive of a definite place of abode.

Oh hell, I have forgotten that it was said that the moon, even though when not in its full shape, it has the ability to severely affect people, some people at least. Perhaps I should have first considered that before leaving our place of rest. Again, it was not fully present, it was obscured by the clouds when I was leaving, Nora reckoned.

Amble Lee had a severe and most frightening episode; reacting to the presence of the occasional peeps. She came to a sudden stop, gazing up to the heaven at the black backdrop. The half-darkened heavens offering to Amble Lee a ton of confusion with the twinkling stars.

"What is it Amble Lee?"

"I can see my mother waving, and the eyes of my siblings winking at me."

"What mother are you talking about Amble Lee? Your mother is dead I told you."

"Well, there she is up there."

"It is the stars and the partial presence of Luna Moon you are seeing darling; your mother is not there. Give me your hand. It is just the swift passing patches of dark clouds passing in front of the stars that made it appear that way as though they are waving and winking at you, Amble Lee"

Amble Lee quietly extended her right hand, clutching fingers with her aunt. The two continued on their journey with Amble Lee still taking occasional glances into the heavens as she made her fumbling steps in the translucent Darkness.

There was a lingering presence of overpowering smell of something drifting across the plateau. With Amble Lee's over sensitive nostrils, she could not bypass the intense presence of what appeared to be perfume, and complained bitterly about it.

"How now I smell her perfume and you say she is not here?"

"You cannot say that you have smelled your mother's perfume Amble Lee, because you never knew her, and you have never seen her in your life. And worse, you do not have any idea of what perfume she had used."

"I know her; I have been seeing her every time. She is with me right now, and there she is high in the heaven looking down. It is you who do not know her."

"I do know your true mother Amble Lee; she was my sister."

"No, you don't."

"You have no sister Amble Lee; she is my sister I told you."

"Then how come I smell her perfume?"

"What you smell Amble Lee, is just the fragrance of the night blooming jasmine, or maybe the presence of a spirit. I see nothing, and I smell nothing. There again, it could be the slight drizzle meeting the asphalt that sends off that perfume like fragrance."

"You are trying to fool me but..."

"Why should I try to fool you my dear niece? What would it profit me?"

In the midst of their verbal tiffs, there came some noise from the adjacent woodland, the sound of children playing.

"And now here are my brothers and sisters who all want to know me."

"Oh, for heaven's sake, they are not your brothers and sisters Amble, you have none."

"Then who are they? And why as I got here, they are saying things to me?"

"My dear, niece, the sounds you are hearing are the creatures of the night in the woods."

"What's that?"

No explanation that Nora could give was adequate for Amble Lee to believe. She quickened her steps in accordance with those of her aunt's as they trek.

"May God grant me the will to deal with this crazy child, for only you know what I am going through?" Nora beseeched.

Nora's lips quivered a little as her tension rose. The problem with her niece confronted her like a living image--- growing from its infant stage to now a giant ache.

"It's hard to explore the depth of her behavior," Nora said bitterly.

More often than ever, Nora pictured to herself what would it have been like if Amble Lee had come into this world as a sane child, and sane enough that she could see all things with a clear mind and understanding. Most naturally, she would not have been encountering all these nagging intervals of torment and discontent.

God knows everything best, *she* mused, offering herself the ultimate consolation.

Several more hours went, and toward the end of the night they came upon yet another cabin--- a place of rest they badly needed. Amble Lee became tired and beaten. She needs to rest her eyes, but with the ever-thriving belief that she was in the comfort of her mother, she tried to sleep but with a little reluctance. She was fearful that her mother would again leave her if she fell asleep. Nora tried valiantly to give her a new personality, but all her efforts fell again on barren ground. And above all, the possibility that Amble Lee may hurt herself made it less easy than said than done for Nora to get a restful sleep.

"There was no way will I be able to put up with this for the rest of my life. If only I knew about a Lunatic house about the place, I most naturally would have taken her there. The cursing child's condition is getting more unbearable, and even worse since she was able to glimpse a few things."

Amble Lee intermittently opened her eyes, and with curious surveillance, her eyes roamed about her confines occupied by that which she believed to be her mother.

"What is it Amble Lee?" Nora asked.

"Nothing"

"Well, I need to sleep," Nora shouted.

"Then sleep!" Amble Lee replied.

In the succeeding period, her behavior simmered when the folding end of Luna Moon again suddenly peered from behind the leaves of the dancing willows. And there came another ultra-taxing moment for Nora when Amble Lee's autism escalated. There were troubling moments of unbearable behavior.

"Aunt Nora there is my mother winking at me again. You have been lying to me--- telling me that I have no mother. Here she is winking at me. Every time the tree shifts itself, she winked at me."

Amble Lee's sudden outburst had the better of Nora, and with a single cuff to the side of her face she was knocked into quietude.

That gave her a short spell of quietness that lasted for about five hours or so.

"I am sorry that I had to do it, but God knows that I was left with no alternative." Nora muttered in her quest for forgiveness, with penitence forming a veil over her face. "It's time for your nonsense to stop," she said calmly, as she pulled the blanket across her body.

Six hours of rest that's all allotted to her by the dictate of Amble and time. They got up; Nora paid the small lodging fee and again headed for the waiting area. There was that slight but constant drizzle that impeded her leaving. She looked around and then gave a hefty sigh.

"What the devil is this?"

Soon she gained a little control of herself and sat on the chair in the waiting area. She rested her head against the high back of the chair, her eyes half closed. And before long she got up and pulled the curtain--- blocking out any semblance of the last peering moonlight. To think of other moment of rest at this stage, would disturbed their comfort, and in any case, Amble Lee would have made it difficult, if not embarrassing for her with the last of Lunar Moon occasionally peeping in.

At the end on this side of things when all seemed to be at ease, Nora seized the opportunity to gain some portion or part or the remainder of her rest. She snoozed off.

They will be taking the road again to be sure, but within the following minute or two, or as soon as the drizzle eased. And while she waited for the drizzle to be abated, she sneaked yet another snoozes, recklessly allowing the confused Amble Lee to fool around with the decorations on the wall. But in the remainder of time, it kept the still mother of Darkness into her usual shape with the once restless wind lulling in gradual form. And by this time, Lunar Moon was no longer a tormentor.

The two at least seemed now ready for the road after some half restful sleep. The Light and the nagging drizzle subsided.

On the very morning before they left their place of rest, they packed their bags and headed out. Nora dropped a sealed brown envelope into the slot of the wall then she slammed the door shut behind her.

The light drizzle ceased and the wind lulled. The daring and miserable Light of Lunar Moon seemed got totally lost in the post-midnight sky. Nora and her niece were well on their way to the next train station they hoped they would find with Nora's trouble mounting before her. There were no train in sight. They continued on foot until for two more days in the variable weather that carried the uncertainty of a long spell of warmth and dry. The deadly lonely road continued to emanate the delicate fragrance from the once warm earth aggravated by the nagging drizzle offered them yet another sense of Nature's breath.

"Come, let's go. Walk up, walk up" Nora said, frustration piling.

All this time Amble Lee was nipping on her fingernails and yet to be aware that she was facing another journey.

Any moment now the sun can come up, for the dawn had drawn near," Nora said.

And so, they continue on their way. Nora was prepared to discuss any topic relating to reality, and about the Darkness, but refrained because of Amble Lee's sickening views. She stilled her tongue with all the floating ideas and the arresting thoughts; that's all she could bear.

It was wonderful, a most pleasing time of the morning with the stars still shining but faintly hidden behind the forming clouds. But as expected, there were no uttering from Amble Lee. Nora tried and introduced a topic that would bring about at least a short sentence from Amble Lee, but none.

"We are going to a place where everybody fond of each other and want to be there," said Nora, who attempted to open a conversation without the use of the word Darkness or Light. "I had every reason to believe that this topic would have generated some form of input from her, at least a simple opinion, but no, none stir her interest. Well, I supposed later in the morning after she entered into her other phase, she will say something. She is conceited, understanding nothing. She has a sick mind and no interest in anything at the moment. Anyhow, perhaps it is good as it prevents any argument," Nora said under her breath.

Chapter Eighteen

THE AUTISTIC CHILD AND THE TRANSLUCENT DARKNESS

Five to six hours went by and the mother of Darkness slowly and softly tapered off with the subtle intrusion of some semblance of the father of Light in the sky by the time they got into Four Seasons. Then there appeared to be some dillydallying before the father of Light emerged fully from behind several billowing clouds, and with the pleasing presence of the dissidents of the mother of Darkness in the far and friendly sky. After that final semi restful night, Nora and Amble Lee with a short spell of abiding peace, they were quick to use the presence of the half-diluted morning to travel the long distant until they came upon what seemed to be the third, another shanty cabin. Amble Lee was much less fond of the transmuted stage of the mother of Darkness. They stopped temporarily at the first opportunity. And there came again a continuous sprinkling of rain, and the heavy roaring of thunder in the distant with the threat of worse to come. The lone cabin master availed himself, and at a guess at least, he must have considered their plight before opening the door at the third knocks.

"Yes, what can I do for you?" he asked. The angry tone of his voice from the ad jarred door was enough to say they were not welcome. Then what seemed to be God's silent rebuke, he later opened the door and asked: "What on earth are you two females doing in these lone woods this time of the morning?" said the heavy gray bearded cabin master who looked at his pocket watch. "It's now minutes after five!" he added.

Nora explained her situation to the seemed to be transformed and heartwarming cabin master, and who with his change of mind he made room for them. After a brief conversation he escorted them to a room adjacent to the horse stable where the agonizing stench of horse urine and compost drifting in with unbearable odor.

"You will hear some strange things happening during the morning, but don't be afraid. It gets even worst in the nights."

"What will that be?"

"I must tell you that you may even feel your bed moving and the sheet being pulled, and if you stay for the coming night there could be even more. There is no need for you to worry though, for my father passed away some years ago and this was his room which he had used each time he visited me," the cabin master explained. "Every now and then he makes his presence known in there you know..." However, this did not deter her. Her sole apprehension was all about the Light that may enter the room through any crevices between the wood's gaps of the windowsills. She was mainly concern about the peering of Light that will sets Amble Lee off. And it made the worst of a situation that may not have been otherwise conducive to the ease she was seeking from Amble Lee and her illusionary antics.

She took the room to catch the remainder of whatever little rest they could get before the sun comes up. Nora, though half prepared, she accepted the inevitable coming of the sun which soon occupy the element with the complete inundation of its whole.

"Thank you. Anyhow, I am not afraid," she said. "My chief concern is about the coming of Light, which this child has no tolerance for."

"Well, I am just telling you just in case," the cabin master explained.

With just one window, she reached into her little carry case for the sole candle she had left and placed it upon the windowsill. Then came a gentle wind that blew softly against the swaying flame, and in its whisper, it leaned the trembling flame against the slow phasing mother of Darkness and the softly flapping curtain. With Nora's gaze fixed on the dancing flame of the candle, she summonsed a thought that aroused her own curiosity. And in her sense of thinking positively, she uttered within: "If air is coming in, then there it is going to be Light when the sun comes up. They always seek and follow the same path, and that would mean more problem for me," she said. With that, her dozed was short.

After an hour and a half, she got up the first time, and begun to take the remainder of her belongings out of her carry case. The only thing she had not removed was her ever-troubled pent-up problem that brought on a frown and the deepest of contours across her brow. She looked tensed, very tensed, and for a while she glanced at the tired Amble Lee hiding behind her bobbing lips.

"What's wrong Amble, are you ok?"

"Yes."

With some surprised of modesty, Amble Lee got up, searched and found the finest feminine bathroom articles she so anxiously needed, and with the assistant of her aunt she went to the bathroom. There was the presence of a slight glow when she first entered. "Aunt Nora what is this?" she asked in a frightening voice.

Trembling like falling autumn leaves, her aunt quickly looked up and answered:

"What do you think it is it?"

"Look!" she said pointing.

"Oh, it is just a faint reflection of the rising morning star that got caught in the window pane," answered Nora.

"Ok."

Amble Lee did what she had to do with the aid of her aunt, both returned to the bedroom. There she ensured that all the possible openings for any seeping Lights are sealed. And for all it worth, she kept the single bedroom as her sole domain--- corking every possible crevice with the remnants of fabrics she found on the bed in the hull of the fast-transmuting daughter of Darkness.

At this quick change of behavior, whatever little conversation she had with her aunt was absent of any semblance of coherence. This inflamed Nora; her annoyance visibly marked the beginning of what to come.

Nora listened with much impatience as Amble Lee continued with her tangential utterances. And soon, it came home to Nora that as soon as the morning star disappears everything would be different. And so, her tolerance restored, but lasted only for some added minutes until the sun broke from behind the clouds.

"I forgot that the sun has some severe effect upon her as well," Nora reckoned. Then she hissed and clasped her hands before sitting at the foot of the bed; her eyes rolling in the slow peeling sheet of the morning sun slowly creeping in to chase away the mother of Darkness.

"It is a great pity that my poor niece will never be able to come to the realization that the Darkness is just one of the mysteries of Nature, and the worse part of it was; the damn child will not sleep for any long time. A catnap every time she supposed to…" Nora grumbled. "I hope that one day…," then a giant sigh.

The dawn of another day came, and luckily for Nora, it came in the daring company of a dense overcast--- the face of the sun obscured by the uniting of clouds that formed a shielding canopy. It was like a blessing for her when another act of Nature temporarily thwarted what would have been another miserable day for her. Then, as the hours went, and another day took its port, the morning star and the quarter moon finally vacated the heaven but bade no farewell to the eyes. They beheld not their seemingly peaceful departure that had set the stage for an uneventful day. Nora and her niece left the cabin and headed for the road.

Nora and Amble Lee in their miseries, caught the beginning of the day while trekking the cool morning on a rugged road to the place Nora called Four Seasons. It was a blessing for her who needed some more time and some soothing moments to thaw herself out from the many days of traveling with all the annoying disconnected utterances from Amble Lee.

And as they took up their task with the long and lonely road ahead of them, the unexpected question from Amble Lee stirred the moment: “when are we going to reach?”

“We still have a good way to go, “replied Nora.

“How soon will the complete Darkness again come?”

“It will finally come after at least another twelve hours.”

“And when will we reach this Four Seasons you talked so much about?”

“Unfortunately, with still two or so days to go, it will take us another night and another day at least.”

“And that means?”

“We will have to wait and see!”

The new day came and was about to end, with several dark hours that came and filtered in with occasional specks of Light, the glare assisted in the guiding of their path. With the courage of Nora, Amble Lee, with little reluctance. She had no alternative but abiding thereto. And as they trek along the docile road, they came upon two men laboring early in their field, burning bushes that send billows of thick black smoke parading in the sky, which helped to shield from their sight, the scorching beam of the morning sun. Under these conditions, they missed the upcoming sun. With the billowing smoke and the slow and heavy forming clouds, Nora was rescued. Thanks to the tillers of the soil. But at snail's pace, gradually returned the dusk formed by the slow passing of the hours. And soon another day ended, allowing another night in.

Nora did not for a moment missed the disappearing day, for before long, the night had again come and as usual, it was tenderly hugged by the mother of Darkness. Then all what would have been visible images during the day, were slowly cloaked by the mother of Darkness that acted in her habits of cloaking the nights. Then the occurrence of the capturing of places, objects became less visible to the eyes when all the dreaded sheet of brightness and the Darkness against the presence of Light once again as they had done many times before, hand their grip on the cycle of time.

After a few anxious moments, there appeared a lone driver who picked them up but dropped them off at the next crossroads. In their struggle with the chill of the night and a cloudy day with blinding fog, they came upon a little township. Amble Lee had now fixed herself in the corner of her thoughts, pulled hard on her makeshift headgear. Together they thwart any possible incoming portion of Light. But if really, she was to be doing any good to herself, she must challenge the task of continue walking, and hope that the Light would show some hesitancy in coming from behind the clouds.

In Amble Lee's ignorance, she would further jeopardize her health by the starving of her body from the well-needed sunlight. She would have to wait for another possible full day, before the swollen body of the mother of Darkness in which, according to her belief, her mother dwells. The revisit of this problem would make Nora's task of coping a thornier one. To make matters worse, because Amble Lee's incoherency, she temporary lack the intelligence and the capacity to understand the severity of any further imminent illness she will be causing upon herself. The not so long ago burst of ungainly insights that rise above her unproductive and irrational judgment must be considered by her aunt. And because of this, several ideas came home to Nora, which she pondered about before voicing any further displeasure, and regretted taking on the responsibility of caring for her niece. "To think of it," she said: "I cannot understand why should I blame her for her action when for all it worth, she had never been for any considerable period in a frame of mind that is common to reality! Now that I have a fairly reasonable knowledge of her situation and the Darkness, I am going to think differently. It is time for me to be much more lenient in my thoughts about her," Nora said, acknowledging her reasonable share of the child's care. "From she was alone in her mother's womb she has been encountering it. And it has been here long before there were any trees or any other discernible objects," Nora said. "It is now all around us almost at all times, starting with the gradual cloaking of the evenings before sneaking into nights, and with which it tarries in the belly of the elongated nights. Now realizing this, I will have to now accept it that it is something she loves and I will have to live with her and her belief."

"The long spell of its presence is behind us, and now that it is gone and we are in another region where it comes in periodic form is something I must learn to accept. All these Amble Lee should understand, but the ability has never been there for her to. So, what's the sense of distressing myself?"

Amble Lee now apparently able to see things much better, and with the ever-growing love and attentiveness of her aunt Nora and her tolerance, she was already taught by this, and well aware that the Darkness finds itself with ease in all unlit passages and does son in a still manner in its immense frame, and therefore it cannot be her mother as she holds in her view.

"After all, what she needs to know is while in this frame, all the casting Shadows of its presence reserved themselves in wait for the faintest appearance of the dimmest glow to make themselves visibly known."

At this point, Nora's old time male acquaintance Crampy, intervened: "Pardon my intuitiveness," he said." Then he went on to say: "what Amble Lee need to learn is, with these acts of the Darkness that prompted her personal belief that the Darkness is real and is believed to be in the body of a physical person is false. She may have measured her cause for such belief as dictated by her illness but we to date, do not know. Anyway, in her personal frame of thinking she seems not to have taken into consideration that even with the appearance of the diluted body of the mother of Darkness, the Shadows sneakily worked themselves in with the twinkling Lights, and therefore, there ought not to be any life within such frame," said Crampy. "It's unfortunate that her ability to understand these actions has never been with her," he added.

"What do you know Mr. Crampy?" she asked insultingly. "You are following my aunt who knows nothing about my mother, except for being afraid of her because of her stupidity. It only tells me that both of you are as fool as duck."

Chapter Nineteen

AMBLE LEE IN HER EXTREME REACTIONS

According to Crampy, Nora, should have known that it was the deluge of this massive blackness that accompanied the Nights and which so often flowered in softly and swiftly with unnoticeable action. Without this awareness that sometimes by the awesome act of Nature, it slowly and lazily sneaks into places before engulfing the ambiance at large; and at which time it posed a problem for the autistic Amble Lee, and worse, it is mainly when fused with Light that it caused more problem for her.

Nora was not aware that long before Light inundating the innocent ambiance the daughter of Darkness in her subtle fashion she cunningly dodged at various places. And during these moments, she often looked so solemn in her appearance, while displayed in an ideal fashion to provide in a figure, a formidable bliss of solitude to some people. And that is why it is so difficult for Nora to accept Amble Lee's ever-funding affection for the Darkness, and cannot imagined how she became so riveted in her fixation.

What Nora should have known at least, was, the mother and daughter of Darkness come in with their clever acts such as rendering themselves to the offering of comfort to some, and mostly at places and time where some people often used it to find solace. But all this meant nothing in terms of ease for Amble Lee who lacks the ability to realize this type of blissful feeling. And only for a second that she Amble Lee, would try to frolic with the Shadow at the base of things that shows the advancing stage of her autism.

In the meantime, the Shadows mending their business stayed within the confines of their limited space on floors or anywhere, the very way Amble Lee remains in the confines of her belief. Her behavior showed how much she has been filled with her loftiest desire from her inception, and nothing seemed able to change her at this stage. No threats or challenges had ever disturbed her or can changed her belief, care not what her aunt or anyone may say. From her stooping posture on the floor, she looked up at her aunt who softly crept up behind her with great pity written on her face.

"I wonder what on earth you were doing!"

"Why were you looking at me like that?" Amble Lee asked in a stern voice.

"I was trying to see if I could offer you something to eat."

"I am not hungry," she replied.

"I think you should try and eat something. It is full time now for you to."

"I said I am not hungry," she barked at her aunt.

"Ok my dear, I was just trying," her sympathetic aunt said in a low tone.

Amid their presence were frequent interruptions caused by the trembling flame of the inquisitive Light that peered intermittently through the vacant openings and the wind periodically teased the unlocked door. By then, the half fading mother of Darkness had already eluded the eyes of the innocents, the non-conversant; most of whom witnessed not the dominant presence and know not the cause of her existence, while to others, it is what subscribes to their misapprehension.

"We've lived our days entirely unaware of the true terrors lurking around us. And only sporadically that our understandings will give cause for us to draw back the veil of Shadows and are able to reveal the horror in our unwitting minds. These glimpses into the supernatural presence of the Darkness can cause us to retract into comforting allies but we are not, and we are not just because of our belief, when in fact we are responding only out of our curiosity," said Crampy.

"There is no such thing as awkward curiosity. It was by whose view that it was arrested or harbored by a few of us through our ignorance, and who was afraid to look at all the awesome acts of Nature, what it can do and had done to the life of man animals and plants. So, it is honestly difficult to know, and I will never understand how my dear niece can ever take the Darkness as her mother!" said Nora.

"It is sad to say that in these days only a few humans seemed to have been betrayed by the Darkness, and are with certain apprehension regarding the validity of its presence when in its configured mode. For whatever it is, the Darkness is a multiple dividable body--- a mass of blackness that is so well adaptable to time, place and condition. And it remained an institution that stands inseparably associated with Shades, Shadows, and Silhouettes," said Crampy.

"What is all this talking about my mother?"

"There is that expressed misgivings that appeared to be motivated by certain people as in the case of your niece Amble Lee and her views," said Crampy.

"I am glad that you said that, Mr. Crampy, for it is the views of those--- another set of people such as my aunt who have their views originated through their ignorance and fear; and they are either wholly misinformed regarding the fundamentals of the absolute reason for the ever coming and the going of my mother, who in her mystifying presence of blackness before transforming herself into the various forms," said Amble Lee. "Then from this comes the view of those who are not, or less aware of the purpose of her presence. You all call her Darkness because of the way you think," said Amble Lee. "But I know that she serves her purpose in some of the most amazing ways, whether it's in her translucent, transparent or opaque form, and mostly at the time when calmness joins the integrated influence of Nights, and at the time when she locked- horns with the passage of change, from uncloaking of Nights, that she can become Day," Amble Lee explained.

What is particularly strange about Amble Lee, is that on the contrary, while others are afraid of mother Darkness, where she is concern even at the period of transforming itself, she adores it. For the average person, to harbor such, it would be for that person to adopt the type of passion or illusion as she does. It has always been Nora's wish that her niece would abandon her passion for the Darkness, which is contrary to the belief of others who believe that everything that is Dark is bad and dangerous. It is quite the opposite belief of Amble Lee who holds such that all that is evil cometh from the mind of those in the transient precincts or places of their darling Light and not the Darkness.

It took Nora with all the guts to tell her that a person who is pregnant with such views and own thinking stands to bring into disrepute the fear name of Nature. Nora wondered if that could have been the reason why Amble Lee took preference for the Darkness.

"Yes, she maybe unkind to a few, but she helped in the flowering of the prospect of billions or more people."

"We differ in thoughts Amble Lee, and we have been separated by our individual wisdom that led to our own view about the Darkness," said her aunt.

"And I must tell you that in my view, you and others only welcome the coming of lights into all the spheres and a vow not to deem them as your enemies, refused to think of my mother and all my siblings Shadows and Shades, and even to the very Silhouettes as being dangerous. You most naturally did not see them in the same vein as I have seen them," said Amble Lee.

"Amble Lee, you are only looking at the Darkness in one way--- a perception you have formed through your unfortunate illness."

"You keep on saying that I am sick and continue to refer to what is my choice as an illusion. It's a pity that you do not know, and seemed not prepared to understand..." Amble Lee replied angrily.

"Understand what? Amble?" Nora asked. "You need to accept one thing, and that is, you are damn sick. I cannot stand here fooling myself that you are not, and I will make no promise that I will ever hide the truth from you by pretending that you are not. I would not be doing you any valuable favor or even myself."

"There may be no specific season for my taking a preference to the mother of Darkness and even for the translucent form as it stands; and even if it operated not in any form, nor with any attempt to display anything, at least not for now, nor for you, but whatever it is, it is my preference while you have chosen the agonizing Lights to be your friend whether it is that of the Sun, the Moon, the Stars or that of man's invention to be your friend. And you can claim no conclusiveness among them while I can for my mother."

"Ok, Amble, I will not argue with you, I know what I am going to do."

Amble Lee do not have the ability to understand that the Darkness cannot hold or demonstrate any power against the father of Lights or even to patronize them in any form whenever they make their presence known. No one in his sober state of mind will take the Darkness to be his mother, although it at times demonstrated as if it is accurate, and even the fact that it is with such enormous expandable ability and not consistent with life.

"He, she, who holds such belief, is with a fixation as demonstrated by you Amble Lee. Poor little soul, you've been taken prisoner by your illness," said Nora. "I have seen your periodic agitation that I often tried to ignore, but…."

"You are hurting my feeling, aunt Nora."

I can only hope that one day you, Amble Lee, will come to yourself that the Darkness is without flesh, sense, eyes, or power and is with no act or willingness to give her the impression that it is her mother, Nora mused.

As much as Amble Lee so well adores the Darkness she called her mother, she is unable to come to grip with the fact that the mother of Darkness adopts and can move with all the speeds of its chosen image and power itself at its will, all in its adherence to the dictate of the movement of portion or semblance of Lights and objects.

Most of Amble Lee's love for the Darkness is driven by her illness and her non-awareness that it will remain motionless at times while awaiting the movement Lights and objects. And it meant all those things caught in the fold of Lights, but not that they are sympathetic to her or how she felt. She is not sufficiently witty to realize that the quickness and frequent lazy behavior of the mother of Darkness affects the dormancy of Lights as it, too, remained in compliance with the act of Nature and not to her bidding.

"Among the things Amble Lee needs to know is that there must only be some glare from the appearance of lights from somewhere that interfere, propel the movement of the mother of Darkness, and at which time it brings on the translucent frame and body when light is lurking on the horizon. She also needs to learn, that it is the light that is the basis on which the mother of Darkness changes her shapes. And through the interference of any portion of light, it is that which promoted her perception and enhanced the presence of something that may be caught in the wandering eyes of the curious. For even though she is so much engrossed with the Darkness, she has no idea that it is rampant at times as appear in some of its reduced frames that lay about at the root of things; trees, the back of branches and in the belly of things whether they are animate or inanimate. She sees the Darkness only as her mother and not knowing that it is a matter of her fixation," said Crampy.

"Thank you so much, Crampy. And it's pitiful to know that my aunt has been so much absorbed in her ignorance about my mother and do not know how she cloaks the Nights, hangs around the Days in sharing her tasks and acts as the hasty steward between human and animals' things," said Amble Lee. "And aunt Nora seems not aware that the phasing color of my mother's body normally gives way in her secrecy, and while doing that she gives people the impression that she vanishes the moment Sunny or any other form of Light that may take over and covered all the folds of things."

That night Amble Lee sat pensively on the patio in her short state of sanity; she employed and used every iota of her reasoning that the mother of Darkness has always been among the living and the dead. She gave thought to such things as trees, twigs, houses, cattle, buildings, and against the pillars of stones. And she could be considered right--- for Darkness was ordained to prevail over places with no Light or any semblance thereof.

"And as often as this happens, to her, it gives all the appearances as though it was hiding from the presence of the mighty Sunny Light."

"In fact, it is my belief that the mother of Darkness should not share company with any person or things but with me, since no one else seems to appreciate her presence anywhere," Amble Lee said.

The moment Nora heard her annoying views, she contemptuously shook her head with a pair of pitying eyes, and in a pitying choking voice she muttered, "poor little fool."

"Those who believe that they are wise will refer to the presence of my mother and her chief role in their lives, but may fail to realize the extent of her varying blackness; her characteristics, and the astounding immensity of her transformable body." Amble Lee said. "And it is known that among some of you it, is your harboring views and your faith imbedded in you why you adore Light. It is, of course, my opinion that it is, which is according to my makeup, and that's the reason why I take her to be my mother and call her the mother of Darkness," Amble Lee explained.

"It is seldom that one with such distinctive opinion will ever change." Crampy said.

It is difficult to understand why Amble Lee believe that we know not of the doing of the Darkness, when in fact, it is just that we do not subject ourselves to it as much as she does. We know that the Darkness is not here as an agent of bantering objects or persons or as a mimicker; it is also here to mark and distinguish the difference between night and day. And we know it also performs other playful antics behind the shaded coats of Sunny Light.

Amber Lee's past darkened path, which she encountered for years in her autistic and unwitting state of occasional jealousy and ignorance, showed that she did not know then, and does not know now, how to rationalize her held concept about the Darkness. Outside of these points of example, to all the sane, things appear crystal clear as so prearranged by Nature before its blackness steps in. And there were numerous sighs at times that came from some of the same people she met with her aunt Nora, some of whom had ventilated in their complaints when Nora told them of Amble Lee's fixation with what she termed the mother of Darkness.

Chapter Twenty

AMBLE LEE'S ARROGANCE INFURIATED NORA

Nora was furious and had no qualms about it when she said: "It is no wonder some people are sometimes called simple and strange. And it is those people that breed the kind of vagabonds who have doubtlessly set out to discredit the sense of the sane. For they have carved for themselves, a view they cherished to achieve their personal goals during the course of the Nights that are always accompanied by what you Amble Lee called your mother. And you are one of those people who should be deemed devious because you are well aware of the ever-close relationship between mother Night and the Darkness you called your mother."

"So, aunt Nora, are you calling me devious?"

"Who the hell is speaking to you?" she shouted.

"Take it easy aunt Nora, take it easy!"

"Oh, I am sorry my niece. No certainly not," Nora replied. "But you have not yet displayed your positive portion. And I know that if I live long enough, I am sure to see you further deteriorated since you are so well occupied with the Darkness."

"Whatever may be in her character and her perception of the mother of Darkness, it must be in her mind. She is an individual who sees it her way. So, perhaps there is a hidden sense of purpose for her coming into this world. Therefore, she is going to see it her way even in the character or in the configuration of the Darkness however frightening it may appear to others but not to her. It does serve a purpose to her," Crampy said.

"It is perhaps surprising to the ultra-wise but unclaimed by the foolish that in all their views they wished they could dispense with my mother and the unwitting greatness of her infamous body," Amble Lee said.

Amble Lee's hope stood out that one day she will physically hold onto it as a tangible and true body with sense, flesh, blood and bones.

"We are to recognize therefore as we thrive among the things most of which we have no control, that among them are the other product of Nature, some of which are in distinguishable form while some are in the docile form with little variation, if any," said Amble Lee.

"Amble Lee, it is evident that you are really somebody with special gifts or some form of blessings. How you came up with these views I do not know. I cannot understand your level of reasoning for someone who did not go to school. Looking back on Jesus as I made to understand, and the way he answered, questions made me wonder, as I cannot recall reading about him going to school, and yet how brilliant a man he was according to my mother," Nora expounded.

Many years of trying to get some understanding of the mother of Darkness in its entirety, will no doubt be revealed at the end that all the enquiries made by Amble Lee are just; and to the purpose that her query will one day bear fruits. It is my hope that it will not be so much as hinted and that it might not be such a tedious task, at least not for her.

"Nevertheless, at the closing stages I will hope that she will reveal the number of awes she has caused among human, and the sometimes confusion in her distortion that was influenced by the slightest residue of or any member of Light, and that we will at the end understand why she is so absorbed by its behavior that she took it to be so real," said Nora.

And there is also that hope that soon it will become further evident how the central portion of the Darkness became a universal occupier of space, the earth, and the open void it generally filled.

"Let peace reign within thee for the time will come when I shall be telling all about that which has caused much wondering about her varying occupation of certain areas on earth, and I will demonstrate too, her tricky behavior in everywhere she often spends her time whether it's with me, Night or Day." Amble Lee said.

"The shift of Nature at times caused perpetual awes and wonders considering the long absence of the Darkness as dictated by Nature, I know, but how well will you be able to explain that to anyone?" asked Nora.

"There has always been unquestionable evidence in the world of her ever presence elsewhere, aunt Nora, in which time she is known to have similarly seized and occupy the places of Lights the instant they disappear. This happened because they are of my blood with similar power. That's why."

Nora looked and listened in amazement at the now seventeen-year-old speaking with such authority as she made the utterances of a person who spoke with such wisdom.

"Amble Lee, you must have been a gift of God, a special gift, and no wonder why you have survived the tragic circumstances under which you came into this world that took your mother's life."

"Care not what I am, and how I came into this world, whether I am a gift of the master or I am a prodigy, I am speaking the way I see things. I know further, that my mother has never been frustrated or late in the mimicking of the objects and the images she seeks, even though she remained unvaryingly with her ever determined but silent characteristics she exhibited even throughout her transient presence. So, with all those characteristics that she has, why should I not accept her as my mother? I would like someone to tell me."

"Amble Lee, you are as crazy as a bedbug. You need to accept one thing, and that is, the Darkness in not, and cannot be of your blood."

"Why should I not speak of her as my blood? The main misfortune is the origin of the belief that all that is dark is evil, and all that is of Light is with purity. I know what you'll say the next time you speak, but how well whatever you I'll be saying be taken, or be seen as something of importance is left to be heard." Amble Lee said. "And whatever you may say will tell the difference between you and my mother. She too will show how gracious and clever she is. She is my mother who has been so well endowed with special gifts as well."

"I think I know what you mean Amble Lee. All sort of negative things has been said about the Darkness I know, but I still do not think you should be so well taken up in its existence and behavior."

"Aunt Nora, you continue to call my mother 'it,' and you are also well enough aware that people in some other regions are well acquainted with her in all her attendance and all the luminaries that made her worthy of thoughts as I have often construed her to be." Amble Lee said and went on to say: "she gave me every reason to respect her and treat her as human being."

"It is not all the time Amble Lee, and not when Silhouette stepped into the holes and caused to create and corrupt the mind and the imagination of people."

"Aunt Nora, for your knowledge, it is only the minds that are as friable as yours that her presence corrupt people," replied Amble Lee.

"That is an understanding, and therefore I can now see Amble Lee's predicament as coupled by the fact that she is with her severe state of mental deprivation."

"You keep on saying that I am ill., but I think you are the one who is ill."

"Was it then in your vision or an act of your autism?" Nora asked.

"My mother of Darkness is equally and unwittingly behooving, but she is treated with a one-dimensional value and approach; leaving no place for her essential features and purpose of her non-perplexing delude in all her global activities as demonstrated by her," Amble Lee said. "Admittedly, she seemed destined to be mischievous at times and was powered with the ability to manifest herself in varying degrees of intensity, and that she acts only through the efforts of continuous disappearance and appearance of your friend Lights, and through certain conditions that forced the alteration of her intent and her organization," Amble Lee expounded.

"It's not so sure if Amble Lee knew this and if she will ever know regardless of her unique autistic ability. She may well know that the mother of Darkness can infuse herself sometimes in all visible order, but at which instance it has no effect upon any other mankind but her. She will never know that whenever it reshaped itself with the presence of Light, it is that time when it often fooled the eyes of people through its quickness that they thought of one beholding a human where it was often not present but appeared to be."

"I might admit that it shouldn't be allowed by Nature, but it is already the way it is. So, since man has no dictate over her coming and going or her action with Light that caused illusions, mankind may well bow to me, Amble Lee, and my views."

According to her, only she Amble Lee cares and knows its whereabouts when the Light comes on." Nora said.

"And aunt Nora, even among the sane who are amongst us, with their intelligence and preliminary knowledge, they can never accurately state the difference between the body of the Darkness and her dissents, apart from the fact that her grand body is much larger than them?"

Answering any or all the questions about how her mother of Darkness came by its name has placed Nora and her friend Crampy in another state of quandary. For not even the wizard of the mother of Darkness, Amble Lee, knows; if she knows, and if she knows, she has yet to reveal it all. There are hidden facts in her that are to be let known according to her, but only after Nora accepts it that the Darkness is a human the same way Amble sees it.

So far, the most straightforward answer to the question that ordinary people can answer is that the Darkness is motionless at times but only when caught in its usually crudest and most non-understanding state of Nature.

"You all are only up to this stage, able to extrapolate her structure regarding her body construction. This is an essential element to consider when thinking about her and me, Amble Lee, which all reasonable people should know as it is evident that only me, Amble Lee know most about it."

"Yes, that may be so, but it is only of man's wisdom that he may determine in his imaginary that may view its end, its path of coming and going, as expected to be so done by you, Amble, Lee," said Crampy.

When we put together all the elements of Nature, we will first realize that there is no specific attraction of the mother of Darkness to anything apart from Amber Lee, or there was any natural affiliation with any other modules apart from Light, and with which the mother of Darkness shift herself in all manner and ways. If there were any other to consider, it is left to Amble Lee, who, through her autism, it would have made sense to explain it further.

"Have you noticed that Lights, even in the most extreme cases of filling the void, dared to occupy all the empty spaces occupied by my mother? Amble Lee asked, "It is this which must have caused frustration to aunt Nora after she was convinced that man cannot eradicate my mother, regardless of how they may try."

It may well turn out to be that it is only this autistic child who will be able to tell us more about the mystic behavior of this mass of frequent blackness that caused to promote the thoughts of a man preparing things with any degree of accuracy, things such as those carved by him in his entire creativeness and which had caused numerous awes within the function of it whole or parts thereof.

"You should, of course, believe in what you believe if, in your opinion, it makes sense to you," said Amble Lee.

"No one should blame Amble Lee for her to be so foolishly but relatively formal in her ridiculous approach to the mother of Darkness who bears her wondrous and most incredible adjustable size. Amble Lee, who remained in her world of belief, should be sympathized with or excused for expressing her frustration to others while creative in her autistic spectrum. She has seen the Darkness and all there in with her bold eyes… they lit up as she glanced around, then curiously, she wondered about the possibility of some strangers for whom she holds no grudge for Shadows, Shades, and the very Silhouettes she loves so much.

"I need no pity from anyone."

It has never been a task for some people who, out of curiosity, gazed at the figures of the enormous spate of the mother of Darkness resting in sight for a year. And amid distance, they see only the barren glare of Lights through glass compartments with glossy streaks floating atop glistening waters, with formed shapes that bear nothing but the carved images or reflections caused by Light, with the occasional casting of the sometimes-angry presence of the somberness of mother Darkness blending in.

From where the sane are concerned, it is only when the casual remnants of the Darkness are integrated with the different links of Lights that we often need clarification. But then, when we, through the act of Nature we wrapped ourselves among the things we have caused to be warped and then referred to them as Shadows, Shades, and Silhouettes. None of these, however, need to be considered a life-threatening danger to mankind although they generally imposed themselves upon the life of man.

In the meantime, there is always that gracefulness in the approach of what appeared to be some semblance of the mother of Darkness as made known by Amble Lee, and in the process of its remnants before establishing its principal integrated designs wherever it may be. And that would be whether it is in its in-transitory state or even when its visits are transitory. It is noticeable that at all times when in its in-transitory frame, it often swells or conceitedly expands its structure, and come the time when it pours itself into a giant magical formation that offers no happiness or any jolts of high and or bright spirit or praise from Nora or her friends.

"Except for you, Amble Lee, you know that there are the felonious-minded who often use their presence to advance their criminal objectives. And even the moments when they came, they used their snail crawl-like speed in forming their size to carry out their devious activities. And not even the wisest of all the wise in all their efforts can prevent them from pursuing their lawless deeds. They continue to use the shaded color of the nights as a shield against their evil deeds."

Only Amble Lee knows that the swelling and unbridling presence of the mother of Darkness hinged here and there at times, and sometimes displaying its fancy patchworks on the half-clustered plain. And on the streets, it clothed vehicular traffic, and even in and out of the Palaces of the unkind and the merciless.

"The Darkness at all times definitely unable to wittingly steer itself with any degree of accuracy, even though Amble Lee hangs onto it as her mother. Its dissidents bouncing their way around into objects like a set of careless and reckless drunkards, though they suffered no abrasions or burses about their ultra-flexible body." Crampy said.

"Amble Lee, I know that you are particularly charmed by the subtle charging body of what you believed to be your brothers and sisters that cause no reverberation on impact and leave no evidence of their presence anywhere after leaving, and particularly when they leave their port at the coming of Lights," Nora said.

The mother of Darkness, as it is fittingly called, has never applied for permission before swathing herself around pillars of stones, wooden or granite walls. Because of the gracious shifting and placing of her grand body, as the mother of Darkness, she easily adheres to the dictates of Light. This action gave cause for various questions asked by Crampy and others. And the first was: "Is it correct to say that all the Darkness around the world are subjected to the same dictate?" Crampy asked.

"Crampy you know so much how come you do not know that?" asked Amble Lee.

"From all reasonable belief, Amble Lee has the answers now all wrapped into her cleverness and showcased them through the frame of her autism. This we all hope to hear when she explains in detail," Crampy said.

"It should be made clear and clear enough by Amble Lee."

"Except for Amble Lee, no other person has her personal view of the coming of the Darkness. And since so, we will continue to ponder the use of the perpetual presence of this vast mass of multifaceted blackness and all the transient and intangible matter Amble Lee sees as her mother."

Chapter Twenty-One

THE GUESTS OF NIGHTS

The mother of Darkness has always been the uninvited guest of Nights, which Nora never seeks to learn more about its mystic going and coming, and whatever the makeup of such, the significant body of Darkness is. It took only Amble Lee's irrational behavior for her aunt to start examining its coming, and at the latter stage, she wondered what its actual presence denotes. People may call it whatever they so choose, but they can only see it as one of the grand arms of Nature and perhaps as one of the many uninvited guests of the Nights whenever Lights are absent.

"I will not stand to hear my mother be so described as an uninvited guest," Amble Lee asserted. "The eyes of the wise may well see her in one form while the minds of geniuses see her in another. Some may see her as matter in a state of self-configuration, but I see her in a different frame. I see her as my mother, and with whom I communicate and direct my many questions and concerns about where my particularly loving mother goes when she is not in my sight."

In Amble Lee's exposition, she labored a great deal on the goodness of the mother of Darkness and repudiated her aunt and friends about their remarks, who referred to her mother as an uninvited guest of the Nights.

"Without question, she enjoyed being in the company of the passionless Darkness she calls her mother, and fumed at any derogatory term that was leveled against her. According to Amble Lee, the Darkness reminds her of the several months of solitary Darkness and water in which she unknowingly spent much time floating around, and at the end… seven months and nine days before she was trampled from her mother's womb, she escaped, but was born to be what she is and has taken her situation as a gift from her creator. She has never asked or cried for pity or hoped that her world was otherwise like that of others. She is the kind of child who, in her youthful days, had already exhibited signs of supreme gift. Not before her time, any other child had ever displayed her predisposition." Nora stated.

Thereafter, a strange tale of promise is the influence of comfort on the staggering mind when one day her aunt promised to take her to the green grotto- where all the fish are blind where the sun never shines. She visited with her amid the changing colors of an evening, just when the evening adopted the usual shrouding of the Darkness. Now seeing around, her, her first question was: "are my cousins and my mother going to be there?"
"Yes," Nora replied to offer her some added happiness.
"Well, take me. I will go with you."

With Amble Lee's obsession with the Darkness, it was never a significant task for her aunt to get her to go with her, although she will not be able to convince her that the darkness is not absolute and that it cannot be a valid personal friend, nor can it be her actual mother. The only thing her aunt Nora will have to do is to advance her secret hope that at such time she will become aware that it is indeed a subscriber to the existence of man, society, its economy, and some things, whether they are in the living form or dead.

Again, using this strategy to explain these phenomena to a person with such a disorder as Amble Lee, she could be feeding into her castle in the sky fantasy. Nora's only hope would be built on no foundation since Amble Lee's understanding is a fixation on a well-built-in illusion.

Nora then had to hinge on further hope that at such time, Amble Lee would help herself to become more aware that all her fanaticisms are in the very extension or expansion of the body of the Darkness that only she alone believes in and adores. Further, all that she sees is the Darkness, and with limited activities in which she is unwittingly engaged, not knowing that it is nothing more than a bliss of false belief. Nora also needs to let Amble Lee learn that the Darkness she so glamorized has within, the ability to shell away dark portions known as Shadows, Shades, and Silhouettes, which are not her brothers and sisters as she believes. How well she will be able to do this is to be seen.

And Nora needs to let her know further that it is necessary to let her be aware that although the Shadows are seen as so natural and have been seen as vitally important to her, they are of less importance and are much less crucial to others.

Although Nora does not know that the Darkness is vital to the economy of the various nations, she is hard-pressed to keep this knowledge away from Amble Lee, and dare not let her ever hear this. Otherwise, Amble Lee would want to use the opportunity to prove to her that she was all along right in believing that the Darkness is really of flesh.

Nora tried everything in her limited knowledge to convince her that the Darkness is unreal and without life. All this time while talking with her in the thick sheet of pasted night, but her explanation was in vain. Amble lee's fixation has a strong hold on her and will continue to guide and direct her through the remainder of her life; it would seem.

"I am happy that you are talking with me, aunt Nora, but what talking with me means?" she asked in a firm voice. "You are of my blood according to you, and so is the Darkness."

"You said it, but it is not of flesh and blood even though it may appear to you, Amble Lee," Nora explained. "It is nothing but a shattered matter of nothingness that made its appearance wherever and whenever Light is absent," Nora, for the hundredth time, explained.

"For all I know, she is my mother and the only mother I have been seeing now for years wherever I go. Like your friend, you are always against her. And even if you are there, I do not see you. Both of you are against my mother, which you want me to accept. I will only accept your ignorance of her, but I will continue to hold her as my mother until she has proven otherwise."

"Amble, you are only imagining things."

"Aunt Nora, how can you say that when she is right here in front of me, hugging me, something you have never done?"

"Where is she, sweetheart?" Nora asked.

"Here!"

"Here where my dear niece. Do you feel her?"

"Right here and over there, behind the lamp on the wall and everywhere."

"My dear niece those are Shadows, which are the reflections of the lamp carved out of the presence of the light. Will you please understand?"

"No, she is not. How then she is always with me, and I see her more often and larger than I have been seeing you?"

"You see, Amble, we are living in a region where the sunlight comes only every day in the morning, and after it comes out it stay for twelve hours."

"That's what you say, for we all see things differently and from different point of view," replied Amble Lee.

The presence of the Darkness hardened more in Amble Lee's belief that it is her mother, and who believe that if it were not so it would not have traveled from home with her to the very hull of the green grotto and back. Such has become an irresistible idea of reference for her.

In the meantime, Amble Lee wrapped her arms around her skeletal like frame, head down, and gasp for breath against the stiff and semi chilly evening wind. This was her first trip with her aunt Nora out of Four Seasons Macula. She had all along the way admired the serenity of the Darkness and the specks of Light from the stars glittering on high. According to her belief, every time she speaks the Darkness respond in appreciation of her presence, but Nora harshly rebuked her on each occasion that she made such silly utterances.

"My dear niece, it is the echoing of your voice that you are hearing."

"How then could it be and she does not respond to you whenever you speak?" "What do you make of that?" Nora asked.

"It is because she is not your mother and she is not obligated to respond to you."

"Oh, silly can you ever be! It is all in your thinking Amble Lee, all in your mind."

"That's what you think," Amble Lee replied.

"What you have not considered Amble Lee, you speak with a much stronger voice than I do, and as a result, your voice carried and echoed through the wilderness."

At that moment there was another sound that came out of the hull of the Darkness.

"Now you see. That's what I told you. Here is my mother and my siblings talking with me. How then can you say that she cannot speak?"

"Amble Lee my dear, it is someone else may be in the yonder talking, but not necessarily to you. You are definitely hearing the echoing of your voice coming from the dark wilderness."

There was no soul around except that which the sound came. And with all the clearance to their ears and their patient listening, the moment soon became calm, then only the sound of the flapping wings of the hanging bats lifted themselves.

No measured portion of empathy could be counted that Nora did not have for her at this sad stage. With that, she only shook her head in disgust and put out the flame of the little torch that sparsely pierced the Darkness an hour or so after they left the Green Grotto.

The instant they returned to their temporary place of abode was another plug of confusion. Amble Lee tried to convince her aunt that her belief about the Darkness bears more factual evidence of reality than that of her presence. Their return in the evening assured Amble Lee that the night traveled home with them.

"See what I have been telling you?" she said. "She came with me. She followed me to the grotto, stayed with me, returned with me, and is still present with me. Now aunt Nora, if she was not my mother, why would she do that?"

"You need to know, Amble Lee, that I am much older than you, meaning that I have been in this world years before you. And yes, you may be endowed with special gifts, but…"

"So, what are you trying to say, aunt Nora?"

"I am saying you know that what you are going on with is complete nonsense which you must stop."

Frustrated and heartbroken, Nora could not devise an effective method to transform, at least, the depth of Amble Lee's illusion even into some semblance of reality. Now she had to be more careful in her thinking and her utterance as Amble Lee grows.

Chapter Twenty-Two

THE HARBOR SHARKS

Nora was watching all the harbor shark-eyed- boys parading the street the following day; young men with their ravenous libido appetites that had yet to know her unfortunate situation were now admiring her. Nora fixed her watchful eyes on her niece whenever she goes shopping is paramount to Amble Lee's wellbeing, as her wisdom to ignore boys is severely hampered. "She may not understand, so it is my responsibility to watch and tell her," Nora said admittedly. "You are certainly not an ordinary child."

"I'm I, not an ordinary child?"

"No, you are not."

"Well, aunt Nora, from now on, there will be no need to wonder who I am. I have already told you that when any of my sibling is found beneath the sole of your feet it is noon time, and if it drifts an inch from beneath the sole of your feet it is about 12: 30 in the afternoon, and 2 inches from beneath it is 1: 0'clock in the afternoon."

"Augh…!"

"Augh what?" Amble Lee asked.

Nora, became awestruck and now more aware of Amble Lee's sarcasm and not interested in anything else she had to say.

"I think I said them in your hearing some time or another, and you…"

Amble Lee, interjected and fumed. "You see, aunt Nora, even from those days, my brother and my siblings Shadows, Shades, and Silhouettes were meaningful wherever they went or were seen."

"I now remember the old man told me that in his days, they noticed that Shadows begin to stretch themselves as the day wears on. We therefore see one of the many acts of the daughter of Darkness introducing Shadows, but not what you have taken it to be."

"Care not what you may say, aunt Nora, she is my mother. And all that you may explain will ever do is strengthen my view that she is my mother whom you are working hard to deny me."

"I am not going to argue with you, Amble. Just come on, and let's go."

The next unplanned journey was completed faster than Nora had imagined.

They are now at another temporary place of dwelling. Amble Lee chose to rest; she sat on the stump beside the barn when came a stiff Shadow.

"Let's get inside, Amble."

"Why?"

"It can be hazardous for you as a little young lady to be alone in the dark."

"So, you are also afraid of my mother? I am not afraid. There is nothing in her for me to be afraid."

"There may not be anything in her Amble, but you do not know! Come inside."

Amble Lee remained sitting, staring into the sky, counting some things she found much pleasure in. According to her, they were the eyes of her siblings peering gleamingly from behind our mother. During those nonsensical utterances, Nora could only watch and listened to her niece's nonsense then shook her head in pity and sighed.

In the meantime, a sneaky shadow appeared in the clustered undergrowth.

"What else is left on earth for me to do?" Nora questioned herself, and looked to the heavens. "Have mercy upon me oh father of heaven," she appealed.

"Twenty- one, twenty -two, twenty -three, twenty-four," Amble Lee continued.

"What are you doing Amble Lee?"

"What do you think?"

"Stop the nonsense," Amble Lee, just stop the cursing nonsense."

"What nonsense? I am counting…!" Amble Lee replied as the shadow slowly advanced.

"What are you counting?"

"Those eyes in the far are winking at me and that shows how friendly my siblings are."

"Stupid ass, they are the stars, and you will never be able to finish counting them."

"You can say whatever you want to say aunt Nora, twenty –five, twenty-six, twenty- seven, twenty- eight, twenty -nine…"

In an attempt to convince her, Nora tried all the tricks she knew. She passed her hand across Amble Lee's face with regularity to determine if she genuinely seeing the stars. "In the meantime, Amble Lee, you must not forget that without the sun, which is the Lord's protector of the days, and without it such distinct act or display of nature could not be possible. You are now seeing those because the sun had long ago left the sky."

"Then where is it now? I saw it just once some hours ago before we went to the Green Grotto."

"It had long disappeared."

"To where?"

"Moreover, you could not have seen the sun. It must have been the moon, for you could not tolerate the presence of the sun. And it is to be borne in mind Amble Lee, that it was not for man, although seemed at liberty, to trace the end of the sun or the darkness, and it is not in his competence to find such, as much as it is not in his competence to measure the amount of water in the oceans," Nora explained. "And moreover, you do not want to see the sun that will make you more miserable, wouldn't it?"

"I am not trying to do that aunt Nora; I am simply saying that the Darkness is my mother and that I would like to know where she went the morning when your darling Sunny Light came over the hills you talk so much about."

"Stupid, it would be farfetched or insanely premature for anyone to harbor any such thoughts that such would be possible for anyone to know. I do not know where it goes when it disappears." And even then, when will such imaginary impossibility ever get close to reality, I don't know," said Nora, with the sound of annoyance in her voice. "And if such become possible Amble Lee, it would have marked the end of life and time."

"I know, but I will not now tell you now."

"When will you tell me?" Nora asked. "The world would be most happy to know, I think!" she added.

"And then I will die, "replied Amble Lee.

"My niece, you will not die because of that. The word Dark, and Darkness, have a long-complicated presence in the world as well as in the history of man, his imaginations and formation. Yet I have never seen or heard of anyone before you who has taken it on as their mother or, using your words, and now think you know where it goes when the Light comes on!"

"You are still with the view that all that is Dark is evil, aunt Nora. You will see, and then you will believe that I know that the Darkness is not evil." Amble Lee replied.

"To date no one knows enough about it. Therefore, I do not believe there is a single living soul apart from you, Amble Lee, who is able to answer your question. It may be perceived as being self-created or self-formed, so it would be most interesting to know where it goes when the Light comes on. I have before told you that I am awaiting your findings on it."

"You have your doubt Aunt Nora, but I shall prove to you that I now know, and I will show you in the due course of time," Amble Lee promised.

"What I do know is that it can well be argued that it is the chief architect of shielding and inhibiting things, utilizing all its powerful authority and its might in its nightly dominance. Yet where it goes, I don't really know. I am therefore with the world awaiting your discovery on its whereabouts the moment any portion or parts of Light comes on." Nora said, pressing home her views, that are totally contrary to those of her autistic niece.

"You will know soon enough that it has never done anything that is evil to me!"

"Yes, I can understand that, but you may not have observed the great deal of evil it is believed to have caused. You are too young and inexperienced to see, or witness the degree of evil it has caused to have done to people. So why would you want to attached yourself so closely to it I do not know!"

"That you will never know nor the feelings of others, aunt Nora."

"Yes, and it could well be one other way of people showing their ignorance, which is just the same as yours but in a different frame."

"You are not saying that I am stupid or crazy aunt Nora, are you? You have said it before. Is it what you are saying again?"

"Oh no Amble, I just want to bring to your awareness that everything in the world has a purpose, and they all function by some form of motion and belief, some of which are not necessarily correct. In the evenings through mornings, for example, and at both time of dusk or twilight, that's when one aspect of the Darkness in motion shows its scary behavior. And when through the presence of Light, both acts in accordance with each other, and behave in frightening manner. Therefore, the Darkness cannot be with life although it so appeared to you," Nora asserted. "And in its act with the presence of Light, it mostly begins its defensive approach while it robotically and slothfully retracted into its domain, or emerged out of its nothingness. And then from its grand acres of places of concealment it made itself known the second the Light disappears."

"Aunt Nora you keep on calling my mother it."

"Well sweetheart, I cannot call it anything else because I know that it is not human as we are. It is a thing Amble Lee, and I will continue to call it 'IT' as a know it to be."

"You don't understand aunt Nora, you don't understand."

"I do understand Amble, I do understand, but you are the one having difficulty understanding the Darkness and all it actions. The things you are attaching to it are just out of your imagination; and what I am seeing is certainly not of my imagination, I can tell you that."

What was missing between both niece and Aunt was, it can well be said that the Darkness has been given such a splendid endowment that as the twilight hours wears on, it cunningly creeps into its coat of ultra-blackness, and then becomes an institution that is radically opposed by man, at least to some. So, it is not so clear, or perhaps we do not yet know what flavor gave Amble Lee the happiness she has found in it.

"That's what I have been trying to tell her all this time."

"As of now I will no longer tolerate your dictate. Get away from me," her aunt barked angrily at her.

"You are opposing my every view."

"Oh no Amble Lee! I am not opposing your views. I am simply telling you that it is the roundabout of Nature that sometimes come in, and in such a conning manner that it provoked a number of people and give them such thoughts and abnormal thinking ---showing the lacking of conventional wisdom. This happens among some people Amble Lee, while others like yourself glorify it for its conniving secrecy it applied at times just as in your case."

"Aunt Nora, you are calling my mother conniving because she has gained my love and my preference, isn't it so?"

"No Amble, I want to aware you how your mother's conniving ability to conceal both large and small images and objects, whether they are wet, dry or weighty; and even in a state of weightlessness, which should make it more difficult for you to keep it as your mother. Something is really wrong with you Amble Lee."

"For one thing, aunt Nora, she is too complex for you to understand. And aunt Nora, she never gets wet, and she never cries about being too hot or too cold like what you all customary do."

"You need to think a bit more rationally Amble Lee."

"Aunt Nora, you earlier on said I am to go away from you and I am going to do just that. I will not stay around to annoy you anymore and allow you to treat me like a child, for I am now a young lady."

"And I'll wash my hands from any guilt of what may happen to you. I told you about what I saw and you took no heed," Nora warns her. "So, you may go wherever you chose."

"I have my mother who will take care of me, so don't you worry."

"Go right ahead Amble Lee, go right ahead."

"Here we go again," said Amble Lee.

"You have this fixation about the Darkness that I'll never quite understand."

"What is there about her to understand? I care not to know anything more about her other than she is my mother, and with my siblings she stays with me closer than you do."

"In fact, while you are holding it as your mother, Amble Lee, it is bearing the burden of carrying the stigma as being the grand agent of harboring evildoers. Would you in all conscience want to place your fleshly mother, even though she is dead in such category? And also, in the depth of its blackness comes the feeling and the perception of others who talk unpleasant things about it such as its mal-facial presence, and how it leads the nyctophobic to tears and fears that often linger within not only their thinking, but in the minds of others; while with all that blamed for stirring confusion and invoking misapprehension. Are you really sure you want to hear things of such be said about your real mother?" Nora asked.

"No, but I think that those who are afraid of her are unwise like you are, and because of that you all will say anything."

While Amble Lee and her aunt Nora engaged themselves in their verbal tiff over the Darkness, there is that open question among those who would like to know the exact role the mother of Darkness played in the pre-life era.

Much could be argued in a variety of ways, and one in which those who favored its presence like Amble Lee does, and that of its dissidents, because, in their view, they allow the progress of a specific set of people to perform all their devious acts, while that state of awes prevailed as others admire its maneuver and what sometimes appears to be someone who is with unvoiced but cogent views, which actions are propelled by just two simply basic causes.

One is the presence of some semblance of Light and an object. Without any form of Light and an object, the Darkness would appear in a still body in a giant form. And without it, Light or any constituent part thereof would have been insignificant. Then, too, it would stand vast and still as it were before God so sought and said "let there be light."

"One should think not of her shape, which may be seen as the inhibitor of all that is bad and evil. For evil dwelled only in the mind of the wicked and in the frame of man, who bears the burden of making the distinction between that which is good from bad, and may adhere to that which is their preference since '*as a* man thinks *so* is, he.'" Amble Lee said.

"Where did you get those views from Amble Lee?"

"Why do you ask that questions aunt Nora?"

"Because your reasoning at this stage would make one believe that you are truly a prodigy. So, I would like to know," replied Nora.

"I got it out of my thinking."

"That's ludicrous."

"There we go again. I do not think that I speak with any of what you so called ridiculous utterance. And even if you think I do, it would be found only within the frame of your personal thinking."

"Ok, Amble Lee, say what you have to say. You just be careful of that shadow I saw there."

"Thank you, but I am not afraid."

"You know Amble Lee, after listening to your latter reasoning, I begin to give some thoughts to some of the things you have said, but still cannot agree to your belief that the Darkness is your mother."

"Thank you, but as I was saying aunt Nora, my mother does not bear any evil thoughts, and she harbors not any grudge, feelings or resentment to me or you or anyone. And she is not inherently bad or inherently good. And even if she were to be deemed inherently bad, it would have been through those who seek and use her as their domain for the purpose of perpetuating their evil deeds, which she is unwitting of," Amble Lee argues. "I am not with any evil deed, nor do I have any intention to pursuc any. So, the fact that I take her to be my mother, let it be so."

"I am so happy to hear you say that, because I know that the Darkness is a neuter gender that sets itself within the bounds of its authority as dictated by Lights and objects and as caused and set forth by God and Nature. And there are times during the days when it hides itself behind turrets and in tunnels and other places, and with no specific preference neither to day or night, man or beast, good time or bad time, hot or cold, or wet or dry. It all along performs its endowed ability in the form of maintaining its transient operation," said Nora.

"Yes, and she is comely too. I know that because there are times when I would desire her to be more than what she is. Since there are times when part of that which is not of herself, such as when she and my dissidents' siblings set themselves before our eyes at various times and places, she looks the same." Amble Lee explained, assuring her aunt Nora that it is not all that she has said that she is against.

Aunt and Niece appeared to be reasoning on common ground, although every now and then Amble Lee differs in views and often resort to her tangential reasoning. It is only when Crappy's untamed occasional interjection interrupts and came into the fold that her argument is increasingly strengthened.

"The mother of Darkness sets in her pattern, and is quick to respond to the dictate of her progressive rulers. How well she gets along with her fused body bearing the name dark, is one thing that needs to be measured and to be weighed in as a startling module.

There are always other objects of delight and interest that often claim the instant attention of a few who may look to the sky and in particular, at the marvelous attraction of Nature, and how meticulous it is when in its state of dictatorship in dealing with the Sun, the empty sphere, the Moon and the Night." Crampy argued. "It can only be ignored when the awareness of man is abducted by the splendor of Nights, and when all the regal appearance of the artificial sparkling Lights takes the mantle of the disappeared Sun of Nature," he added.

Mother Darkness without doubt, is neither a pitying nor an unpitying vanguard that acts on its impulses. It acts in all its efforts that it makes when seeking to take the opportunity presented to it at the slightest shift, as dictated by any portion or part of Sunny Lights. And that's what made it appear to move from one place to the other. First, mother Darkness as she is called, respond to the temporary appearance and disappearance of any semblance of Lights and thereof; all of which contribute to the achievement of her end. When fused with what is believed to be her daughters or dissidents, it is here that she is to be blamed for the unshielded areas that are left alone?"

It could be assumed and perhaps argued that the mother of Darkness fused herself with no hesitancy at times, with any other form of blackness of her kind through the open act and order of Nature's influence. She has never, cannot, and will never carry out any of her acts independently. She acts on silent order, and by virtue of her ubiquitous ability, she acts both instantaneously and simultaneously.

We should, however, hold firm that by the action of her dissidents, from time to time she sometimes appears in minute proportion while they all act in response to dictate. Despite all that, what is certain is, she usually opts to rest herself in places where Lights are lacking and encouraged the warped mindedness and the deceitful characteristics driven by man's own will and self-determination to act in his area of preference.

In her contemplation, Nora wondered about Amble Lee and the Darkness. Little, if anything, she knows about mother Darkness herself, at least not more than what she has so far explained to Amble Lee. And in her thinking, she would occasionally throw in her sometimes-disconnected views about mother Darkness whether she has any influence upon anything but that of itself.

Nora's plain to the eyes raising veins and curving wrinkles have now made their visible pronouncement in her face as she aged from the stress of coping with her niece's ongoing situation that become more burdensome. Seeing those, Nora was kicking mad at the idea, the fact that there was nothing more she could do apart from acknowledging a couple of things. Half the time she was upset with Amble Lee, and would have liked to reverse her decision to take on the task of caring for her, at which time she was thinking of long years of healthy life and happiness.

Nora acknowledged the sacrifice she has made thus so far, and at which time it gives her pleasure at least sometimes, but she did not foresee the stress Amble Lee's condition would have placed upon her, even though she was prep before about her illness but not to the degree of stress she is now undergoing. For not only that Amble Lee is getting worst as she grows, she is becoming ultra-verbal combative and problematic.

"I know that mother Darkness has an imagery decor of the sometimes-wayward ambiance all in its pervasive act while it remains in its state of stillness. What I cannot understand, and as I have said several times before, is how this child has taken into her feeling that it is of her blood," Nora said. "That I do not think I will be able live with any longer."

"It should not be too difficult for you to understand that the child is autistic, and as a result you should have expected a number of strange behaviors," Crampy said.

"How long can I take her behavior? That's my question," said Nora.

"And you are to expect even worse. She will be like the wind at times. Sometimes in turmoil, and sometime she will be as mute as a door post," explained Crampy.

"I observe that. And I have noticed that unless she is told to do anything, even to herself, she will remain still and move only by instruction, just like the Darkness waits for the order of the Light before it moves. Other than that, she will remain as dormant as a tombstone. I have noticed all that much about her."

"To put it mildly, you have a problem on your hand Nora," Crampy said.

Chapter Twenty-Three

NORA, IN TWO MINDS

Wearing a pale blue chiffon and white dress, Nora stood blank in the autumn draft; a low bale of cloud formed slowly, and a spot of Darkness seemed unmoving behind her. She was still speaking with Crampy when suddenly was an uproar in the shaft of the element that drowned their utterances. "Perhaps I could use what happened here which is the behavior of nature as an example in this respect. Did you hear it?"

"Yes. Have you noticed the immediate action of the wind and how quickly the Darkness in the clouds disappeared?"

"Oh yes, I have noticed that. Otherwise, if it were elsewhere, it would have, at this stage, waiting for the first action of a leaf in the company of wind and some semblance of Light for it to shift itself in a similar fashion. The child's behavior is as unpredictable as the weather."

"I guess you have noticed this ---while quite to the contrary--- the dissidents of the Darkness entrenched themselves in places we would least expect," said Nora.

The mystic acts of the grand body of the mother of Darkness supported the smooth shifting of Shades, Shadows and Silhouettes from place to place at the mere appearance of any form of Light. And through their frequent and conceited behavior, they are able to sustain their adoptive ability to fit themselves in voids that are disgustingly depleted of Lights.

And, as often as it happens, on any clear Nights when the clouds are nowhere to be found, and the hovering of Lunar Moon is in its majestic form, they seemed now to be hiding behind the willows might even down to the hidden garden tools. Then next to step in, was the number of spotted blackness that appeared angry at the hasty wind that caused the leaves to aimlessly flutter themselves about with the passing of the wind and time.

"The Darkness clashing with the Light of Lunar Moon brings on another admirable splendor."

"Yes, I know. And it shows you the outstanding ability of my mother, "said Amble Lee in her jubilation at Crappy's example.

"The Nights in the meantime, appear smooth and quiet with the glow of Lunar Moon, who sometimes half inundates the open sphere, but offers no visible spasm of fear or horror to most. And that is the sole reason why Amble Lee can tolerate her for now. In any case, for some inexplicable reason, with the force of her gravitational pull, she should affect whatever little coherent functioning that lies in Amble Lee, which she sometimes displayed."

"What do you know?" asked Crampy. "And I said, because it is the opinion of some people, she subscribes to the twisting of jaws, while she has scientifically proven to have subscribed to the rising of tides and the wreaking havoc of the mind.

"The degree of control she has over the ocean seemed to be much above all that is to be understood."

"So, are you saying that since it is something so often happen on a clear Night, with the presence of the diluted Darkness there should be no fear?" asked Nora.

"It could be, yes, since it seemed to be comforted by the sheer presence of Lunar Moon, but only until Night bears itself in, then transformed itself into a spate of ultra-brightness."

"How such beauty to behold in the atmosphere when my mother falls in her misty acts, and as she settles beneath the leaves and branches across the hills and along the plain; yet often enough she cannot be appreciated. Nature at these times seemed to have set the stage for her happiness and comfort of man and for us to live in accordance with it as observed in the behavior of my mother, yet some people often fail to appreciate her. It is understandable, though, that not all human is blessed with such gift to appreciate anything, more so, the awesome beauty of my mother."

"Amble Lee you are talking crazy."

"That's what you believe, aunt Nora."

There are superstitions that derived from the lacking in originality and reality that are in the figure of the presence of its often-dissident images all in the form of Silhouettes, that markedly subscribed to some great extent, confusion of various degrees. But not all are the result of the mere presence in trueness, since Amble Lee sees things differently.

There are other things that should be observed and cast into the fold of the imaginary minds; things such as the figures on the wall as well as in the soft whispers of the Nights, against lampposts, hidden studs, and columns of various sizes.

"I believe that the contention leveled against her mother Darkness, was in fact prompted by just a sense of poor confusion- causing mixture of the deformed mimicked images that lead to all the flawed imaginations and beliefs, which are purely of those who beforehand made to believe and accept the formation they caught sight of. And I say this because of what I have observed in Amble Lee. And one need not guess the result. Yes, in the presence of these they obviously distort both the eyes of man and their minds, and often robbed them of their ability to think cognitively and realistically," Crampy said.

"I agree with you Crampy, but never mind, it is to be understood that not all the accusation placed upon its existence is with any factual reasoning. For although they were all caught in the focus of the eyes, that personal view and irrational calculation could well distort their actual formation caught in the imagery pattern of all things that are all about in the open field or in the path of the Darkness, said Amble Lee."

In the meantime, the behavior of the Darkness gave cause to the arresting of the curiosity of three women standing by the wayside, and in their strength of mind one asked the other: "have you ever heard anyone said that they have seen ghost during the daytime?"

"To think of it, no, I never heard that."

The woman's question flew open the door for a detail explanation that led to the importance of some accurate information, which is essential to the development of the mind. At the same time though, it thwarts the building up of any inauspicious curiosity of Crampy and Nora, as well as the other women standing on the periphery.

"Merciful father," one shouted. "What a question!"

"What I do know is that we often fool ourselves and so often carried away by our imagination, and as a result we have adopted idiotic views through our unawareness of the simple things around us. And we further succumbed to our superstitions, which are often induced by our ignorance to the behavior of the master of Lights and the mother of Darkness, who both carved Shades and Silhouettes," the other woman replied.

"Amble Lee, as she is well known, has no fear of such as she intermingles with all three, Shades, Shadows, Silhouettes, she claimed to be her siblings. And she also said that there is human who are routinely garbed and locked themselves with her mother for their personal reason," said Crampy.

The blistering dialogue, however, was not meant to destroy the notion that there is no such thing as ghost. In their argument, the pronouncement of the visible presence of what is so-called apparition is less commonly used in all ghost tales about seeing them in the Days over the Nights, both of which are in opposition to Amble Lee's thinking. It can also be inferred that since mother of Darkness has always been accompanying the Nights visa-visa, it is only at such time that evil traversed.

"Now here comes that insensible side of the argument, which lies within the flawed belief that ghosts walks only in Nights and not during the time of mother

Days, only because the Night are always cloaked by my mother,"

"That's not the case Amble Lee."

"Yes, it is so, for you have all placed my mother in that frame of thoughts because of how you think, especially you, aunt Nora," shouted the angry Amble Lee.

"Amble Lee, it is not true that your Silhouette, has created havoc?"

"Oh no! It is the eyes and the minds of idiots such as you that brought on all the distortion you are talking about."

"Well, if you believe that you are bemused by what is said, you must understand that the cause for this quagmire is indicative of the degree of illusion caused by opus mother Darkness and all her dissidents, since no one has never stated that they have seen ghost during the time of mother Days. So, if one harks onto such belief that ghost are only seen during the Nights or in the hours of the coming or presence of the mother of Darkness, it would be more logical to hold such belief since it is more comprehensible, the fact the Silhouettes have the capability of playing such tricks with the minds and the eyes, and can be accepted the way Amble Lee accepts it," Crampy argued.

"Are you saying Crampy, based on what the woman said and accept it? If you are thinking along that line and agrees with it, you would be saying that it is because that are afraid that they will be easily seen during the hours of mother Day," Crampy asked.

"Your argument is stupid Mr. Crampy, All you are trying to do is put my mother down. You all hold the belief that the tone of her skin is responsible for all that is evil, and as a result, I deemed it as nonsense which should not be in discussing my mother?"

Amble Lee was blatantly ignored fearing that she would blow her top hearing the title of her mother so loosely used, but she already heard and blurt her annoyance.

"So therefore, on a based perception of something with this temperament, it can be taken that ghosts are intelligent enough to know that they are more likely to be seen in the days, and as a result take the preference to walk during the course mother's presence?" asked Amble Lee.

"It is a fact that you should accept Amble Lee, and without any hard feelings."

"No, I cannot, for in that belief, will again find a place in discussions, since the minds of the wise also holds it that because my mother may conceal or inhibits things, she is the chief reason why more people believe that they see ghost whenever she is with mother Nights."

"It is probably true, Amble Lee, the fact that mother Nights have the tenancy to do a lot of things when in the company of your mother; and people depend on her a great deal do evil and conceal things," Nora said.

"Oh no, here we go again. All blames are placed on my poor mother because of her who she is. What I have heard in that foolish discussion is, all that is Dark or appeared Dark there is evil within, a blatantly vocalized course of your confounded dialogue laced with ignorance and hatred," said the enraged Amble Lee.

"There is no need for you to be angry Amble Lee. All you need to do is think that because mother Nights are invariably accompanied by your mother who is the Darkness, and both she and Nights are somehow synonymous to each other. And there is by a hair's breadth, a mark difference or distinction between them and there can never be mother Night without your mother of Darkness. It is only occasionally, when at such time, your mother of Darkness will come alone without the presence of mother Nights," Crampy said. "And you as an unerring young lady, Amble Lee, and with your unerring instinct, you should have known that," Crampy added.

"It is my belief that because of that feeling without any unerring wisdom, people like you and my aunt Nora do not understand that my mother Darkness dwells amongst us in dwarf proportion at times, or conversely, we dwell at times in her body, depending on the circumstances," said Amble Lee. "My sibling Shady Shades, for example, you all use him to shield yourself from the beams of your friend Sunny Light, yet around the bend you have the worst thing to say, and with much disdain."

"Amble Lee, I have noticed that you did not mention Shadow, is that a deliberate act?" Crampy asked.

"Even though you may think that I have forgotten him, I am asking you not to concern about his name of his presence, for he is of our own mimicked formation as well as that of things. So please, don not worry about him."

These marvelous happenings that stay with mother Days and later herald the coming of the evenings, are slowly transformed through to mother Nights. They are all part of the giving of the master, and all in the acts of what He sets in the form of my mother among all other things with which we live.

The integrity of the confusion caused by its presence can be seen, but only as far as one's power of thinking may take him. Amble Lee's action can well be taken as an example, although in all her beliefs and her behavior, she never mentioned seeing a ghost herself, and not even since she has gained some sight.

"To think or to assume that ghost does not traverse during the presence of Days would lead any ardent believer of the opposite view to hold on strongly to his view? The core fact remains that the mother of Darkness plays a number of tricks with the minds of man, not to mention his eyes and all his imaginary well-driven personal opinion, which are primarily formed as a result of his way of thinking and belief. And that is what made it so extraordinarily strange if not surprising that Amble Lee has never made any alarm of such. There is no doubt that her action is a result of the close bond she has with mother Darkness, he proclaimed mother and a bond seemed that it will never be broken.

Chapter Twenty-Four

THE TRUE AUTISTIC AMBLE LEE

There are those dual presence of the mother of Darkness, which gets in action at times. The mother of Darkness, Shades, Shadows and Silhouettes, are all of which seemed to have caused more negative perception among people, and in particular, those who are embedded into their self-driven nocturnal fears. It is acknowledged that in accordance with the dual-purpose and mission of the mother of Darkness, the mighty Sunny Light stood firm during the time of mother Days, and in time of his ruling, there are occasional shifts in his pattern to display his authority over all earthly things, hence the birth of Shades. So how Amble Le gets it to be her sibling is not known.

"We can argue as much as we may choose, but the foundation has been laid for any challenge that may come about. And we may learn from the preceding reasoning of the women, that even though seemed somewhat convoluted, their views can well be taken as important, and knowledge gained about the acts of the mother of Darkness and all her dissidents. The discomfited behavior of Silhouettes that often caused the quandaries and illusions we often tied ourselves in, is a needless cause that frequently breeds contempt, and with such severity that often promotes the most dreaded fear," Crampy argued.

"I know that some people have it that this frame of belief is a simple act of caught up ignorance, which can be found only among those individuals who through the extent of their perception of my mother," Amble Lee replied. "It is therefore reasonable to say that the first requirement for self-assurance is trusting in oneself, as well as confidence in self just as I'm confident that mother Darkness is my mother."

"It is to be noted that the mind holds that which is the perception of the bearer," said Nora in her sarcastic response."

When the mingling of the floating drifters with the mother of Darkness takes place, the giant body of mother Darkness has a way of shifting itself quietly with the coming of daylight hours, and as if the master had opened the door, its splinters once again seemed to hasten themselves in single unit and will maintain in this casing until come some form of disturbance from somewhere interferes. They will then noticeably speed up their action, and in their act of mockery they go berserk in their response to the self-driven motion with the hasty Wind, Sunny Light and objects.

The actions of these are particularly noticeable when they are responding to the movement of the Wind while the mother of Darkness lies behind the objects. The most astonishing act of the mother of Darkness comes when with all the fury of the Wind, the mother of Darkness stands her ground and moves only the splinters with the interference of Light that have them dancing, on the sole order as dictated. Then, gradually, into these peaceful settings, the mother of Darkness moves away smartly with a silent clatter leaving Light to seep in.

The margin between mother Day and mother Night is marked off by all the imaginary meager lines formed between them when caught in the path of the still and half translucent body of the daughter of Darkness with specks of light peering in.

"The mother of Darkness though sometimes is like a giant monster!"

"I know. And that is what I know my mother to be. And whether it rain or not, I know that during this period, among the many small bands of fork lightening and beams stretching through her endless frame, there are fragment of added colors cloaking the ambiance that create such visible splendor, though none of such can disrupt her presence apart from Light. And it is to be remembered that the realization of such splendor lies only in the eyes of the beholder who had the ability to see but in the distant mind, and who can recognize her as a priceless gift with the ability to present her portion as a blessing of the master, and whose creative wonders carved out of the frame of his handy work," Amble Lee explained.

"It would be only then that this whishing prospect would offer any glimmer of hope that such could be possible. And then, again, such would have been the case of wishing hope that should be banished purely by the degree of the impossibility of such."

"Are you saying Crampy, that my mother should be viewed as an insubstantial matter that has no binding ground on which she can stand?"

"No, I am not saying that, Amble Lee."

"Then what are you saying?"

"What I am saying is, in her immortal presence which, in the sometimes-long hours of Nights, even in her transitory stay, she is forsaken by the wise and the fearful as if they had a mandate to vacate anywhere, she may make her temporary appearance. I do not blame them. It is also understandable because it is impossible for man to withstand the anguish of her perpetual presence at home or the time in the wilderness where it is difficult not to expect her during the presence of mother Nights. Knowing this, I do not understand how do you managed to take it on as your mother," said Nora.

"The fleeing thoughts of man would have then been my concern. And in the face of the universal dominion that my mother seized in her periodic acts, it is impossible to illustrate the countless activities that she has carried out beyond any fragment of a doubt, that her awe-inspiring authority contributed to the shaping of the mind and to the end the destinies of man, his action at any part on the globe, and even beyond the un-imaginary spheres."

And now, when considering the high sense of implausibility and the fact that one knows not the time when the earth will again re-surrender itself to the fullness of the mother of Darkness, all harbored thoughts of such should be shattered and let alone the perpetual mysteries of the coming or formation of all names of Darkness or of her kind, and all members thereof will remain the ever causing of awes.

"Why is there such an argument about my mother?" Amble Lee asked. "I am aware that there are several distinct assortments of tragedy that happened because of her presence and those of my brothers and sisters. And I know you have placed your own judgment and name upon them by calling them Shades, Shadows and Silhouettes, but it can only be assumed that they have done various manner of things thus, the blame is often placed upon them both in my mother's absence and in her presence," Amble Lee argued. "And for all I know, there should not be much accountability placed upon her, because man has eyes to see, ears to hear, and an intelligent mind that is fit enough to guide him away from all perils and danger; against the things he cannot see, and the things his eyes cannot pierce and to behold because of her. He should therefore stop putting blame upon the often-formed opaqueness of my mother."

"In my view she is purposeless," said Nora.

"Aunt Nora, you said that because you do not know that she has an unwritten purpose to serve mankind, and in all her purposeful fullness, she has before measured her duties and always accompanying the mother, Nights. Then with the dawning of Lights, for which she obviously has a phobia, she begins the thinning of herself as he is about to depart from the mother of Nights; leaving room for the coming of mother Day, and she would then follow with similar behavior just as when the coming of the outgoing mother Nights."

"Will you admit that she is awesome most of the time, and in particular when she is with mother Nights?"

"Yes, but while it is true, it is by the way of her occasional slothful march that she has given mankind the opportunity to be mentally prepared for the unknown that may be inhibited within the unseeing frame of her ever-flexible body. And that's the moment she draws herself into twilight and remain there as an invited guest of Night." This is what the autistic child was trying to get across to Crampy and her aunt Nora, but both of whom opposed her views.

"And before the inundation of the atmosphere, I imagined how she measured her texture; cloaking all the spheres and objects while Lights danced gingerly about. Then as she watches for such dancing, Light slowly disappears and caused her body to change from one state of her transient visibility to another and gradually caused her to slump into an opaque body that habitually engulfed the whole of mother Nights. That is how great she is," said Amble Lee. "So, what is this argument about her I do not know? I can only suppose that it is because at this stage she makes it extraordinarily impossible for man to penetrate her with his naked or unaided eyes, and leave him only to the mercy of his sensitive feeling to touch; then he is only able to traverse by using his wits and his hands as feelers to penetrate her blackness with comparable safety, which he should at the end be proud of because she gave him the aid to a comforted mind."

Well, so far, the emphasis has been on the mother of Darkness and how well in her movement she performs, in particular, how amazingly she does her stunning maneuvers the moment her ground judgment tells her that mother Days is drawing nigh. And then, because of her diverse ability she believed to have retarded progress sometimes, and then makes her presence more complex than one could ever imagined.

"For some people she is assumed to be with such severity, and to the extent that her name is often used to denote all the fear and the struggles that promote evil. And at these tenuous moments inside people, their anxiety increased with revolving imagination that often perplexed their minds. And I know that it is with her presences that caused the glow with the slow alteration of the ambiance that draws no comparison, while the eyes of the fearful rolled in their sockets as they imagined, and nothing that could be more absurd than her solemn sheet of blackness that filled their view," said Crampy.

"Yes, I am aware of that, and that is the bone of my contention, because I know how people have perceived her, but I am aware that one knows that in another view she has reshaped herself and is held in the minds of others. It has been said that it is only within the hearts and the minds of the wasteful thinkers that such is harbored. And it is only in the bearer of each heart that knows its own bitterness. Therefore, it is in such hearts that lay the feeling of the individual, since one sees only with his own eyes, and hears only with his own ears. I see her as my mother and so what? I have heard all the unkind utterances made about her; and some of you even refer to her as 'it.' There is nothing that could be more insulting. What you all need to know is that because I was blind, I learn that no man can see through his father's eyes, and no blind person can ever accurately count the colors of a rainbow, nor can he accurately describe the antics of horses in a three-ring circus," Amble Lee. "And I understand, because it is evenly and ultimately impossible for you to determine the next action and the absolute purpose for which she came. Therefore, I will not accept the views of all, because I am not obliged to adhere to them," Amble Lee added.

"You are upset Amble Lee?"

"Yes, I am upset, because of what you people are saying. I know that according to specific views and her purpose, and based on the individual perception of man and the many who carved in their frame of mind their views; to them she is not worthy of any attention much more any consideration of this magnitude. So here comes then a host of some brighter views that may further arrest curiosity and promote a wider range of concern about her and her purpose for coming into existence."

"What are they?"

"The shifting of her presence for one thing is the first example of the wonders of her action. With her given ability to do an abundant of wondrous things, she first swathes the element, and in her mystic poise and subtle approach she thinned herself the moment Light made the slightest appearance."

"So, what?"

Chapter Twenty-Five

ASSESSING THE COMPLEXITIES OF MOTHER DARKNESS

The constant negative utterance leveled against the mother of Darkness has given cause for the summonsing of a wide array of other views that were brought into Amble Lee's thinking. "My mother has such diverse characteristics in all her regions, and the fact that she sizes the frequency of her presence vary a great deal. For example, from time to time she has been periodically coming and going into her fullness, and at the time of her departing she has made it more problematic for some people to understand her, that I can understand," admitted Amble Lee. "And that is the only flawed action, which is called Dark, and was misconstrued by the ignorance of some people that caused the problem. I must admit though that she and her Dark dissidents can, or may cause confusion to the weak-minded. In any case, the duty she performed on her own will be for a mighty long time, and will continue to place you all in a state of awe each time you see her. There will be much more action from her dissidents."

In the assessment of all the degrees of complexities regarding the coming and going of the Darkness, it has become necessary to question the absolute usefulness with in-depth thinking about her fused body and all what is believed to be her dissidents or her breakaways we so called Shadows, Shades, and Silhouettes, and what is in their existence and the purpose of their transitory but randomly bonded body serves in its entirety.

"Now that these rudiments in your thinking have caused to set forth this quagmire in understanding or determining their placement and their duties, they have also given rise to the frazzling of some of the fundamental issues that are germane to the knowledge of man about her fused multifaceted phenomenal behavior; the purpose of both the grand body of her presence and her breakaways serve in society on a whole you don't know."

"Amble Lee you are as crazy as a bedbug."

"I have heard that before, but as one of the hosts of awes in the frame of Nature, people like you are often struck and almost completely dumb at intervals in amazement at the awesome wonders she has caused by the demonstrating of her share of splendor when she caught your friend Light at dawn or dusk. If she were not real, how then some people become unbelievable and speechlessness when they see her action at those times, and which last for minutes, and yet so refer to as the unwittingly deceitful host, why?"

"Amble Lee, I know that you do not take calmly to whatever I have to say, but to begin, the Darkness is known to be the chief architect of seduction, and it is the solo two-in-one module in the world of blackness in which the employed terminologies continue to create doubts and confusion. In fact, Amble Lee, it could well be dubbed and become known as the trickiest black woman for man to fully understand," Nora said.

"You all will not understand her, for her unique quickness, her movement and her ubiquitous ability should really allow everybody to realize how amazing she is. And the fact that she also has the ability to remain still, and in her grand and unterrifying spell of her blackness she is able to anticipate the coming and the interference of the slightest manifestation of Light. I have to admit dough, that before the appearance of your friend Light, the stunning presence of her imperishable blackness seemed vexed at times, which should be understood. For who the hell wants to be unduly disturbed during the time of comfort?"

"And Amble Lee, you must not forget that it is at those time mother caused more fear in me and scared even the very devil out of my wits, more so people with fragile mind."

"Yes, one can understand those weak minded as you are, who are so well caught up in the fervent belief that there is always danger lurking in the often-thick broad spread of her blackness. And I know that it's a well-held view that is riveted in the minds of almost all none Dark human, that all that is Dark is the cistern of evil. Nothing could be further from the truth, for it should be realized that your friend Sunny Light is much eviler, considering his harshness to the skin of the non-Dark. And he has never separated himself from the scorching ability he comes with unless when the floating drifters in their vast layers are using themselves as protective shield between man and his burning rays. So now you see, Aunt Nora, why I take such stance."

"Yes, but..."

"But, my foot, just say what you have to say aunt Nora."

"You should be reasonable and ready to admit that in the absence of Light, there is the action of your mother, the everlasting sheet of blackness, and at which time she carries out her overwhelming presence in the atmosphere and fused herself with the dark spots and all thereof. And, as an immortal being, they sometimes defused themselves and spread such daring phenomenal acts around things and objects that some human will, in an incalculable time, continue to live in a state of interminable awes and fear," said Nora.

"I am so pissed, for I do not know why the most unsavory reputations are leveled at my mother!"

"When it comes to you Amble Lee, it's needless to assume anything. I am sure you have noticed that in the name of the family of Darkness and all that are related to her according to you, it is your mother who displays the most unsavory reputation owned to her frightening blackness and vastness, even though she can unreservedly boast her non- vicious acts against anything. This makes me agree with Crappy."

"Aunt Nora, you are lacking the wisdom that several intense observations of her presence revealed that apart from her, nobody else can be said to be the easiest going and harmless. The fact that she offered not, and presents no threats of any kind to the life of man or beasts. You are aware of that. It is only to some form of plants that she may have caused to deprived of the nutrients and the energy your dear friend Sunny Light offers."

"That could well be so Amble Lee, but you may not have observed that in the forest glades where the gleaming brightness of Sunny Light fails to shine continuously, it is because of her. And as a result, the soil is depleted of grass and many other herbs and creeping vines. And whenever she takes hold of these places, she offers no purity or nutrition to anything. Will you agree with that?"

"Yes," replied Amble Lee.

As aunt and niece argued over the value of the Darkness and the likes of Sunny Light, there is some sense of uncertainties whether these spots of mother Darkness we call Shades in this respect, are hiding from the brutal onslaught of the giant mighty Sunny Light. It is not quite clear if they are seeking refuge from the objects they cover.

"For whatever their reason, what is clear is, the position they took demonstrated another simple and amazing act. It could well be viewed that the leaves beneath devoted themselves to the shielding of the delicately fine herbs from the scorching Light."

"So, now that it has come to have surpassed man's wildest dream, that apart from the interchanging of oxygen and carbon dioxide with us, and that they breathe and help in the sustenance of the plant, no one truly knows what other direct purpose they serve apart from the outlined."

"The mother of Darkness in the spirit of semantics, she is the host to all that seek refuge from the mighty

Sunny Light, and at which stage the product of her acts is called Shade, said Amble Lee."

The concept of mother Darkness may be contrasted in this respect with all other modules of Nature, and in particular, those that are purged of the ill will against man and all living things. In any case, there will never be any found among them since mother Darkness has been known to be the sole shield and the friendliest module of all modules.

"There are lines of reality that marked this of course, because in essence, outside of my mother, the acts of all other modules can be very devastating as seen in a variety of ways and for quite a number of years," said Amble Lee. 'Overall, I have found her to be amazing, and so are all those who represents her. As a result, we may look at her and all that she has offered to us in an assortment of ways. Her vastness and her displaying array of antics has caused staggering opinion on the stateliness of my mother and all the skills and dexterity she demonstrated in the world of herself."

The adoption and lauding of the presence of the mother of Darkness by Amble Lee, is one distinct example of how much it has compelled one to take it into his or her fold, and to the point that it has been seen as something with natural life. Man may travel as far as he can go with his imagination about the mother of Darkness, but he can rest for sure that all he will see in the distance is something that carried him far beyond the eyes of his mind; the unending presence of nothing but the mother of Darkness in her existence, filling all the unlock spaces in the absence of Lights. There has never been, and there will never be a situation caused by the simultaneous absence of Sunny Light and the mother of Darkness.

"After all, it has shown where my mother has never been said to be all that unkind to man, notwithstanding all the likely pitfalls it may cause to some who claimed that she has," said Amble Lee.

"In all our thoughts of life, or anything thereof, we should in all cases approach them with an open mind. And within such frame of mind, or within our mental scope, it will make it much easier for us to carve in those unoccupied space the imaginary things about mother darkness. Leaving alone that vacuum that harbors no frame of thoughts that nature is a gift as you yourself are a part thereof, can be very troubling. And it may never come home to you that through your employed imagination that the Darkness is an entity and a constituent part of life makes it more troubling. This is the way Amble Lee thinks, but too extreme.

It is a known fact that when some of you think of the coming and the presence of the mother of Darkness, you think of danger that may be hidden in her. You should know by this that Sunny Light rules mother Day and all the hours within her time, while my mother shares all the hours with those of mother Nights. Sunny Light in the meantime with his authority dictates his rulings over mother Days and her daily functioning. And because of the degree of threats, she is afraid that her character might be impugned, and as a result she routinely caused to carve and mimicked images influenced by the towering presence of Sunny Light, in his finest intermingling spell with her daughter, she made her daughter of Darkness loafs about.

On the imaginary, the penetrable ability of the simple frame of mother Darkness who in her lurking manner, without any foundation she gave her observers a view of her routine behavior.

"It is only the good judgment of a few, and in whose strange eyes and minds they are formed and are forced to accept the reality that my mother has yes, a complex gift and too complex for all to understand what happens to her the moment Sunny Light or any other type of Light appears why she disappears."

"She will continue to play all the unbolting tricks and antics around the globe, whether in the sight of man or behind him. And she will always mesmerize the minds of those who need to be more conversant with all her acts and antics. A good look at the sometimes hide- from-view action of the mighty Sunny Light and Lunar Moon, shows how quickly she finds herself between them and even sometimes temporarily obscuring the face of Lunar Moon," said Amble Lee.

"Amble Lee, would you agree with me if I say that those acts are enough frightening spells of unbelievable swiftness and the constant awry behavior displayed by what you called your mother have caused people to be scared?"

"No,"

"Even though she at times obscure things in the meanest of form?"

"No."

"The endless observation of the action of your mother of Darkness will always be treasured by you Amble Lee, for there is that pattern of her behavior and her eager to find herself in the places where Lights failed to control, which gave cause for some people to observe her and wonder. And by their observation, she clearly shows that at such stage she presents herself in a most frightening fashion. And that is what caused the level of mirages that lead to anxiety and fear. It is only you Amble Lee, who at this moment, watching her, would not be at awe and fear."

"Then aunt Nora, doesn't she show her ubiquitous ability and her obedience? In the numerous acts of my mother, she causes amazements, and shows how well without force she gets from one place to the other, and how effortlessly she demonstrates her ability to mystify people. And without any known act of pressure from anything that motivates her action or caused the acceleration of her movement, she shows her true ability."

All answers seemed to be resting in the gifted wisdom of the autistic Amble Lee, and who will reveal all, as she has previously stated.

"It can only be said in short, that my mother does migrates and imports herself very swiftly from place to place. And the degree of her swiftness, and the speed at which she moves in and out of places made it tricky for the eyes to behold the split- second, and the movements she demonstrates in her appearances and disappearances; the awe-inspiring coming and going of my siblings further propelled the cause for amazement. So, it bothers me to know all those, neither you or your friend Crampy has ever showed or voiced any appreciation."

"Then Amble Lee, have you ever thought that the reinforcement of the type of fear she caused, it is reasonable for us believe that within all her movements and presence there are some forms of danger lurking somewhere even at such brief span of her presence?"

"No, for it was observed that it is the movement of your friend Lights that caused the mysterious appearance and disappearance of my siblings. And although they are parts of her being, she has no control over their doing. It is your darling Light, who has all the dictates. In fact, they are all at his mercy," said Amble Lee.

"Actually, Amble Lee, to be frank with you, the way you talk about your mother and your siblings, I thought they would have had control over their action," Nora said.

"What else can she do after my siblings chose to become dissidents to showcase their magical maneuvers?"

Amble Lee has created a host of extraordinary and stunning observation wrapped in her speculation that the Darkness is exceptionally fond of places that are void of Lights. These familiar actions, according to her, the mother of Darkness has never before been questioned even though she had an immeasurable period of time appeared on the horizon long before man's intelligence and his wisdom became known.

"Oh, such extraordinary character is my mother, that you all spend your time talking about her!" Amble Lee said. "Don't you all are tired of spending your time thinking and talking about events of the past and the presence of my mother while she has shown no sign of fatigue or vexation?" Amble Lee asked.

"My dear niece, don't you think it is reasonable for us to be scared, realizing how she can disappear in a whisper and so often limit the vision of people?"

"What you do not know aunt Nora, is that the restricted visibility that she may have caused at times depends on a number of factors. When she is in her territorial limits for example, she is controlled by your friend Light at that time, and that's where a seeable process of integration of the two takes place, which depends on the intrusion of your friend Sunny Light. And it is at these times that many strange things happen. In the meantime, all the confusing breakaways, and dissidents find a secret place somewhere in the solid-state or stillness of my mother and made their acts unfathomable. For in their acts, they tarry not as Shades often do, which is unlike Shadows who sometime takes the task of trailing, leading or even at times flank and cloaked moving objects.

"There has not been any known forerunner of the mother of Darkness as we could say about your friend Light."

"Is that a statement of factual reasoning?"

"What are you talking about Nora?"

"Sunny Light is believed to be the first form of Light, seconded by Lona Moon and all the Twinklers that followed."

"So, what is your argument, Amble Lee?"

"Because had it not been for my mother, there would have been endless trouble."

"That might be so, Amble Lee, but you will accept one thing; your mother scares the hell out of a lot of people."

"Is that a charge against her?"

"No, but...."

"So, you agree that the underlying principle behind this whole thing is that my mother has been here before all things and will remain so until the closing, or at the end of all things and time?"

"Yes."

"I am glad that you are in acceptance of the fact that before all things there was her presence."

"Yes, and it's no wonder why you gravitated toward her."

"Yes, but even though she has no station or fixed place as we can say for your friend Sunny Light, who is said to be fixed in the heavens and we watched his effortless motion as he slothfully move from one side of the heavens to the other. Then at the end of his journey your mother in her massive frame languidly engulfed all areas and leaves no trail of his long presence in the face of mother Days."

Crampy with his repertoire of knowledge, has led the way in the execution of his authority that offered much challenge to Amble Lee and her views, but little did he know that she was blessed with a multitude of flawless knowledge as a compensation for her autism. Crampy thought he knew as much and went on with his challenging knowledge against Amble Lee and her endowed wisdom, only for him and Nora to later embarrassed themselves the moment Amble Lee points out to them where her mother hides herself the second their friend Light appears.

"The might of Sunny Light will forever temporary vacating all his occupied spaces on an often-cloudless time, that mother Days at her closing, seemed happy that she is being released of his tight biting rays. And it is only in these periods that we conceitedly and irresistible accepting his passive action."

"The fact that the two together often form a union with shared responsibility in the forming and the shaping of Shadows, Shades and Silhouettes made the difference. They start their defusing action from the presence or the brightening of Sunny Light in the face of the azure, and to the very end when came the time for mother Darkness to slowly, but surely manifestly shows herself in her adherence to Nature's suggestion."

"While I may not agree with you in essence, Crampy, I will agree with you in part; and from a more practical view point that wherever your friend Sunny Light is, if he does not harshly present himself with his authority, my mother some sometime becomes the master of that time and place."

"What I will agree with Amble Lee, is, the observed action of Sumy Light which reveals further that the unpitying behavior of what you call your mother is so compelled by him, that she has shown all the composition of all spirit of the age and stands as the vanguard in space and the void, but without authority or power."

"I agree with you, Crampy, but you must have noticed that the recurrence of her portal and non-portal occupation, she leaves her mark upon the astonished eyes as she vanishes or vacates all occupied space at will, even when she is in her slowest motion with time, and even at the closing hours of mother Nights," volleyed Amble Lee.

"Yes, indeed, Amble Lee, but Sunny Light recaptured its place in the exigency of his duties and exercised its authority from dusk to another day into the next twelve hours or so!"

"Crampy, the time will come when I will prove to you and my aunt some of the strangest things you'll never believe."

Chapter Twenty-Six

AMBLE LEE AND THE VOLATILE MODULES

Earthly Ground has contributed so much to the sustenance of life, and more often than ever, although appeared calm and dormant as a tombstone, she would at times, acting on her impulsive displayed her unwelcome behavior that are almost similar to that of Amble Lee's. She is a sneaking, dangerous, and volatile module that spreads herself beneath our feet. And with unpredictable behavior she revolves with her unforgiving unpredictability, and would sometimes shudder in rowdy rage with her often dry and thirsty crust, with her hidden layer at the base of the ocean deep.

The bygone example of one of her impulsive acts and what seemed to be a calm and peaceful module, one day she made it known that man should not place all together his trust in her regardless of her harmless appearances. For while appears to be in her often stillness, she suddenly rocks, shifts, slides, and often open cracks and craters. And in the act of her rowdy unforgiving rage, she obnoxiously and cruelly topples infrastructures.

In every aspect of her behavior there is a perceived action that must be followed, for she was designed within the frame of all things as dictated to her staged the possibility that at any time there can be an action carved out of her clout with various degrees and intensity.

There are cases when the passive ravagers of her peers such as Roaring Streams and Norman Wind, both of whom slothfully and gradually erode portion of portions of her face. And within such acts the passive ravagers become increasingly destructive that they change considerably, her physical appearance leaving alone the mother of Darkness who adopts her portion accordingly in responding to dictates.

“We are from nature’s cause ourselves, and we act by his order. We are living among the unspeakable things that often stand with us at times at a standstill, yet dangerous in their entire disturbing encounters. And in displaying their hostile behavior, they wreak havoc not only of human lives, but that of animals and plants,” Crampy said.

“Why don’t you talk about their unbarring acts accompanied by tumultuous sounds that tumbled in, they set the shattering stage for the wrecking of nerves and evoked the quivering of the lips of the frightened. Then as a people, we unwittingly find ourselves under continual disquietudes and seldom relish any lasting moment of pleasure,” Amble Lee expounded.

“That’s a good point!” said Crampy.

“There you have it; you have now come to my point of reasoning that my mother is not a warrior as she has been so perceived. The often-unlearning acts of Earthly Ground’s delicate tremors that followed the ravishing force of her wrath are more than enough to scare the daylight out of the very devil. You agree?” Amble Lee asked.

“Yes, in a sense.”

“So, therefore, you see that my mother is not an evil woman!” said the artistic progeny Amble Lee, who maintain her hold on her belief, while drifted off into a more convincing example, challenged the stance she has taken in procuring the integrity of her mother. And as we all know, there are the good side and the bad; the positive and the negative. We have also inherited and reaped so much from her that it might even sound ungrateful for the rest of us to cherish the idea of escaping her by following those who are taking off for space perhaps in search of solace somewhere on Luna Moon or even Mars,” uttered Amble Lee in her cynicism.

“You will agree that Earthly Ground provides a host of good as in the case of producing, preserving, and sustaining the fundamentals of life such as minerals and the propelling of the growth of plants, weeds and trees," Nora suggested.

"Yes, aunt Nora, but I will try to explain to you by demonstrating some of the debacles that has been caused by her and Salty Ocean. And I will hand to you or, placed them in a reasonable and straightforward characterization of the most equally dangerous characters known. And there is no mistake in characterizing them as being similarly dangerous as Tom Wind, Sunny Light, and even Luna Moon, all of whom have their own subtle form of danger they frequently hand out to us."

"What have they done you Amble Lee?" Nora harshly asked.

"Aunt Nora, I can't believe you have the audacity to ask me that! You definitely not conversant with the acts of Earthly Ground, who will grumble beneath Salty Ocean, shift herself, and propel him to soar in sudden rage. And in one of her silent and brutal acts, she caused the savage Salty Ocean to whale. And as he whales does that, he leaped into hasty rash of tempestuous behavior; and in his fury, he tossed himself in a state of utter tormenting act that ravished the shores," Amble Lee argued. "Therefore, you tell me aunt Nora, when have you ever heard of my mother doing things of such?" she asked. "Then further, in his act as if dictated, he demonstrated what appeared to be his anger, and carried it to the bitter end of destruction that leaves all those who survived in frightening gapping awes," Amble Lee reflected. "And while Earthly Ground in her state of restlessness, Salty Ocean whaled and howled, and raced to the open land where he chased and claimed down to the lives of thousands of the innocents and ill prepared. Then with his ravenous appetite he gorged himself with the young, the old, the black, and the white, the yellow, the pink and the brown, leaving them no time to think of pigmentation or specific status," said Amble Lee.

"She is right in her reasoning, for her mother really never display much, if any definite love or likeness for anyone or an ethnic group."

"I wish not for any of you to tell me that I am right, for I know I am."

And in her state of unrest, she harbors not any hand down or any mercy for the already dead, as in his monster like behavior of Salty Ocean who gulped even debris and all that came in his path; acting out his bellicose behavior all through the influence of the often-passive Earthly Ground and her obedience to mother of Nature. The difference is, with my mother, no one needs to worry," explained Amble Lee.

"Amble Lee you have so much talk now as you have grown eh!" said Crampy.

"Yes, for with the wrathful attempts of Earthly Ground and Salty Ocean, they together try to reshape of the face of towns, cities, and adjoining course lines. And their show of force demonstrates to the contrary the calmness of my mother, and how well she goes and comes, appear and disappear all in her comely presence without cause for undue concern. In fact, the sole social evil that she may present, lags purely in the minds of the idiotically pretentious people like you and aunt Nora, in whom harbored the type of fear that drove others into a state of illusionary pickle. And while doing that, my mother is as harmless as a lamb and is as docile as a door jamb unless being interfered with by that friend of yours, Sunny Light."

At this time Amble Lee's aunt could only listen while Crampy plugged in his every now and then patronizing views.

"Regardless of what you may say Crampy, there is no reasonable equation between those wicked modules, and any example that can draw any reasonable parallels between my mothers and all the other modules, for they are dissimilar to an immeasurable extent. For one thing, my mother is much more sympathetic and friendlier, that in her entire act she adamantly refuses to separates herself from them despite their entire blatant act in the wrecking of life and the habitat of man, animal, and plants."

"Yes, but she has scattered her wasters across town and villages and sliced through crevices and offering her frightening specks to man all the time."

"But how would you compare that to all the devastation done by Tom Wind, Earthly Ground, and Salty Ocean? And on top of it all, in the midst of all the ravaging acts of all other modules, she maintains her saintly presence in the furnishing of the ambiance. And there is no semblance of anything that may bring to mind any comparable evidence of such danger that has ever been experienced, or offered by her in the history of her whole. In fact, the only exception that may be considered about her to be dangerous is her unfathomable weight or lightness, her density and her inaudible but acknowledged intelligence that have led man to be fearful, or perhaps because man is apt to be fearful of the unknown."

Amble Lee's argument has much in it to think about, for we know that man often use the presence of the darkness, and chiefly when it is in its most dense form to hide or seek it as a place of refuge, and often enough used it to perpetuate their evil deeds. And, he may use it as his heavens at times although he knows not its next action that maybe hidden within the belly of its blackness, which could be one of the secret places of God.

"You can only assume to distinguished whatever there in her after the twilight's hours descended, or even during the measured time of her configuration in preparation to cover mother Nights and all things that fall within her path. And man may otherwise sheer her blackness with whatever form of Lights that he might use in finding his own path through the belly of her spongy blackness as she masked mother Night."

"And my mother, in her acts, she maintained her ability to do a number of things such as the concealing of things that fall within the cover of her sphere, even though she has never attempted to, or displayed anything such as harming anyone, and not even when at a trifle above or below what the world has seen of her. She has been fashioned with numerous endowments, but there is only one shorthanded form of a bequest that was not given to her by her resourceful creator, and that is her physical ability not to cause the death of human. In the literal sense, she has the inability to shield things forever in her often-opaque body but with no promise of eternal hold. Yes, she may have subscribed to some unfortunate situations, but man was given the ability to craft things that are able to repel her ultra-blackness to some degree."

"Amble Lee, you for the first time has acknowledged that there are aspects of evil done by what you so called your mother," Nora blurted.

"Again, yes, it maybe so, but the fact that there has always been some form of your Lights wherever she is absent, yet it shows that regardless of her duration of stay, it makes her less likely to render any harm to mankind since your friend Lights are in most cases so inquisitive, he always avails himself. The veracity that there has always been some form of Light whether it is by that of him, or those Lights invented by man, made her task much more impossible to deal any act of evil. Do you all agree?" Amble Lee stated. "And do you agree that the non-vendible value of the Darkness tells a lot?"

"I don't know about that Amble Lee, but are you aware that your mother and all that are synonymous to her, or in her likeness are without vendible values?"

"Give me an example, will you?"

"Sure."

"They would shield themselves and their apparatus from the glare of Sunny Light with the object of inviting my mother in for them to go about their clicking. Outside of this purpose, whether my mother is in singularly or in a bonded body with her dissidents or not, she remains without promise or noticeable problem to society."

"I am not so sure about that," said Nora.

"Then if that what I told you do not show vendible values, then you may need to look twice at her worth," Amble Lee said.

"Unlike her counterpart Sunny Light and all other form of Lights which are vendible, shows the importance and the purpose they serve in society, marked that clear distinction between your mother and Sunny Light."

"That maybe so aunt Nora, since your friend Lights overall, excluding that of the mighty Sunny Light, who is now a vendible matter easily acknowledged. Looking around us whether we are at home, in the clubs, churches, tabernacle, kingdom hall, the theatre, office, or any other place of entertainment or worship, we can see where he is often harnessed and placed in a manner to combat the presence of your mother. Therefore, base on observation, he is definitely more a vendible agent who is contrary to the value of your mother," Crampy asserted.

"You are to realize Amble Lee that the swiftness of your mother provokes the mind and offer tricks the eyes each time she is interrupted by him," Nora said.

"That's the way she is," replied Amble Lee.

The mother of Darkness teases curiosity, but keeps her amazing maneuvers silent. Questions about such acts were never asked until Amble Lee mysteriously came into the world. And then with her steadfast half sad and diluted spirit, she joined forces with the Darkness and with which she set the stage for all the awes.

We may sit and gaze at the difference in the use of these modules, accepting the fact that only synthetic Lights that can be harnessed to temporarily disperse the Darkness, although only in limited proportion. It is in the creation of things, and as attempts are made to suppress it that the sneaky Shadows are left alone to occupy any space they choose. Then at these stages amazingly, they would stay wherever they are unless when any semblance of Light jumps out upon them. And in their encounter with Lights, they demonstrate their obedience to their presence and shift themselves accordingly. And like a saint, with the interferences by Lights they shaft themselves in direct focus in crevices and vacant spaces.

Then these spots of Darkness called Shades at times and Shadows at other times are quick to shift themselves into corners or beneath the body of targeted and untargeted objects. And their quickness is immeasurable, tricky, and is very loyal to the objects they rest themselves and cover them to the extent that even at the disappearance of Lights they stand their ground in the offering of greater coverage.

Here now set the confusion in determining the veracity in this that Lights are a much more vendible module, but the simple examination of the charge of our everyday living is more than enough to quell the quandary poised between these two fundamentals of Nature.

"Mankind pays for the synthetic kind of your friend in his attempt to thwart my mother, and he even temporarily use your friend Light in his home while he is spared the cost of that which is provided by Nature, while for the cost of the use of my mother or any part of her, you will notice that there is no charge. So, in the name of my mother Darkness, whether she is in her Shadows or Shades form, there has never been any charge. It is only when we stand in our unstated state of blindness indirectly that there is a charge, and only for the repelling of her presence. So, standing alone in this sense, the only incurred cost that my mother placed upon man is to have her repelled instead of utilizing her in this respect."

"I will again admit Amble Lee, that in her presence we turn our improvised Lights on to disperse her and to see around us. And we use our own invention in providing his use or used the invented synthetic of various form to pave our way through darkened path caused by your mother. And yeah, doing that we unwittingly provide an income through her slightest presence and even in our quest to see our path through her often thick and densely still and opaque body."

"And yes, I must admit further that as usual, my mother sometimes locks herself in her soldierly like precision. And during these times she leaves no stone unturned when in her wadding presence. And I will acknowledge that she is one of the main invaders of man's personal space, but while her casting, she offers much wooing to the evildoers who set sails in the woods in the company of mother Nights to perpetrate their devious acts. This could be all the dangers to which she may have subscribed, while it would be wise for you to note even though there are no acts that are of her personal willingness to carry out."

There has always been that unvarying change or vacating of space in the split of a second by the mother of Darkness the moment Sunny Light or any other form of Lights comes around or otherwise turned on. How do your account for that?" Crampy asked.

"By this we should boomingly well know that we do not need the use of any form of Lights to find her or any of her constituents. And there should be no harboring of thoughts or any imagination of such about her."

Chapter Twenty-Seven

YOU NEED NO LIGHT TO FIND THE DARKNESS

There is more to it than the purpose they serve, thinking that Light does not need assistance to find any members of his own, the mother of Darkness, or any of her dissidents. And we all too well know that we do not need any form of Light to find another apart from that which is in the mind of the bearer of such. "You should have known that it is only in man's view and his wits to develop and discover things that he may consider to be up against the placid black giant you all styled as black and antagonistic. I cannot see her as described in her un-intended confrontations with man and Light. She is my mother and I will endeavor to protect her integrity."

"If you are considering any such views that we need Light to see another, it would be like a utopian dream," said Nora.

"That argument should be between you and Mr. Crampy, because I am not prepared to be in any wrangling with you. My mother has never been knowingly tied together. And not even when she spreads her vast opaque body on the plane, as wherever she may be present, she commissioned herself to the order of Nature. To date there is no known visionary, genius, or geniuses, that can pattern or act out her characteristics. The thought of such would also be another wander away opinion that would have locked itself within the mind of a lone bizarre thinker."

"You said it."

"My entire family of Darkness is one set of enduring people and is certainly not known to be of any threats to mankind. My aunt and her friend Crampy saw her and referred to her as a nonmaterial and non-spongy structure, which claim I will not refute. And I know that she is definitely unlike that of her darling Sunny Light or any fraction of his luminaries that glow in the mantle of his frame. Therefore, after looking at those, she deserves to be treated with much reverence. You have treated your Darlin Sunny Light with much more reverence than her. I have noticed that. In my view, my mother in most cases, is by herself, existing through the application of words. Yet, she is an enduring body who no one is likened to her or her gauged body except her often-fused dissidents who are my siblings, and are of my blood," said Amble Lee.

"Amble Lee has a strong argument here; for through the use of semantics there gained the title dark at times, and of course is one of the strongest adjectives that draped it around all things. All this came in the name of things in relation to the thinking of man, and in whom all views on their existence are considered bad or ultra-devious," Crampy again asserted.

"At proper intervals all over the world, these evildoers built their lives simply around the presence of my mother as the bulk of their heavy labor in misdeed are carried out during the course of their nocturnal activities. And be it known that this is the custom of not only the vagrants, but also those who set about to make their heavy haul in the opaque path of my mother. Then they placed all blames upon her because she is as dark as Darkness. No one should speak negatively of my mother who speaks not of evil or good about anyone. I will admit yes, that she presents herself at times as an ultra-innocent giant clothed in blackness, yet she is as harmless as an unborn lamb."

"You can go ahead with all your sophistry Amble Lee."

"I am aware that there are frequent skirmishes between you and your darlin Sunny Light. In fact, some of those skirmishes are sometimes at noontime and even sometimes in the presence of mother Nights. And I know that there are frequent skirmishes amongst others, but none of which my mother provoked or participated. Stormy Wind may blow with all his strength and fury, but my mom has never offered any opposition, physical hinderance, or obstruction. She tends only to her duty, clothing all objects in the absence of your friend Lights."

"Go on Amble Lee, go on."

"No, you say what you have to say!"

"In our portion or lot, Amble Lee, I observe that the word Dark stands out the most in all common usages as she is often so used to describe things in the most negative form. In any case, to the contrary she remains the most sparsely used of the entire family of mother Darkness and her family. I also observe that she stands aloft in abundant form as she awaits the unuttered dictate and unuttered order and movements of things as well as all other silent elements before she acts."

"Yes, that's her, that's the way she is," replied Amble Lee.

"I have observed how much she is absolutely resolute in all her nightly presence."

"Yes, but you should notice that at which time she yielded in restricted portion as dictated by the influence of your darlin Light barging in."

"Now I see!" said Crampy. "Therefore, I will no longer wonder why Amble Lee in her autism, is so engrossed with her; and holds fast to her view that the Darkness is her mother," said Crampy.

"She is like a magician in her personal world of antics. And it is needless to say, she is indeed the imperial portraits of that of mother Nights, and at which time she planted herself at the base of things and hoods from the stationary to the traversing objects. Yet there is that unfeeling logic of her behavior that sinks deep into the wondering minds of the coward who pondered restlessly about her existence," explained Amble Lee.

The pondering and the amazement came as she feels not obliged to refrain from the offering of her scary presence. It was only the mere presence of Lights that may in their secret dictates that had forced her removal or part of herself.

There are those groups that were before mentioned, and one of which bears that infinite similarity to her grand presence. On the other hand, they are sometimes slightly lesser in pigmentation as well as in characteristics. This then made their presence known when Sunny Light takes the mantle in his faintest of form. Then they made their presence with their slight pigmentation, and come into the spirit of focus when Sunny Light is in his dim phase; skirting himself in the far distant or in the foreground with time.

A little later in life, time makes the difference. The passing of time with mother Darkness, and mother Night is when semantics becomes more a transforming figure, and through which it created the placement of title or name upon the color of the evenings, mother Days, and mornings.

All these times Amble Lee in the other phase of her autism is helpless and unhelpful in making any decision. She listened without understanding the calling of time and the maneuvering of the colorful evening's mixture of Sunny Light and her mother spreading herself across the azure. Such is chiefly beholding during the coming of the twilight hour, a moment she dislikes most. The second Amble Lee heard this she burst out of her room like a reckless brute as if to challenge Blow Wind peering through the window. And straight away she was caught in the midst of that regular friendly battle with her mother and Sunny Light, and blew fewer skirmishes; Shadows prevailing over the wayward Blow Wind. This went on until the evening in its stillness, slothfully slumped into an uttered spate of translucent blackness until her mother gained the upper hand, she believes.

It was Amber Lee's pleasure to see her mother stretching across the dell and against the doorpost on which she leaned. The magic of her mother stood still as Sunny Light slowly disappeared, leaving alone Amble Lee's half-cocked smiles that radiated the evening's sphere.

"Some moments in life should be remembered when we think of the mother of Darkness as the agents of deception," Nora muttered. "These together form a single body, but are individually gifted in their magical art of mimicking man and all objects, whether the objects are with or without life. The Silhouette itself is known as the chief architect of deception. In as much, when in the company of the Darkness it magically invoked perpetual awes and illusions, and guides all the frail minded into frantic moments. So, it makes me wonder how could Amble Lee managed to placed herself with the Darkness and say it is her mother!" said Nora.

These though, are the matters of individual blinkered views that are formed or arrested, and are observed chiefly at dusks, or in the presence of mother Nights when the presence of the mother of Darkness is half shattered by the infringement of Lights.

"There can be no Shadows without any fragment of Lights, which is also true for Shades and Silhouettes, but at this stage, these depend largely on the magnitude or the strength of Light. And the degree of whatever form is vitally important to the shape of the formed imaged. Whenever Light is scanty, the mimicked image naturally going to be as scanty or is in a state of indistinct formation. There are times when patches and remnants of Faint Darkness are determined to be no more than extracts of the vast body of the mother of Darkness would sprawl herself on the ground and against walls, which unexpectedly appears during the course of time when mother Days is in her periodic fashion."

On these occasions, objects such as Floating Drifters sailing crosses the face of the source, and so cause the frequently quick shifts of the mother of Darkness. And at this transient moment, curiosities are commonly arrested, causing eyes to roll to the heavens. Then with the occasional accompaniment of deep annoyance that often last for short period when it follows its transient pattern and flows about.

"When we are caught in one of our conscious moods about nature, we sometime observe the intermittent appearance of Sunny Light during the course of the day. We would then wonder how brilliant nature can be in its many adorable displays with the Darkness in the evening sky. In this form, and with the featuring of its characteristics, and with the presence of Sunny Light, the two often present a joyous spectacle in the heavens, creating much splendor to the eyes and the consoling of hearts."

And, as you would imagine, it depends chiefly on how well the sometimes-brief appearances of the Floating Drifters that cause to obscure the view of Earthly Ground, which can be sometimes frightening to the eyes. The result of such then, again, brings in the transitory presence of the mother of Darkness. And at such stage and time, when it is caught in any of its thinnest phases, there are those moments when its transparent state of thinness quickly transformed into that of a vast sheet of blackness, thick enough to cause concern to lives below and about.

"Although sometime comes the expectation of terrifying cries and yells of surprises and self-driven fear from the terror of my mother through the subtleness of her blackness, I am here to say that she has no physical strength to hand out harm to anyone. Therefore, all expected shouts should remain silent in the gullet of the frightened beholders of the Night, while the fearless night in this instant run silent to its core."

In the neat of time, with the day changing, things happened. Sunny Light with his powerful rays habitually dictates its might, but fail intermittently to pierce the Floating Drifters even with its needling forklike beams. So here comes the troublesome one-dimensional view that "the sun is hiding its face behind the clouds." Nonetheless, in the true sense of such tale of fallacy, it is the Floating Drifters that move themselves across the broad face of Sunny Light, which is ultimately contrary to what the notion bears. For neither the self-feeling threat that seemed to be hanging, nor the notion challenge or disturb the peaceful presence of the subtle mother Darkness that roams about with the Floating Drifters all in their occasionally aimless canters.

"Filled with its loftiest desire as set by Nature, and acting on its own self-driven impulses, this phasing out of the mother of Darkness blackens the face of the azure before transforming herself in various dimensions, then tumbling to Earthly Ground sometimes in fine strewn mist. And more often than ever, it tumbled in a form that sprinkled on hills, forests, and in the common as rain, while in the valley beneath appears the unpleasing shifting of the wild billows of mists parading in the atmosphere."

Amble Lee hates all moments of brightness, and declined every offer that they may make with Sunny Light. During these moments the countenance on her face bears a temporary disfigurement and showed her displeasure as Sunny Light permeates the heavens. And all through this time, Nora was gazing in an element that was temporarily deprived of the mantling mother Darkness, leaving alone the barefaced of the azure and the blistering rays of the raging Sunny Light.

and at these Times she frocked herself unwittingly in dreaded shrouds like apparel that seclude her already undistinguishable shape. And while in her dreaded but then, as the day wore on, gradually came that grayish layer of cloudlets, a band of mystically formed darkened Drifters floating aimlessly above the too far- to -reach heights of the atmosphere. And further, by the cause of nature, the darkened bulges progressively came in larger construction with the Floating Drifters, and then spread themselves across the heavens forming a blanket of dark gray and somber brown.

"And, in frequent changes, it often drew them across the face of the endless formation before mercilessly releasing from time to time, the fluidal substance of life so-called Rain," Crampy said.

"Admittedly though, contrary to this period, my mother sometimes sets herself in some of her most dreaded form by stretching or intermingling herself beneath bales of mushroom Floating Drifters that also create fears and anxiety among some people. But in accepting reality, there were some passion and delightful moments for their coming by a wide cross section of the occupiers of Earthly Ground."

Another area of frightful moment came when Luna Moon, obscured the face of Sunny Light, and how at which stage a gradual spate of the mother of Darkness occupied the atmosphere. Then the eye-catching apparition they formed created awes of great magnitude, though not to Amble Lee. For to her, it is her preference to be with mother Nights and in all their presence, so much was the better for her. Guided and controlled by her autism, Amble Lee believes not and fears not any evil except for Lights.

"It is indeed an unpleasant thing to know that this period of time, when Sunny Light and Lunar Moon choose to offer their scary appearance, the face of Sunny Light has never been obscured for 24 hours at any single spell."

"And thank goodness, for had it last for any considerable period, no one knows what would have been the ultimate outcome; considering the unpredictability of some other modules of Nature. I cannot understand how Amble Lee tolerates this."

"When any modules act out in this form it brings on such a scary feeling, and not only among human, but to the very lower-level form of animals who become restless, while the birds of the air seek early roosting as they become confused with the Time of the day. Looking at the behavior of the birds and other forms of animals and their confusion, it is enough to say that your mother Darkness, unquestionably impinged on the lives of some living things. Do you agree with that Amble Lee?"

"Let it be said that I need no pity. I am happy with the choice I have made," Amble Le replied. "In fact, no, for my mother offers no toxic threat or any form of danger to anyone. And so, will be the case forever that the restlessness and confusion she might cause, they are but the only known physical danger she posed in all her mystic forms or function in all the years of her periodic presence. They will be here always, and with all her imposing order and figure she passed on in her existence in time with no known danger to man," she argues.

"Dark and all the sometimes- fused family of the mother of Darkness operates on order and dictate, and have no particular style or taste of their own. Whenever they are operating in oneness, within that bond they carefully defined their acts of mimicry; and neither by choice do they offer any grand flourish or embellishment in the carrying out of such acts. And, their behavior even remains true when carrying out their individual acts. They are perpetual, yes, in all their deeds with man in his optimism preparing for any abatement that may be instituted by them at their leisure. In any case, the prospect of such leisure will only be achievable when life on Earthly Ground for all has ended."

"Thank goodness, you have again accepted the truth that your mother can be a nuisance to people."

"It is to be realized that as long as there is the mighty Sunny Light or any other body of his Lights around, there is going to be various acts of my mother, which will only become permanently latent only when all Lights ceased to be present."

"The presence of any semblance of Sunny Lights, whether it is in the distant or in close proximity, it infinitely serves its purpose. For one thing, it encourages the action of some sort of your mother wherever she may be present, regardless of the degree of her density. In the still of the Nights, and chiefly when she is more visible in her state of oneness, and at which point she makes it more noticeable; a Time when she is pierced by a form of fork Lights that caused her to disperse, but only in constrained portion with the presence of lanterns or any other restricted form of shaded or unshaded Lights," Nora explained.

"Aunt Nora, if you are perceptive enough you will see during the day time how the multitude of Dark spots on the ground dancing sometimes happily under trees, where the limbs may span a limited or vast area. And if you were enough observant, you would have also seen in the presence of the splintered spots of my mother, and how well she and my siblings in concert identify the individual sense of their purpose, and in particular, when your mighty Sunny Light is shining in his glory," Amble Lee in her sarcastic articulation said to her aunt.

"At this Time, there is no ground for thinking as it should be widely recognized that these spots of blackness were otherwise in cluster. You will perhaps—agree--- that it is strange that they are called Shades when in the presence of Days and even into twilight. Then the moment mother Night descends their presence are called Shadows!"

"I do not have a problem understanding that. It only demonstrates the amazing ability of my mother and her splinters all of whom are of my blood."

"I quite follow you Amble Lee, but there still stand those amazing aspects in their acts."

"Astonishingly, the cries you are making over them are titled by you and all those who are against them. It is they who named them when the said sets of leaves are in scanty formation and gives a scanty mimicked reflection. Then they are seen differently, and being referred to in varying terms as Shadows and Shades. But it is only when in the overall formation starting at dusk through the Nights that they are referred to as simple Shadows. Is it not you then and your people who are causing the confusion?" Amble Lee asked.

"Yes, the word Shades disappears from the lips when your mother, Darkness, according to you, aligned herself with the evenings; forming that gradual coating of the Nights. What propel this shift in describing the same set of clustered leaves in their reflection of Sunny Light, which is contrary to when in their daily reflection as Shades I do not know?"

"All blame is set upon my mother because of her pigmentation," Amble Lee said,

It is in this shift of name that drastically brings on the power and the glory of semantics that instantly transformed their names and action. And thus, observers of their behavior proclaim their convoluted maneuvering acts that bolster that figment of imagination. Thus, the type of nocturn-phobic behavior some of us exhibit.

"The wilderness holds the key to the answer. At these Times when the mother of Darkness is in her compactness, there is no guided mark that offers any semblance of separation or act of confusion. Light then separate itself, and only in the distant far where their maybe glow of some sort filtering in, and which may bring the presence of apparition in those folds of the Darkness," Crampy replied.

"As Time wears on there comes a sense of appreciation by some people for their presence, although during these periods they distort the true shape of their objects elsewhere. In the interim they create laughter caused by their mimicked objects in the formation of animals of different species against the background of white walls."

"What about them and the wall?"

"To make the case, it would be interesting to know how you feel about the images they form on the wall. If you found yourself curious enough, or feel that you have an adequate amount of mischievousness about you, you may place yourself in front of a bright white Light whether it is at home or in your office, then look at your body formation against the wall. You are sure to see with Light behind you, how your body will form a dark Shadow, which will graciously give the amazing appearance as if she is pasted against the wall. That's one of the amazing acts of my mother. And you may even extend any of your hands with your fingers energetically moving around; and relying on the degree of your creativity or your imaginative ability, you will see anything that your ingenuity allows you to form," Amble Lee explained.

The autistic Amble Lee's example demonstrates the fact that her mother Darkness, is somewhere even when Light is present. It is only she who will, through her autism can tell where it is. Her example to some extent soon to, hopefully, provide the information, and also proved that it is the presence of objects and Lights that are the basis of the formation or creation of any mimicked objects.

She has proven that although seemed estranged; these two modules when fused, they play a formidable role in the mimicking of things. And interestingly enough, they do not, and cannot mimic themselves or act independently in the creation of images even of their own liking. So then, it is to be perceived that only in their fusion that images are formed.

Listening and observing Amble Lee's view of the Darkness she calls her mother, shows that whatever the position you may desire, you are sure to see some formation of an animal ranging from a cat to a rabbit, a guinea pig or the head of a dog.

Mother Darkness in her cleverness adopting your body image on the wall is surely in reminiscence of those old days when you were a child, and at which time you would spend hours playing with such formation making images of the various animals.

"Whatever your pleasure was during those days, it is unquestionably that at the end you must have found some form of virtues in the presence of my mother, at least, even for those moments when you were young. So, even if you were then afraid of her grand body of blackness, there were those moments when she would indicate to you that there is some form of desirable quality within her, although to date there is still not very many people carry any striking quantity or preference for her. And I said it because I know that my aunt Nora is one of them."

"Amble Lee demonstrated how the grand body of her mother Darkness and or splintered siblings sometime takes into their formation, a complete replica of the image they sought, and then shrouds and mimics all that came into their path. But it can be stressed that the Dark and or the mother of Darkness overall, are often found in one global body, though differentiated in verbal application, hence, the separation enforced by language that caused to separate or fused the Dark and mother Darkness into intermingling," Crampy said.

"So, because they are fused in standard form but severed by description in singular usage, it has become more difficult to accurately extrapolate any absolute difference in just one single thought. It is through man, and through his wisdom that he has coined words that placed the Dark and the Darkness in all the wide range of application as the case may be."

"Naturally, man, if it were at all possible, would do everything to understand and prevent the ever presence of my mother whether they are used in the amalgamated or alienated phrase or not. She would have been alone with her special gift; and had it been in my power to do all manner of things with my mother such as commanding her, only though, if she would have abided by any of my order. And only then would you believe me that I now know where she goes the moment Light comes around."

Based on the strong dictate of Nature, they are still a non-substance that often adopted themselves to the act of configuration; an object that intermittingly occupy the environment and have altered the lifestyle of a vast majority of people on a daily basis. Amble Lee has just technically explained that not even she has any control over the Darkness she so-called her mother. And further, the more mother Darkness spreads herself is the more the complications there would be.

Because of this often vastly presence of the mother of Darkness, Amble Lee would have to produce proof that she is her daughter and that she knows where she goes the moment Light comes on. Then Nora would have the tedious task of proving that Amble Lee needs a psychologist, and she would need the involvement of a trustworthy psychiatrist to say otherwise that she is not acting on her own knowable will. But, sad to say, it would not have been the end of her miseries.

The Dark or the Darkness as they are called, are immeasurable and their age incalculable. With their years of fused presence around the world set on the edge quite a problem in determining how much they have affected and distort things in their pre-life formation, and the pre-life of things and the cause for Amble Lee's problem.

"Considering all their amalgamated form and in particular their amazingly non-intentional procedures of formation, what we are seeing today obviously sets off the type of quandary we are faced with in our efforts to understand much more about the mother of Darkness and why Amber Lee so chose it as her mother. It would have been best for us to try to understand that her choice is measured and made by the nature of her illness, and not an arbitrary preference," Crampy said in his appealing quest to Nora and others to sympathize with her.

"Leaving alone the mystery brought on by Amble Lee and her belief, we know that together the mother of Darkness and the Dark evidenced by their routine occupation of some of the strangest places one would at least expect. As is usually the issue with the word Dark, it is more often used in conversation as its scope has more modification in languages than the word Darkness.

In this factual sense, the Dark is used in much fewer instances than the mother of Darkness. Maybe they were scared of hurting Amble Lee's feeling.

When Nora heard the discussion about the usage of the word Darkness, she raced out of her room like a drunken sailor; and garbed only in her thin cotton nightgown, she pierced the dreaded mother of Darkness to the terrace where she stumbled upon the empty old chair. And in a loud voice she cried, what the hell is this?"

"Oh, fool, look and watch your steps, all of you, for there is my mother in her dense state with her caring blackness. She is hugging the Night in the absence of your darling Sunny Light, who had not long changed from a blistering ray to now."

And if Darkness had in any way an absolute relation to man, it is in the way in which sense that Amble Lee sees it.

"But then the same could be true for that of Dark but without real life in the true sense of the word. And we would, as usual, pay little if any attention to all the yapping about its formation and its actions as it spreads itself across the sky and over Earthly Ground."

"The only trouble that I am having with the mother Darkness, is that I don't like it because I haven't been able to see what is in it," Nora said.

"There is nothing in it. It is just a vast sheet of blackness stretching across the vale," A voice from the wilderness uttered.

With all these non-reflecting appearances and utterances about the mother of Darkness in the dialogue, Amble Lee took it that the aforementioned examples were not meant to inflame her or the heart of anyone in any way. It was by far a statement of fact, and which should not go unnoticed or treated with any simplistic views, or for it to be treated with any degree of misunderstanding or warp mindedness.

There is that hope that it will be construed and treated, as it deserves in frankness, and in practicality as such that there are no views above and beyond this idea that can ever be embraced as being more factual.

"Why then should we not adhere to the explanation given about the word Dark and Darkness as Amble Lee's mother? Well, I supposed that only she knows so well why, and in all her life she still chose to refer constantly to it as her mother. To us we can only assume that the reasons she so chose to adopt it as her mother is in keeping with the order and dictate of her autism."

"Based on these elements of noticeable fact that we have often allowed to go unnoticed, the qualifying placements upon these fused modules of Nature are indeed troubling, and makes one wonder why, and how can Amble Lee hold so fast to her idea and belief about it."

"The central role the mother of Darkness plays often falls in the formidable task of blanketing all unlit things. And it could well be meant for the shielding of things and all surroundings and cloaking all areas and things during the absolute absence of any or all form of Light, said Amble Lee. "And as a matter of fact, as a young, artistic blind child, I have always been fascinated by the concept of the Darkness. And while I have never been able to see with my own eyes, I have always been able to feel it in my own way. It surrounded me, enveloping me in its mysterious embrace, and yet, it always eludes my understanding. Growing up, I learned to navigate the world around me using my other senses-touch, taste, smell, and sound. These senses became my tools, allowing me to explore and discover new things every day. But despite my heightened senses, I always felt like there is something missing. Something intangible but elusive, that I could only sense the quiet moments when the world around me was still and quiet, but now that I have discovered and understand the trueness of the darkness, I will tell you and your friend Crampy and all the world where she goes the second your friend Lights comes on," Amble Lee explained.

"Perhaps that could be one other reason why she sees it as her mother. Then again, the mass confusion the presence of the splinters caused to human when they are in their separated form is startling, the fact that because of such they have made the task of knowing where do they, or the Darkness disappeared to and so quickly when

Sunny Light comes out, and even in its mega fullness made it more puzzling.

"It is only Amble Lee who knows, and knows so much that she will soon explain where her mother, the Darkness, according to her goes when the light comes on. Her strong view on the Darkness remains in her and continue to infuriate her aunt throughout. But Amble Lee determined to hold her stance and will at the end, according to her, let it known where she found her mother and siblings the moment the Light comes on."

"We are living in a world that is filled with things we cannot change. Therefore, it is prudent that we peruse with our enquiring minds the task of knowing, or seek from our creator the added wisdom that may guide us through, and before long that we one day learn the way to our own destiny; and that we may see our path through the deep channel of our term on Earthly Ground. Perhaps, we will be able to see ourselves the way we are as one in terms of our purpose, and not long before we will learn to tolerate the things we cannot change and therefore accept the mother of Darkness as part of the convoluted system of the mother of Nature by which we are governed. We are all a component in the essence of creation, and an entity that was created to occupy the path of both Sunny Light and my mother Darkness, and both of whom are with unlimited dominion over us and things. And when the master of mother Days is in his shining glory, he takes pleasure in alerting Earthly Ground of his presence and his purpose, although at such time my mother squeezes herself in crevices and vacant holes, behind doors and beneath logs and timber and all things that are at peaceful rest. And to add, at such time my mother will be showing so much of her virtues, yet she will seek not any reward for her acts of kindness to mankind," Amble Lee outlined.

"So, Amble Lee, where do you say that your mother Darkness goes when the Lights come on?"

"Aunt Nora, you have been calling me stupid for years, yet you cannot realize that I have outlined almost all the places where she goes except for behind the sources of your darling Light. And because of your ignorance to my unfortunate situation, you constantly describing me as a damn fool and stupid idiot, which has been proven to be the opposite."

"You said you know Amble Lee, therefore what I am asking you to do is to tell the world where does your mother go the moment the Light comes on," beseeched Nora.

"It is simple aunt Nora, very simple."

"Yes, but for how long should we wait?"

"Because of her high level of flexibility, and worse, the frequency of the indignation you aunt Nora and your friend, she and her dissidents' children my many siblings, always rushes to hide themselves behind the sources of your darling Lights and all their targeted and untargeted objects."

"After all, you know Amble Lee, to think of it, it's true, I agree," said Nora.

"Thank you," replied Amble Lee.

The End

www.ingramcontent.com/pod-product-compliance
Lightning Source LLC
LaVergne TN
LVHW010546160826
845677LV00013B/3011